A Summer to Remember
in Herring Bay

D1407457

A *Summer to Remember* in Herring Bay

Angela Britnell

Where heroes are like chocolate – irresistible!

Published 2022 by Choc Lit Limited
Penrose House, Crawley Drive, Camberley, Surrey GU15 2AB, UK
www.choc-lit.com

A CIP catalogue record for this book is available
from the British Library

ISBN 978-1-78189-040-0

Printed and bound in Great Britain
by Clays Ltd, Elcograf S.p.A.

Acknowledgements

An abandoned Methodist Chapel in Cornwall was the inspiration for a crucial part of the story and I loved the idea of a community's attempt to pull back together and bring new life to an old neglected building. A big thank you to the Tasting Panel members who embraced the idea that appearance isn't everything. Cornish fishing villages don't have to be chocolate-box pretty and that Ruan and Essy needed to see beneath each others' glossy surface before they could love completely and honestly. Special thanks goes to those readers who said 'yes' to the manuscript and made publication possible: Lauren McCafferty, Jenny Kinsman, Gillian Cox, Lorna Janette Baker, Carole Rowsell, Alma Hough, Fran Stevens, Jo Osborne, Cordy Swinton, Anne Eckersley and Gill Leivers.

Chapter One

If the stupid satnav with its oh-so-superior British accent shouted at her one more time to make another sharp turn Essy swore she would rip it out of the car. The narrow winding lane left her no choice but to turn unless she wanted to crash head first into one of the massive hedges flanking this Cornish excuse for a road. She jabbed her finger at the screen to turn Annabelle off. Essy bestowed that nickname on the system after acquiring her at Heathrow Airport yesterday because it amused her how polite the mechanical voice sounded, rather like the cute queen inviting someone to tea at Buckingham Palace. Her mother had tried to warn her that driving to Cornwall was a mistake but had she listened? Had she heck. That wasn't the only thing her mother had reservations about, this whole discovering her roots escapade had made Paula Williams frown and shake her head.

You're making a big mistake, honey. I had good reasons to leave and better ones for never going back. Sometimes it's wise to let things be.

But Essy had a mile-long stubborn streak running right through her. On the plus side it was the main reason her business back in Tennessee was blossoming because Eureka! promised to find anything a client desired. Over the years she had had some strange requests but hadn't been defeated by one yet. She had been toying with the pros and cons of visiting Cornwall for ages but when a request came in that required visiting this remote part of England, the decision was a no-brainer.

According to the map she should reach Herring Bay in about another five miles so she would read the signposts like other folks. An hour later, when she must have explored every nerve-wracking back road in the county, she gritted her teeth and stopped to ask for directions.

'This *is* Herring Bay, my 'andsome.' The woman smiled, fighting a losing battle to control the boisterous spaniel she was attempting to walk.

'Really? But I thought it was on the coast.'

'The heart of the village is, my love, but over the years its spread out and most of the newer houses were built up here. You want to turn left over there and the harbour is about half a mile down the hill.' She pointed further along the road. 'If it weren't drizzly this morning you'd see the sea from here.'

Drizzly? Essy would call it persistent rain but didn't argue. Her assumption that the middle of June equalled summertime in Cornwall was another misstep.

'The weatherman said it'll clear later, but I'd say it's in for the day.'

The stranger's soft rumbling voice held similar hints to Essy's own southern drawl and she idly wondered if the people who lived here also got mocked as ignorant country bumpkins by those who didn't know any better?

'We don't get many Americans around here. Are you looking for a B&B? Mary Warren might have a room and she's got a nice place down near the quay.'

'Uh, I'm not sure yet, but thanks anyway. I'll head down that way to park and have a wander around.' Hopefully it shouldn't be difficult to track down Tregrehan Road but if she mentioned her Aunt Molly's address that would set off a bunch of questions she'd prefer to avoid. 'I sure do appreciate your help.'

'You're welcome, dear. If you do go to Mary's tell her Sue Masters sent you.'

'I will.' Exchanging names couldn't hurt. 'I'm Essy Havers, by the way. From Nashville, Tennessee.' It was always easier to mention Nashville rather than the small town of Franklin south of the city, where she lived and worked.

The woman's face wrinkled in a thoughtful frown. 'Well, isn't that a funny thing. A girl I was good friends with here growing up went over that way to live. She's never come back to visit though because she had a big bust-up with her family. I often wonder how Paula's doing. I suppose she's proper American now.'

A rush of heat flooded Essy's face and a wave of guilt swept through her. 'That's interesting. It's a small world.' Much smaller than Sue Masters realised. 'Thanks again, I'll leave you to your walk.'

After holding her breath driving down a steep hill she couldn't believe was designed for two-way traffic, she discovered that there didn't appear to be any sort of designated car park. She followed the locals' example and squeezed her car into a narrow gap between two others parked along the street. If an officious traffic warden gave her a ticket she'd play the clueless American card and plead her ignorance of the local regulations. She popped on a lightweight rain jacket, yanked the hood up over her head and set off to explore.

Essy sniffed at the fresh salty air and picked her way carefully down the cobblestone street to a tiny harbour. It was sheltered on both sides by sturdy granite walls but there was no sign of any working boats and only a few dinghies with colourful sails bobbed around in the flat, grey water. She strolled along and hesitated briefly outside The Smugglers' Arms pub but the faded black paint and salt-stained windows didn't entice her to go inside. The only signs of life she spotted were a few people going in and out of a small shop that also had a sign hanging up outside for the post office. If the weather wasn't so lousy she might be tempted to buy an ice cream that the display board promised was available. No doubt the weather didn't help but no one was beating the doors down of a gift shop that had a display of colourful plastic beach toys sitting out on the pavement.

She walked around the corner into a narrow side street and checked out the name to get her bearings. Hendra Lane. A display of stunning pottery in a shop window stopped her in her tracks. The sign said Designs by Tina Cloke – Local Artist. Whoever she was Tina clearly had talent because they'd absolutely nailed the elusive colours of the coastal scenery around them.

'You're welcome to come in and look around.' An elfin-faced young woman with spiky pink hair poked her head out of the door. 'I promise I won't hassle you to buy anything you don't want.'

Essy almost said she didn't have the time but couldn't bear to disappoint the girl who must have been watching out for potential customers. 'Okay, thanks.' The tiny shop wasn't the overcrowded jumble these places often were so she was able to wander around and admire the carefully selected pieces on display. Unable to resist buying a memento of her visit she chose a miniature oval dish whose sleek curved edges evoked gentle waves breaking on the beach. 'I'll take this.' She smiled. 'I'd love a whole lot more but I've got to get it back to Tennessee. Your artist is a genius.' The woman's face turned bright red.

'That would be me.'

'You're Tina?'

'Yes. I've had the shop about two years now but… I'm not sure how much longer I'll be able to stay in business.'

'Why not? Your stuff is awesome.' Essy pulled out her purse and checked the price of her dish. 'This is ridiculously cheap. You should be charging a whole lot more.'

'People won't pay it.' Tina shrugged. 'You're a rarity. I don't know the last time we had any Americans in here. Our season only runs from Easter until maybe October and it doesn't bring in enough money to keep me going for the rest of the year, so I have to teach pottery at the local college to pay the bills.'

'That's a pity.' She took her purchase from Tina. 'I sure enjoyed meeting you.'

'Me too. Maybe we'll see you here again, although I suppose you'll be off to see other places.'

'Maybe. I'm not sure yet.' Essy brushed it off and said goodbye.

Back outside she kept on walking past several more shops that were closed, permanently by the look of their dusty windows and dark interiors. The next turn found her in Wesley Street and Essy stopped outside an old Victorian building whose faded noticeboard proclaimed it was the Herring Bay Methodist Chapel. By the rubbish piled in front of the padlocked wrought iron gates and the boarded up windows she guessed it hadn't seen a congregation in years.

Most of the tiny houses she'd seen so far were jammed together like peas in a pod and the soft ice-cream colours of the paint they all flaunted and hanging baskets of scented colourful flowers outside most of the homes gave an air of faded prettiness that appealed to Essy. Out of the blue she glanced up another of the steep hills leading away from the harbour and a sign for Tregrehan Road stopped her in her tracks. A nervous cramp gripped her stomach. She tried to put it down to the greasy breakfast she'd consumed on the way down here but the truth had nothing to do with bacon and fried eggs.

There was still time to turn back. Her aunt would never know.

Ruan leaned on the harbour wall, ignoring the damp seeping through his shirtsleeves and stared out to sea.

'What's up, boy? How're you doin'?'

He jerked around. 'I'm all right, Mr Hawkey. You?' He'd known the older man all his life and his deeply-lined face was weather-beaten from a lifetime of working outside.

'Got to be, time enough to complain when I'm six feet under.' Hawkey chuckled. 'Even when the sun's not shining there's no view like this.' He gestured around them. 'You never had nothing like that up-country now, did you?'

'I suppose not.' Ruan could see the man's point. The sweep of rugged coastline barely visible through the heavy mist, dark brooding skies and unrevealing sea had a unique beauty of its own. It suited his present mood rather than a more typical day at the beginning of summer when the sun would shimmer over the surface of deep blue water reflecting a clear cloudless sky, resonant with swooping screeching seagulls.

'Better than money in the bank any day. You made the right choice, boy.' He grasped Ruan's shoulder. 'There's no shame in comin' home.'

Wasn't there? It depended on the circumstances. 'I'd better get on.'

'You're off to Molly's?'

No surprise there. Everyone probably knew he was working for Miss Barnecutt and he could imagine the comments floating around.

She's got Vera Pascow's boy in to do some decorating. Feels sorry for the poor lad, I expect. Everyone knows he's always been an odd one and his mother isn't saying what happened to his fancy job in London.

'Yes, I'm working on her kitchen.' He pushed away from the stone wall.

'That explains why you're not giving that Michael Portillo a run for his money today.' Hawkey's face creased into a broad smile.

It wasn't the first time Ruan had been compared to the colourfully dressed ex-Conservative politician turned TV presenter, but the paint stained T-shirt and old jeans he wore today were depressingly ordinary.

'Our Kit's bringing his family down from Bristol next week on holiday. You'll be able to catch up on old times. Have a drink together, maybe.'

'Maybe.' He and Kit Hawkey were good friends at school. The best. But he wasn't a fan of rehashing the past. 'I'll see you around.' Ruan shoved his hands in his pockets and hurried off. He saw his mother talking to Jim Speight outside the convenience shop and dove into Hendra Lane out of sight. They had yet another set-to last night when he refused to join her at the pub for a quiz night.

You chose to come home. Make the best of it instead of moping around.

Vera didn't know the full story behind his sudden decision and if he had his way she never would. Ruan trudged along with his head down through the narrow back streets until he reached Tregrehan Road.

A strange woman stood on the pavement outside Molly's house and his eyes were drawn to her red and white spotted mac, skinny red jeans and sunshine yellow sneakers. A colour loving soulmate. A flash of panic shot through her startled gaze when she jerked around. It would take a talented painter to capture the ambiguous grey-green colour of her wide-set eyes.

'Sorry, didn't mean to creep up on you.'

'Well, you sure did.' She pushed a swathe of thick auburn hair out of her face and sized him up. There was no other way to describe her provocative scrutiny and the touch of devilment lurking in him returned the favour. He awarded himself a point as a deep blush spread over her pale skin to throw her bright red lips into sharp relief.

The American accent surprised him. Herring Bay's resemblance to popular tourist spots like St Ives or Fowey began and ended with the fact they were all located along the Cornish coast. Hordes of visitors trekked through those spots on a daily basis from Easter until October but the few people Herring Bay attracted were the bring-their-own-sandwich and flask types, serious coastal walkers who weren't interested in boat trips around the bay or souvenir shops.

'Miss Barnecutt doesn't do bed and breakfast.'

'She might for me.' The enigmatic reply intrigued him. 'Why don't you get on with whatever guys in Cornwall do and leave me to my own business?'

'Willingly.' Ruan stepped around her and pushed open Molly's gate. 'After you.'

'Didn't you get the hint?'

He waved his canvas bag of painting gear in her face. 'I'm

in the middle of doing some work for Molly so do I have your permission to come in too? She's expecting me.' A flicker of uncertainty crossed his adversary's face. 'Are you going in or not?'

'Sure.' She flounced up the path but before she could ring the bell Molly opened the door and stared at them both.

'Aunt Molly? I'm—'

'Scarlett? Oh my Lord.' Molly clasped her hand over her mouth. 'I never thought I'd see the day.'

Aunt? Ruan's heart thudded and a wave of nausea swept through him.

Chapter Two

Essy struggled to reconcile the most recent picture she'd seen of her aunt, taken around nineteen-eighty, with the older woman smiling warmly at her. The youthful Molly had embraced the fashionable big perms, high-waist ripped knee jeans and white lacy shirts with more frills than Princess Diana's wedding dress. Now in her late-fifties her aunt's greying hair was cut in a straightforward bob and her baggy black T-shirt and leggings hinted at a few extra curves.

'Don't stand on the doorstep, come here and give me a hug.'

Essy was swept by an unexpected rush of emotion as Molly wrapped her arms around her.

'Oh my dear soul, I don't know if I'm coming or going.' Her aunt's pale blue eyes were the disconcerting mirror image of her mother's. Now they were shimmering with big fat tears. 'Ruan, go and stick the kettle on, love.'

For a second she'd forgotten the man was there. A few years older than her maybe? Not conventionally handsome but there was something arresting about him that drew the eye. His fashionably short black hair was shot through with grey and intriguing hollows shaded his pale, lean face while the dark, hooded eyes revealed nothing of what might be going on behind them.

'Happy to.' His fleeting smile turned on her. 'Milk and sugar?'

'Excuse me?'

'Your tea. How do you take it?' The soft burr of his accent resembled her aunt's so she guessed he must be local. After decades of living in America no one would guess her own mother hadn't been born there, something Essy suspected was deliberate on Paula's part.

'Usually iced with lemon but I'll give it a try however you fix for yourself.'

'Fair enough.' He disappeared through a door on the other side of the small cramped room and she checked out his solid, muscular body with mild interest.

'Come over here, and let me have a good look at you.'

Her aunt's request put a swift halt to her drifting thoughts.

'You'm a pretty maid but that makes sense. Our mother always said Paula was a proper Tregenna and they're 'andsome women. I take after our father's side of the family and the Barnecutts are all short and dumpy, more's the pity.'

She wasn't rude enough to agree but her aunt's knowing smile told her she'd been rumbled.

'I'm some pleased to see you. I'd about given up because Paula hasn't ever come back home in all these years.' A wave of sadness deepened the lines in her aunt's round, freckled face. 'Sit yourself down and tell me what's brought you here now.'

Essy sank into the well-worn sofa and couldn't help comparing its misshapen cushions and faded pink floral loose covers with her mother's ultra-modern décor. Paula's restless spirit led her to replace everything outdated at regular intervals, including furniture and husbands. Tony Havers, her own father, had long ago been ditched for a younger model. Number four, Brad Williams, had passed the five-year mark but she hoped he wasn't counting on celebrating another anniversary. She'd recently spotted the telltale signs of discontent sneaking in, small but significant things like Paula 'forgetting' to buy his favourite brand of coffee. Essy remained stalwartly single partly because of her fear of following down the same unsettled path.

'No one calls me Scarlett, Aunt Molly. Mom says when I was learning to talk I ran both of my names Scarlett and Caroline together and somehow it evolved into Essy.' She played for time. The impetuous decision to finally visit Cornwall and perhaps be able to make sense of the mystery surrounding her mother's refusal to talk about the past wasn't easy to explain. 'I'm sorry I didn't call to ask ahead if I could come and visit.' It was on the tip of her tongue to say 'stay' instead of 'visit' but that was jumping the gun. 'It's been on my mind for a while and when some work cropped up for me to deal with here at the same time as a cheap airfare offer it seemed—'

'Meant to be.' Molly patted her hand. 'Well, I'm some glad you came. My spare bed is all made up and yours as long as you want.'

'I couldn't possibly impose. I'll get a room—'

'Don't be daft. You're family. People would think it peculiar.' The edges of her smile dropped away. 'I've had enough talk to contend with over the years after all the to-do with your mother.'

It struck her as an interesting choice of phrase. 'Thank you.'

'Tea's ready.' He carried in two blue and white striped pottery mugs and set them down on the low wood table. How much of the conversation had he overheard?

'I'm forgetting my manners.' Molly chuckled. 'This is Ruan Pascow, he's doing a bit of painting for me.'

'Pleased to meet you... properly.' They locked eyes for a moment and she thought she picked up a hint of amusement before it faded away. 'Those are unusual names.'

'Not around here.'

Essy held her ground and waited.

'They're Cornish.' His face tightened. 'Ruan was an ancient saint and Pascow can be spelled a few different ways but comes from the word for Easter.'

'Interesting.'

'Essy's my niece. She's our Paula's girl and come to see me from all the way over in America. She's going to stay awhile with me.' Molly beamed at her.

'Right.'

The terse response sounded jarring. Maybe he thought Essy was taking advantage of her aunt's kind nature but what business was it of his anyway?

'I'll have my tea in the kitchen. I finished the prep work yesterday so I'll make a start on the painting.' He disappeared again and she almost asked her aunt what was up with him but held her tongue.

Molly picked up her hot drink. 'I want to hear all about what it's like over there in America and all about your mum.'

The first part of her aunt's request would be far easier than the last. Giving herself a moment to think she took a sip of tea and fought the urge to spit it out. That was one of the nastiest things she'd tasted in her whole life. Who in their right mind put cold creamy milk into hot tea? Essy pushed the mug away and prepared to answer Molly without giving the complete truth or lying too much either.

Chapter Three

Ruan stared moodily into his tea. When his mother discovered that Paula Barnecutt's daughter had arrived in Herring Bay she would be furious. It was doubtful the American woman had a clue of the wasps' nest she had poked. He tossed the stupid idea of broaching the subject with her to one side. Tangling with Molly's attractive niece in any way would be foolish and he'd done foolish enough recently.

He pushed his mug away and prepared to desecrate Molly's kitchen. She'd asked him to replace the pale cream paint that suited the traditional old fisherman's cottage with dark navy blue paint on three walls and bold navy and white striped paper on the fourth. Ruan blamed the crazy plan on the hours she spent watching home renovation shows. The exuberant hosts scoured the country for houses to suit their enthusiastic clients only to spend the rest of the show ripping them apart. Statement wallpaper was the new buzzword. An ironic trend in his view when papering one wall in a more distinctive design had been popular back in the nineteen-seventies, then abandoned as old-fashioned a decade later.

Ruan shoved his fingers through his close-cropped hair. The recent steel-grey streaks that had sprung up horrified his mother and he suspected that for two pins she'd douse him with the same dye she touched her own up with at regular intervals. She complained the other day that women must assume he was older than he really was. Vera saw that as a negative, and a further obstacle towards getting the grandchildren she longed for. After all the trouble Helena Carter put him through in London he intended to keep a low profile around women for a bloody long time, so the more that were put off the better.

'Where's the dishwasher?' Essy held out two mugs and brought with her cheery smile a drift of distinctive perfume. He guessed the official description would be far classier but to him she smelt like a delicious cup of rich roast coffee with cream and a splash of vanilla syrup. His standard daily order back in the heady days of his London life.

Without thinking he made a grab for her hands, noting in the back of his mind that they were good hands with long, strong fingers and sensible nails instead of work-preventing talons. 'These are.' When his meaning clicked her tantalising smile broadened.

'Oh right. I'll wash them up if you let go of me.'

'Sorry.' Ruan dropped her hands like hot potatoes. 'Are you planning to stay here long?'

'Yeah, you wanna tell me why you've a problem with that?' The good humour left her. When she crossed her arms that drew attention to the tempting cleavage peeping out from her scooped neck yellow T-shirt, a rash of heat prickled his neck. His lack of response made her shake her head. 'I'll let you off for now but we're not done. You'll discover I'm persistent.'

'You might be but the Pascows are renowned for being stubborn.'

'We'll see.' She plonked down the two mugs. 'For your cheek you can wash them and then I guess you'd better get on with your work. We don't want my aunt throwing a hissy fit which she will if she's anything like my mother.'

'Throwing a what?'

'If you take me for a drink tomorrow night I'll give you the rundown on the meaning of a few important southern phrases. I'll also let you show me the bright lights of Herring Bay.'

'I've got plans.' The lie slipped out.

'Another night then.'

'I'm busy all week.'

'Yeah, I'm sure you are.' She swept a dismissive glance over him. 'Fine. Be like that. I'll hang around here with Aunt Molly instead. I'm sure she's plenty of stories to tell me.'

He refused to rise to her bait and after holding his gaze for a few tense seconds, Essy swung away from him and disappeared towards the door with a tinkling laugh.

Usually her first impressions were spot on and she'd no reason to doubt them now. Herring Bay was a dull, has-been sort of place. Her aunt Molly was the sweet and kind-hearted older sister her mother had described. And Ruan Pascow? She would bet her bottom dollar that he was no ordinary painter and decorator.

Molly patted the seat next to her. 'I want to hear more about our Paula.'

It hadn't been hard to spin a tale about Tennessee and Nashville. Not a tale in the sense of telling outright lies but she'd fudged the truth. It amused her aunt when she told several funny stories about Eureka! and the quirky things she'd been hired to find.

'Mom's doin' real well. She's made a great life for herself.'

'I'm pleased. Does she miss Cornwall?'

'She never says so. I guess she's too busy?' That sounded lame. 'I don't mean to be obtuse but it's... kinda difficult to explain. Mom never talks much about growin' up here but I'm curious to find out more. I'm hoping you'll help.' That met with dead silence. 'Something made her leave home before she turned eighteen and never come back. Other than the usual desire for a change, I mean.'

'Yes, something did.' Molly's reluctance was obvious.

'Maybe if I ask around the village someone else will be happy to tell me?'

'I wouldn't do that.'

'Why not?' Essy tossed her head. 'I deserve to know.'

'Don't be silly! You're not a child. You've got your secrets. Why shouldn't Paula keep hers if that's what she wants?' A shadow flittered over her aunt's face. 'Tell me a bit more about what she's doing these days.'

She'd made a huge mistake and been too forthright again,

several boyfriends had complained about the same negative trait in the past. It would've been wise to ease around to this much later, perhaps in a few days instead of less than two hours.

'Sure. She's working as a realtor and sold over ten million dollars' worth of real estate in the Nashville area last year. Did you know she'd gotten married for the fourth time?'

'She mentioned it in one of her Christmas cards. She's done her share of marrying for us both.'

Essy pinpointed a trace of jealousy in the quick response. 'You weren't ever tempted?'

'I didn't say that.'

Another piece to the puzzle?

'Is Brad Williams a good man?'

'Yeah, he's decent enough and adores her but—'

'She's getting bored again?' Molly's twinkling smile returned. 'Sticking with anything was never Paula's way.'

Essy chatted on about the excessive number of house moves her mother had made over the years, the redecorating she set in motion at regular intervals and the designer clothes worn a couple of times before being sent off to the consignment store. 'She's a wonderful Mom though and I love her.'

'I can tell you do. So do I. I've missed her something awful.'

Her aunt's eyes filled with tears again, sending a surge of guilt flooding through her. 'I'm sorry. I sure didn't mean to upset you.' A couple of loud bangs reminded her they weren't alone. 'You're having some work done?' It struck her as a wise move to change the subject.

'Yes, but I'm having second thoughts. I know my home is old-fashioned but it's comfortable. On the telly no one's house looks like this any longer.'

'See, you're not that different to my mom after all.' The teasing gibe made her aunt smile. 'Your decorator isn't very chatty.'

'Ruan's a good boy. I don't know all the details but he hasn't had an easy time of things recently. Or ever, to tell the truth.'

Essy clamped her lips together. She mustn't press any further. Softly, softly needed to be her new byword here in Cornwall.

'The weather's brightening up.' Molly peered across at the window. 'How about we take a wander down on the quay? I could show you around a bit and then we'll get a pasty for our lunch?'

If she admitted to already sampling the limited delights of Herring Bay she might miss the chance to get to know her aunt better and possibly discover more about her mother. 'Sure, that would be awesome.'

'I'm going to comb my hair and find a pair of shoes. Pop in and tell Ruan where we're off to.'

'You're leaving him here while we're out?'

'He's not going to steal the silver is he?' Molly chuckled and waved her hand around the cluttered room. It was crammed with a mismatch of furniture and dotted with every kind of ornament from cheap travel souvenirs to a monstrous collection of Toby jugs. 'I won't be long.'

Essy pushed open the kitchen door and gasped. 'Oh my Lord.'

'Not to your taste?' Ruan paused up a ladder with a brush in his hand. Despite the dots of navy blue paint splattering his face, his teasing smile made her stomach flip. 'And that's for the wall behind the Aga.' He pointed to a roll of dark striped paper.

'Talk about dreary. Is she gonna issue flashlights when people come in?'

'Don't let her overhear you.'

The shared conspiracy sent a jolt of heat zipping through her. 'Uh, what are those?'

'What?'

She reached down to hike up the hem of his jeans' leg. 'These.'

'Socks? Don't you have them in America?'

'I know they're socks but... paint pots and brushes?'

'You express your personality in bright clothes and red lipstick.' The colour deepened in his otherwise pale face. 'Do you have a problem with me doing the same...' he grinned '... minus the lipstick?'

'No it's just... unexpected.'

'Yes, well, a lot of people around here will say the unexpected is my thing. You'd better go.' Ruan's voice turned raspy. 'I promise I won't do a runner with Molly's valuables while you're out.'

'Do you always listen to other people's conversations?'

'Your voice isn't exactly quiet.'

'In other words I'm a mouthy American and you were curious.'

'Phrase it that way if you want.' He dipped the brush back in the paint. 'Bring me back a pasty if you're looking to make amends.'

She ignored him and stalked away but Ruan's deep, rumbling laughter followed her all the way out.

Chapter Four

'I could do with a packet of salt I'm starting to run a bit low. We'll pop in to see Jane Moody.' Molly shook her head sadly. They were standing outside the small shop Essy saw earlier. 'She's struggling to stay in business these days, poor soul. She has to order in smaller quantities, which makes her more expensive than going to the supermarkets in St Austell so most of the locals do that instead. We don't get enough summer visitors to boost her profits either and they won't come if Herring Bay doesn't buck up. It's a vicious circle.'

A bell jangled as her aunt pushed the door open. Every inch of available space was used and the narrow aisles were packed with everything from crusty loaves of bread to hair dye.

'Hello, Jane.'

The big-boned woman arranging plastic wrapped bunches of flowers in a bucket on the floor glanced up and her weary blue eyes brightened. 'Hello, Molly love. Who's this?'

'My niece Essy, Paula's girl.'

The shopkeeper's mouth gaped open. 'From America?'

If she'd said the moon the woman couldn't have sounded more shocked.

'Lovely to meet you, dear.' Essy felt herself being assessed and sensed a million questions Jane Moody would love to ask.

'I was telling her what a struggle you've got to stay in business. It's not like when we were girls, is it?'

'More's the pity. Did you hear Tommy Hicks is closing the garage? Can't make ends meet and his boy isn't interested in taking it on.'

'No.' Her aunt shook her head at Essy. 'See what I'm talking about? Now people will have to drive several miles over to Penwarren for petrol, that's the next village along this coast.'

'Do you want anything else?' Jane asked.

'Not today, love. We need to get on.' She paid and shooed

Essy back outside. 'See those old shops?' Molly pointed to two empty premises standing side by side. 'That one used to be a lovely little dress shop and next door was Dunn's the Chemist.' Molly's voice resonated with memories. 'Now we've got to go to Penwarren to get a prescription filled and down to Truro to buy any decent clothes. Wakeham's Bakery doesn't do too badly but John's older than me so I'm not sure how much longer he'll be able to keep going.'

Her aunt's love of Herring Bay ran bone deep and seeing the village through her eyes gave Essy a clearer picture of her mother's childhood. When they walked out on the quay she'd been given a local history lesson, no great surprise because her aunt's love of the subject was obvious judging by the contents of the overflowing bookcases scattered around her tiny house. In the nineteenth century Herring Bay was a thriving fishing port until the pilchard industry declined. The crabs and lobsters other Cornish fishermen relied on to make a living weren't as plentiful in these waters, which was why the harbour only contained a few pleasure boats, their colourful sails fluttering bravely in the light breeze.

'I haven't seen any school around here so where did you and Mom go?'

'There's one about halfway up Pengolva Hill, that's the road you drove down to get here. It's the primary school where the kiddies go up to age eleven. I don't know how much longer it'll stay open though if we don't get more young families living here.'

How sad was it that a community could lose its heart that way?

'We caught the bus into St Austell for secondary school.' Molly looked thoughtful. 'You'll think I'm a right old misery and Herring Bay is a dump but that's not true.' A sliver of her warm smile returned. 'Well, you can decide on the misery bit. This village might've seen better days but there's good people here... It just needs a boost that's all.' She struggled to sound positive.

Now the rain had cleared the village's charms were more in evidence but so too was the lack of amenities. Tourists and locals alike needed places to eat, shop and conduct business. A beautiful setting on its own wasn't enough.

'I don't know where that's going to come from but I wish it would hurry up.' Her aunt's laughter sounded forced. 'Let's walk back to The Smugglers' Arms. It's not great but there's nowhere else to sit down for a bite to eat since the fish and chip shop went out of business.'

Neither of them said much as they wandered along the harbour.

'Coo-ee, Molly, I need a word.'

'Bloody hell. I might've guessed,' her aunt muttered under her breath as the woman who had been waving at them started to cross the street making a beeline in their direction. 'Ruan must have rung her as soon as we left the house. Daft boy.'

'What's it got to do with him?'

'Oh, love, it's a long story.' Her aunt stopped and heaved a weary sigh. 'Ah, Vera, I haven't seen you in a while.'

Essy received her answer when the stranger joined them. The resemblance lay in the straight jet-black hair, dyed in the woman's case to disguise the grey Ruan didn't bother to hide, the hooded dark eyes and full shapely mouth. If this wasn't the Cornishman's mother she'd eat the hood on her redundant raincoat. Sue Masters had been wrong and the weatherman right for a change.

'I won't bother asking who this is.'

'I'm Essy Havers.' She plastered on a smile. 'You might remember my mother, Paula, Molly's younger sister.'

'I remember her all right.' Vera ignored Essy's outstretched hand. 'You could've warned me she were coming.'

'My aunt didn't know.' Being rendered invisible didn't suit her. 'I turned up out of the blue this morning to surprise her. I'm doing some work over here and I've always wanted to get to know my mother's side of the family so I guess you'd say I'm killing two birds with one stone.'

'You're staying?'

Another negative reaction. The lingering effects of whatever her mother had done clearly still remained in Herring Bay. If her curiosity hadn't already been stirred, it damn well was now.

'All that business is water under the bridge.' Molly stared the other woman down.

'You might think so.'

'I'm sorry but Essy is family to me and she's more than welcome here. I've heard you stick up for your Ruan enough times over the years.'

The other woman turned pale and she couldn't help wondering what that was all about.

'We're going to have a bite of lunch if you'd like to join us?' Molly's innocent tone didn't fool Essy. Underneath her aunt's amiable surface she was as steely and determined as her sister.

'No, thank you.' Vera visibly recoiled. She settled her hessian shopping bag in the crook of her elbow and marched off down the street.

'I don't know about you but I could do with a drink after that.' Her aunt tugged at the hem of her stretchy black tunic to settle it back into place and pushed open the pub door.

'Sure. Lead me to one of these pasty things.'

'It's not pronounced "paystee", dear. Didn't your mother teach you anything?' Molly shook her head. 'You're talking about the sticky things strippers stick on their boobs. We say pasty to rhyme with nasty. Not that they're nasty unless they're made by certain companies no self-respecting Cornish person would touch.' Her aunt pointed to a table near the window. 'If we sit there we'll get a nice view out over the harbour.'

Yeah, if the windows were clean you might. The dingy low-ceilinged room with its cigarette smoke stained ceiling sorely needed repainting, the scuffed furniture hadn't been polished in forever and if she was dumb enough to run her finger over the frame of any of the dreary prints decorating the walls it would doubtless come away thick with dust.

'Your usual, Molly?' A burly man with a straggly grey ponytail leaned on the bar exposing glimpses of his ample belly through the straining buttons on his checked shirt. His gimlet eyes brightened as they landed on her. 'Who've you got here then?'

'My niece Essy. She's our Paula's girl and come all the way from America to see me.'

Several people around them craned their necks to take a look at her and the general noise level abated.

'Hello, my 'andsome. Welcome to Cornwall. I'm Jackie Webb, landlord of The Smugglers' Arms.'

Being in charge of this dreary place didn't strike her as much to boast about but she struggled to appear impressed.

'We'll have two halves of Tribute and two pasties, Jackie.' Molly slapped down some money. 'Give me the change when you bring our drinks.' She made a beeline for the window. 'He's a nosy old bugger.'

'But he'll pass the word around, right?' The impertinent remark brought a flush of colour to her aunt's round cheeks. 'That's a smart move. Mama would totally approve.'

'Does she really never talk about Cornwall?'

'I wouldn't say never but not often or in any detail.' Essy softened her tone. 'Mom is a forward-looking woman who doesn't believe in looking back.'

'Are you the same way?'

'If I was would I be here now?' She toyed with one of the cardboard beer mats, stained with dirty rings left by too many wet glasses. 'I believe the past shapes us and want to understand Mom better… and myself.'

'Here we go, ladies.' Jackie Webb set down two brimming glasses and pushed a few coins across to Molly. 'Pasties will be a few minutes.'

When he shuffled off again her aunt sniggered. 'In other

words he's sent Ruby, his poor wife, over to Wakeham's Bakery because they've run out. Typical.'

Essy wasn't sure which surprised her the most, the fact the disagreeable man had talked some gullible woman into marrying him or that he managed to stay in business at all. If he ever got any competition The Smugglers' Arms would be toast.

'Cheers, and welcome to Cornwall.' Molly raised her glass and a broad smile lit up her face making Essy glad she'd braved her mother's displeasure.

Ruan pressed so hard it was a miracle the paint roller didn't go right through the wall. He should never have rung his mother. Of course she would have found out the news eventually but he should've tried to delay the inevitable for all their sakes.

The sound of the front door opening broke through his thoughts.

'Here you go, my 'andsome,' Molly said as she bustled into the kitchen waving a paper bag in his face. The delicious aroma of warm pasty conquered the smell of fresh paint. 'My girl told me you'd be hungry so I brought it on back with me because she wanted to walk around a bit longer.' Her eyes widened as she glanced around. 'Oh Lord, it's very—'

'Dark?'

'Yes.' She slumped down on the nearest chair and groaned. 'They said on the telly that navy blue will be *the* in colour next year. I wear it a lot but...'

Architects got used to questioning their clients' intentions a certain way. 'It can be difficult to visualise these things and there's no harm in changing your mind. Weigh up the cost of a new pot of paint against cringing every time you come in your kitchen.' Ruan trod carefully with his next suggestion. 'Grey is still a very popular neutral so you might consider pale grey walls with white trim. You could still use navy as your accent colour. Paint over your wood chairs and cover the seats in blue and white striped sailcloth. Introduce a pop of navy in a new canister set on the counter and a roller blind for the window.'

She stared at him as though he'd morphed into an alien from another planet and he could kick himself for forgetting this was Cornwall not London. As a boy his artistic interests were looked on with suspicion and even his continuous string of girlfriends never totally quieted down the rumours about his sexuality.

'How about *I* make *you* a cup of tea for a change and we can talk about it?'

He took his time making the drinks and once they were settled at the table quickly sunk his teeth into the pasty and chewed slowly. It gave him a breathing space to mull over whether to mention the enormous elephant dumping its load in the corner of the room.

'We met Vera outside the pub.'

Ruan felt his cheeks burn.

'What in heaven's name am I going to say to Essy?'

'Did Mum tell her anything?'

'No, but she wouldn't speak to her and made it clear that she's got a long memory. Poor girl must be puzzled.'

'Maybe it'll blow over.' Why didn't Essy Havers stay in Tennessee where she belonged? he thought. She'd only arrived in Herring Bay this morning and already upset the person he cared about most in the whole world and stirred *him* up in other ways, ones he couldn't handle right now.

'Don't be daft,' Molly scoffed. 'I've only known the girl a few hours but anyone can see she won't rest until she digs it all out.' She managed a faint smile. 'When she told me about her job it made me even more certain.'

They hadn't got as far as any career-swapping talk because it wasn't a conversation he wanted to initiate.

'She owns a business called Eureka! that specialises in finding things for clients. Usually it's things like a missing piece from a set of china but I expect it could apply to long lost people as well.'

The words dangled in the air between them.

'Why don't you go on home and see what your mum's got to say? She weren't too pleased.'

'What about all this?' He gestured at the half-painted walls.

'Let's change them to what you suggested. Buy whatever you need but don't come back until next week. Let things settle down some.'

'You're the boss.' Ruan tossed his empty pasty bag in the bin and rinsed out his mug in the sink. 'It'll work out. Things usually do.' In his experience that wasn't always true but he was struggling against his natural instinct to sound optimistic.

'I hope you're right.'

'I'll be off.' Being at a loose end for a few days didn't suit him. Out of sight wouldn't be out of mind where Essy Havers was concerned.

Chapter Five

If Essy was of a suspicious turn of mind she might believe certain people were avoiding her. Her intuition was the main reason for the success of Eureka! and she'd learned to pay attention to it, like a racing driver to the sound of the car's engine.

Her unusual career path started when a friend was desperate to track down a replica of her husband's much-loved but disintegrating high school letter jacket. When Essy blithely asserted that it couldn't be that difficult Suzanne challenged her to prove it. After hours of trawling the internet and multiple phone calls to perfect strangers she hit gold and stumbled across an alumni group with a swap shop for old school memorabilia. It gave her a massive thrill to see Pete's face when he opened the box wrapped in dark green and silver, his old school colours, and she then horrified her mother by stuffing her maths degree in a metaphorical drawer and using every dollar of her pitiful savings to start her business.

Ever since their run-in with Ruan's mother several days ago she had been pretty much on her own.

'I'm afraid you'll have to amuse yourself. I'm behind with my work and need to get caught up.'

Molly's excuse could be genuine because her aunt did provide bookkeeping and admin services for several local small businesses remotely from her home and hadn't done anything since Essy arrived. The suspicion still lurked, though, that it was partly an excuse to avoid any questions about Vera Pascow and her apparent dislike of the Barnecutt family.

The mysterious Ruan hadn't returned to work on the kitchen either and she doubted her aunt's change of mind over the paint colour was the sole reason. Incredibly she had strolled around Herring Bay multiple times without ever seeing him or his mother, something she would've thought close to impossible.

They would all find out how patient she could be. The plan

for today was to visit Fistral Beach at Newquay on the north coast. An elderly lady in Memphis had hired her to pull together a surprise for her husband's ninetieth birthday. Gordon Snell was a dyed-in-the-wool ex-pat Cornishman whose health prevented him from travelling any longer but he frequently reminisced about the beaches he loved as a small boy. Essy's task was to collect a vial of sand and take pictures at each of his six favourite beaches. When she returned to Tennessee they would be matched up with family pictures from his old albums in a suitable frame.

She debated taking Annabelle but lost her nerve and left the car parked outside her aunt's house. If she was too much of a coward to drive again she should save her money and return the rental but admitting defeat wasn't her way. For today's outing Essy joined the half a dozen or so people waiting at the bus stop outside the convenience shop.

I often wonder how Paula's doing. Sue Master's words popped into her head, probably because her mother was never far from her thoughts these days. If she could track the woman down again she could kill two birds with one stone. First Essy would apologise for lying on the first day they met and hopefully that might pave the way to discover if her mother's old friend was willing to share why Paula left Herring Bay.

A small green bus rumbled down the road towards them and she made a swift decision to step away from the queue. Fistral could wait.

Ten minutes later she wiped beads of sweat off her face and stopped halfway up Pengolva Hill to catch her breath. It hadn't struck her as this steep when she drove down it on Monday morning but of course the words 'drove' and 'down' were massive clues.

She leaned on the old stone wall and ran her fingers over the rough granite while she stared out to sea. Silver tipped waves shimmered in the sunshine and the occasional puff of white cloud enhanced the deep azure blue sky. The light breeze blowing around her face and trying to whip her hair out of its loose ponytail brought with it a hint of salt and faraway places hiding over the horizon. People couldn't live by stunning views alone but it helped to make up for other deficiencies. The conversation she'd had with her aunt nagged at her brain. This area needed something to bring it back to life, but sympathetically, and therein lay the conundrum.

The area needs bringing back to life or you do?

Essy mentally shook herself. She was here for two specific purposes and debating the ins and outs of her own life back in Tennessee wasn't one of them. She hoisted her bag back on her shoulder and trudged off up the hill again. At the top she stared up and down the street and prepared to discover how good a 'finder' she really was. For all she knew Sue Masters lived several miles away and was simply walking through that day with her dog.

'You haven't lost Herring Bay again today, have you?'

'Wow, I don't believe it. Are you psychic?' The woman she was looking for materialised out of nowhere, again being nearly tugged off her feet by a rambunctious brown and white spaniel. 'I was hoping to track you down.'

'Why?'

Face to face she was uncertain how or where to begin. Their first meeting started with a lie, not a good basis for inspiring confidences. Maybe this was a ridiculous idea. 'Is there somewhere we could go for a coffee... or whatever?'

'A café? Up here?'

Cornwall was supposed to be a mecca for tourists and they always needed places to eat and drink so was it really that bizarre a question?

'What about a bench to sit on then? Somewhere to chat for a few minutes... sort of private.'

'I suppose we could go to my place.' Sue sounded dubious. 'It's over there.' She pointed to a neat white bungalow a few metres across the road from where they stood.

'Thanks, that would be great but had you finished your walk?' Essy crouched down and patted the dog on the head. The friendly animal licked her hand, jumped up and down and wagged its tail. She hoped its acceptance of her would reassure Sue because dogs were notoriously good judges of people.

'Don't worry about that. We had our long walk first thing this morning, this was a quick one. Bongo has a lot of energy, don't you, boy?' Sue ruffled the dog's fur. 'Come on.'

'You sure do have a pretty yard.' Essy admired the neat flower beds lining the narrow path. 'Your azaleas are amazing. We grow a lot of those in the south but ours flowered much earlier and they're over and done with by now.'

'You're a gardener?'

'I plan to be one day when I'm not living in an apartment with barely room for a few pots on my balcony.'

'I'll stick the kettle on.'

Essy copied her new acquaintance and kicked her shoes off outside the back door.

'Do you prefer tea or coffee? Nothing fancy. It'll only be dunking a tea bag in a mug or pouring boiling water over a spoonful of instant coffee.'

'Coffee with a splash of milk or cream would be great. I tried a mug of y'all's tea but I wasn't keen.' The butterflies in her stomach flapped like mad things. 'I've got a confession to make.' Sue stopped in the middle of taking a jug of milk from the fridge. 'When you mentioned an old friend of yours who moved to Tennessee there's something I should've told you... Paula is my mother.'

Sue Masters stared as if Essy had grown two heads.

'Paula Barnecutt is your mum?'

'She sure is, although she's Paula Williams now.' Essy quickly ran through the whys and wherefores of how she ended up in Herring Bay. 'I know there's got to be a bigger reason why she left other than wanting to see the world. She never came back and never brought me here. Why?'

'This shouldn't come from me.' A deep frown creased Sue's forehead. 'Your family need to tell you.'

'They all shut up tighter than clams when I raise the subject.' Her exasperation burst out. 'Please. Give me something at least.'

'All right. Sit down and let's have our coffee.' Sue set two mugs on the table. 'Try a Cornish gingerbread.' She dumped several dark, hard biscuits with large cracks all over the tops of them on a plate.

They didn't look very appealing but Essy obediently picked one up and bit into it. 'Wow they're really good.' Crunchy, spicy and different than anything she'd tried before this could become her new favourite thing.

'Don't sound so surprised. Cornwall has a lot of great food. We're not just pasties and clotted cream.' Sue toyed with a biscuit herself then let out a weary sigh. 'Vera Pascow, your aunt Molly and I were all born here within a few months of each other. We played together as little girls, went to the village school and then on to the secondary school in St Austell. Vera and I both got married before our twentieth birthdays and had babies right away.' She studied Essy. 'You're ever so much like Paula I should've seen it. You need to remember your mum was a lot younger than us, about eight years I reckon, so I really didn't know her that well, but she was pretty and ever so lively. Molly told us Paula drove them all around the bend because she went on and on about wanting to leave Herring Bay and see the world. Caused a lot of trouble at home it did.'

'People leave where they grow up all the time and they go back for visits and so on, but that didn't happen. Did Mom get into some sort of trouble?'

'You could say that.'

'Was she into drugs? Drink? Boy trouble?'

'There was a boy involved... a man really.' The words sounded as though they were being dragged from her with a pair of pliers.

'A married man?'

'Yes.' Sue's face closed down. 'I'm stopping there. I've said more than enough already.'

At least it was a start. Now she had something concrete to challenge her aunt with when the timing was right.

Did fresh paint count as a commitment to stay? His mother thought so, judging by her contented smile when Ruan started to redecorate his old bedroom. He would argue that it was simply an effort not to be wasteful because he couldn't return the paint he'd bought for Molly to the DIY shop. If he added the perfect amount of white that should tone it down to the muted shades of the brooding sea on a late December day. Before he tackled the walls his first step was to rip up the purple shag carpet, unbelievable that his mum ever allowed him to cover up the beautiful old floorboards. Another thing to go would be the colourful space mural he'd painted one day when Vera was out shopping. The final methodical painting should allow time for his mind to drift away from everything else.

'Everything else' covered a multitude of things. Essy with the lush red mouth, smart remarks and a mother whose decades' old feud with his own family still festered. The looming question of his future. It wouldn't be difficult to find a job with another architects' firm but could he honestly stand the idea of designing more soulless buildings? Ruan wasn't at all certain. His bank balance was the only healthy thing to emerge from his decade in London but at least that gave him a breathing space. He could spend the money on renting a place of his own in Herring Bay but better to hang onto it for when he made a decision on his future. For now he looked on staying here with his mum as the chance to make up to her in a small way for twenty years of infrequent visits.

He prised a lid off a pot of paint and picked up a brush.

'You were a clever lad to paint that space thing.'

'That's not what you said at the time.' He grinned over his shoulder at Vera. 'I was grounded for a month.'

'I might've been a bit harsh.'

'You were raising me alone. If you'd been too soft I would've run rings around you.'

'And you think you didn't?'

'Do you still want company tonight?' His offer surprised her.

'At the bingo?'

'Yes, I won't be playing but I'll come with you for a drink.'

'That would be nice.' A deep frown settled between her eyes. 'She won't be there, will she?'

Ruan didn't need to ask who she meant. 'I wouldn't think so but I haven't seen Essy since Monday, so who knows? We're not hiding out here any longer.' He had gone along with his mother's request to lay low for a few days but was tired of it now. 'I should get cracking.' He made a dramatic swoop of paint across the mural. 'Good thing Michelangelo's mother didn't make him obliterate the Sistine Chapel ceiling.'

'She probably would have done if he practised in his bedroom first.' Vera laughed as she walked away and he returned to work.

Several hours later he glanced around the room, satisfied with the transformation. Time to get out of his painting clothes and cleaned up.

Showered and changed, Ruan slipped on a new pair of tan leather slide sandals before running downstairs.

'You're looking... smart.'

Vera must have given thanks multiple times for school uniforms because even he couldn't alter them drastically without getting into trouble. As a teenager he discovered that it polarised his peers' reactions to him when he strayed from the standard out-of-school uniform of T-shirts and jeans. The girls in particular were either fascinated or laughed at his flamboyant clothes choices. Luckily there were more than enough of the intrigued variety to keep him happy.

'Let's see if you can win our fortune.'

His mother scoffed. 'You know how mean Jackie Webb is. I

expect the star prize will be an out-of-date box of biscuits from the Poundshop.'

They strolled down to the harbour and as he pushed open the pub door Ruan caught a hint of Essy's distinctive husky drawl and spotted her propped on a stool at the bar. The slinky white top and miniscule yellow flared skirt showed off her shapely figure and the gold gladiator sandals did the same favour to her bare tanned legs. Her surprised gaze rested on him. Fascinated or amused? He couldn't quite nail her reaction and hated himself for wanting her approval. The only thing he should want from Essy Havers was for her to leave Cornwall as soon as possible.

Chapter Six

Through the soft edges of her second lemon gin cocktail Essy caught sight of Ruan and almost toppled off the bar stool. The quirky socks she caught him wearing a few days ago should've been a clue but tonight was another story. Slim-fitting bright orange trousers and a white shirt rolled up to the elbows topped off with a dark plum silk waistcoat embroidered with gold flowers. Not regular Herring Bay attire from what she'd seen so far.

Vera Pascow treated her to a long, cold stare before she joined a group of loud, giggly women gathered around a large table in the centre of the room.

'Oh, hi.'

Ruan squeezed in between her and the toothless old man perched next to her who hadn't shifted since Essy arrived.

'You'll die of thirst waiting to be served. The landlord would lose a race with an arthritic turtle. Although he won't find it easy to overlook you.' She touched his bare forearm. 'I never had you marked down as ordinary. This suits you.'

'Careful. Was that a compliment?' His voice turned to gravel.

'Take it as you like.'

'You don't shy away from bold clothes choices either.'

'A compliment?'

'Definitely.'

She fidgeted under his searching dark eyes.

'Do you want to join me? A chair might be safer,' he asked.

'I don't want to piss off your mom again. I'm fine.' She tossed her head and almost wobbled off the stool. Ruan made a grab for her right thigh to hold her steady and his tight grip sent a bolt of knee-trembling desire scorching through her body.

'I'm not so sure about that.'

'Why thank you, my saviour.' She flailed a hand in his direction. 'Help me down and we'll shock the natives together.'

'You're offering to be my partner-in-crime?' A rich thread of amusement ran through his gruff voice. 'Beware. Most who know me are either lovers or haters. Very few are indifferent.'

'I've never been a fan of wishy-washy.'

His warning expression morphed into a broad smile and kicked her attraction for him up a few more notches.

'Off you come.' Ruan snaked his arm around her waist and hoisted her off the stool. Out of the corner of her eye she caught the measure of Vera's annoyance when he didn't loosen his hold on her until they reached an unoccupied table.

'You never did manage to buy a drink and I left mine up there.'

'That can wait.'

'What for?'

He touched a finger to her chin, lifting it so Essy met his challenging gaze head on before his hand dropped away again. 'That will give them something new to gossip about.'

'Apart from my mom and the… trouble she caused.'

'You know?' He turned pale. 'Who told you?'

'Sue Masters.'

'Let's get out of here.' Ruan grabbed Essy's hand and hustled her out through the crowded pub. 'We'll walk out on the quay.'

'Okay.' She wasn't sure why he was so obviously rattled but finding out things was her speciality, he was up against an expert.

Ruan noticed her shiver. Summer evenings here often brought with them a cool breeze in off the sea, welcome after a hot day but unexpected if you weren't used to it. 'Sorry I don't have a jacket to offer you.'

'Your warm arm would do the trick.'

Terrible idea. The thought crystallised as he slipped his arm around her shoulders. There it was again. Her distinctive scent teased his nostrils. In an instant his body betrayed him as she pressed against his side.

'Let's sit over here.' Ruan whipped off his waistcoat and smoothed it over a granite bench built into the sea wall. 'I'll be your Sir Walter Raleigh tonight.' She looked puzzled. 'I'm taking a guess we had very different history lessons in school. Raleigh was a famous explorer and close to Queen Elizabeth the first, some say very close. He was rumoured to have spread out his cloak one day to prevent her stepping into a puddle.'

'Well, the backs of my cold legs are extremely grateful.'

Talking about her legs didn't help his discomfort one bit. He tried looking away from her and stared into the star-scattered sky.

You never had anything like that up-country, now did you? he remembered Mr Hawkey's comment.

'What's Tennessee like?' His question clearly surprised her.

'Beautiful, in a totally different way from here. We're nowhere near any coastline but we still get stunning clear skies up in the mountains. If you choose the right spot there's nothing for miles around. Zero light pollution.' Essy's warm laughter seeped into him. 'I'm not talkin' about downtown Nashville. That's full-on neon and loud music every day of the year.'

'How do you stand it?'

'I don't.' She brushed a lock of hair away from her face. 'I live in Franklin, it's a quaint small town about twenty miles south of the city. I enjoy the occasional night out in Nashville with friends but that's enough for me. I guess it's like you goin' to London sometimes?'

'Yes.' His short, snappy answer earned him a quizzical look.

'It's been a long day.' Essy sounded thoughtful and he waited for the pertinent questions to start. She wasn't the sort of woman to hold back. 'How about we leave the rest of it for another time?'

'Suits me.' Ruan struggled to hide his relief. 'I'll walk you back to Molly's if you're ready.'

'What about your mom?'

'I'll meet her again in the pub afterwards.'

Essy's smile turned mischievous. 'To face the music?'

'I'm thirty-eight, I don't have to explain myself to her or anyone.'

'Come off it. We both know that's not true. I'm a few years younger than you but if it's any consolation I'm no better with my mom.' She jumped back up and held out his waistcoat. 'Here you go or I'll be unjustly accused of making you strip off.' The darkness must not have hidden his smile because she giggled like a little girl. 'Behave yourself.'

Sue Masters can't have told Essy the whole truth or she wouldn't be speaking to him still. Eventually she would discover the unsavoury connection between them and then the axe would fall.

Essy's tired eyes felt full of grit. All night she ping-ponged back and forth in her head whether a brief fling with Ruan was a crazy bad idea? The last few years had been something of a desert where Essy and men were concerned but perhaps he could be her oasis? Sort of a brief stop before she refocused on the road ahead. Ever since her first crush as a shy fifteen-year-old on Dwayne Parks in her high school biology class she had learned to be wary. Essy refused to follow her mother's example of running down the aisle with every man she believed herself in love with. If she made vows of life-long fidelity to a man she planned to mean it and be damn sure he did the same in return. She guessed that made her unrealistic. When she was in a rational frame of mind she understood that no one could be one hundred per cent certain.

'I'm cooking breakfast if you fancy some,' Molly yelled up the stairs. The announcement was hardly a surprise because she'd been sniffing the heavenly aroma of bacon cooking for the last few minutes.

'Sure, that would be great. I won't be long.' She rubbed at her gin-induced headache, dragged herself out of bed and trotted along the narrow landing to the bathroom. The heating was turned off for the summer and the early morning chill in the air made her shiver. That brought back memories of last night on the quay with Ruan. Now she was grateful for the cold room. Essy smoothed down her hair but it was futile to imagine her fingers would have any effect on the tangled mess hanging like limp strands of spaghetti around her shoulders. She decided to abandon the effort and try for a major overhaul after breakfast.

'Didn't you sleep well?' Molly turned around from the sizzling frying pan where she was poking rashers of bacon around with a fork.

The bags under her eyes must be dangling all the way down to her chin. A giveaway sign. 'You could say that. Do you have anything planned for today, only I've got to go to Newquay and I thought we could maybe go together?' She rattled off a quick explanation about her sand collecting mission. Essy didn't mention her plan to pump Molly about the mystery man her mother was involved with who was the cause of her leaving Herring Bay all those years ago. Sue Masters had refused to divulge his name but surely she could get her aunt to cough up the information?

'That's a funny thing to want but I suppose I can understand the poor old chap.' Molly shook her head. 'If you're Cornish born and bred it's in your bones. Unless we're talking about your mum.'

She ignored the sly jibe and fixed a smile in place. 'So are you up for a road trip? Or in our case it'll be a bus trip because I'm not drivin' again anytime soon. The journey down from London freaked me out.'

'I don't blame you, lovey. I was only going to clean around the house a bit and that can wait. It'll make a nice change to go out. I'll pack a picnic.'

'There's no need I'll treat us to lunch out somewhere.'

'Don't be daft. Save your money you'll need it one day.

39

Paula always frittered her pocket money away on rubbishy stuff. Cheap clothes that fell apart after she wore them a couple of times. Gaudy jewellery. And make-up.' Molly's mouth twitched. 'The make-up that girl had was nobody's business. Our dad would try his best to make sure she didn't have too much on before she went out the door. Of course she got the measure of him and learned to sneak away when he went in the bathroom.'

'I'd love to know more about my grandparents. How about you start by telling me their names?'

'You don't know?' Her aunt couldn't have looked more horrified if she admitted to being a cannibal. 'I'll get our breakfast on the plates then tell you everything you want to know.'

Essy doubted that very much but anything would be a start. Baby steps. If nothing else this visit to Cornwall should teach her patience.

Chapter Seven

The smell of fresh paint lingered as Ruan stretched out, rested his hands behind his head and admired the shafts of early morning sun filtering in through the new curtains. He'd replaced the star-spangled ones, now stuffed in his mum's charity donation box, with simple lengths of gauzy material draped over the existing wood rail. The walls were a deeper shade of blue this morning but when the light changed so would they. That satisfied him no end.

'Tea?' His mum poked her head in around the door and held out a steaming mug.

'Thanks.'

'I'm getting the half past nine bus into town then catching the connecting one on to Newquay. I haven't seen Uncle Dick in forever and he sounded a bit down last time we spoke. A couple of fresh saffron buns should cheer him up.'

Ruan wasn't convinced of the mood lifting powers of saffron but kept that to himself.

'Why don't you come with me?'

'Me?'

'What else are you going to do? Mope around here?'

He considered arguing but mentally flipped a coin and it landed on the side of being agreeable. Last night she'd been irked when he refused to discuss Essy with her on his return to the pub.

'Fine, I'll come. I'll drive us if you like?'

'I'd as soon go on the bus. Makes it a bit more of an outing.'

Without thinking Ruan swung his legs out over the bed and a rush of colour shot up his mother's neck. She tutted under her breath and bustled off back downstairs. To her sleeping in the nude was a nasty habit he'd picked up in London.

He made, at least for him, relatively conservative clothes choices because his uncle was old-fashioned and he didn't want to aggravate his mother again. Ruan slipped on slim dark jeans, a plain navy T-shirt and three-quarter sleeve bright orange linen jacket. From a young age he loved colour and never understood why grown-ups, especially men, dressed in such a dull way. Occasionally these days he wondered if one element of his fashion choices came from an urge to stick one to all the people who made fun of his artistic leanings growing up.

'All set?' Before he set foot in the kitchen he could've predicted what his mother would be wearing; her summertime uniform of a calf-length patterned cotton skirt, pastel T-shirt, flat sandals and a coordinating cardigan. Today's outfit was in varying shades of blue but she had them in different colours for every day of the week.

'If we see Dick today that'll be it then for the summer.' Vera shook her head. 'Soon enough the kids will be out of school and the buses will be full and the roads a nightmare.' She had the same love-hate relationship with the tourists as most native Cornish people. A lingering resentment that they needed them to survive economically mixed with pride that so many people appreciated their beautiful county.

They strolled down towards the harbour and his mother's steps slowed when they reached the abandoned Methodist Chapel. Rubbish was piled up in the alley to one side of the elegant old building and he noticed one of the beautiful stained glass windows had been broken by vandals and boarded over.

'When I was young we went every week. Mother and Father never let us miss. I took you to Sunday school when you were a boy too.'

He heard the wistfulness in her voice. 'I remember. Didn't Jackie Webb buy it years ago?'

'Yes, but only to stop anyone else snatching it up. It's wicked he's allowed to leave it idle this way.'

A raft of ideas ran through his architect's brain. A community centre. Perhaps a café. A theatre. It could become the centre of the village again with the right person at the helm. Ruan saw her face brighten and realised too late he'd been speculating out loud. 'Not me. Don't get any ideas.'

'Why not?'

How many reasons would you like? 'We'll miss the bus.' He strode off and as they rounded the corner into Cannery Street his mother sucked in a loud breath.

'I don't believe it.'

'We're not turning around and going back home.' Ruan grabbed her elbow. Molly and Essy wouldn't be any happier when they spotted them. 'It's a public bus there were bound to be other passengers.' Now she probably wished she'd accepted his offer to drive.

'Didn't have to be them though, did it?'

The bus rumbled along the cobbles and hissed to a stop in front of him. They stood aside for the people who had been waiting longest to get on first.

'Fancy seein' you here.' Essy's low smooth drawl had its usual effect on him and the heat rose in his face. 'Are you off to experience the delights of St Austell or going on to Newquay with us?'

'Newquay to visit my uncle.'

'Come on, lovey, I don't want to be stuck at the back of the bus,' Molly chided. The fleeting smile she threw in his direction was better than the silent glare his mother tossed at Essy. 'Always makes me proper queasy. I never have been a good traveller.'

'Are you still that way?' Vera asked. 'I remember you'd be white as a sheet by the time we got home from school.'

The two women smiled as the shared memory briefly brought them together and Ruan found it a challenge to hide his disappointment when it was their turn to get on.

Essy joined her aunt on the first row and sneaked another glance at Ruan as he followed his mother down the aisle. She admired the juxtaposition of his undeniable masculinity with his flamboyant side but it didn't take a genius to guess he'd taken a fair amount of stick from people here when he was younger. No wonder he'd chosen to live and work in London but why had he suddenly moved back? That was the million-dollar question.

'Here you go, ladies and gents.'

The driver's cheery announcement came as the bus shuddered to a halt and she followed her aunt across to claim a couple of seats on the other bus. They had left Herring Bay in brilliant sunshine but it soon clouded over and by the time they navigated what seemed like endless miles of narrow, winding lanes and pulled into the Newquay Bus Station it was grey and miserable. Heavy drizzle in Sue Masters' book. Persistent rain to most other folks.

'It's some pity about the weather. Won't be much for your picture taking.' Molly made a dash for the covered shelter and rummaged in her hessian shopping bag. 'Here you go.' She shoved one of the thin bright yellow plastic raincoats she'd insisted on bringing at Essy.

For once she put aside her reservations about how fashionable she would, or rather wouldn't, look and dragged it on.

'This is typical of Cornwall. One coast is often the complete opposite of the other. We should've checked the forecast.'

It took about twenty minutes to slog the half mile or so through the town and make their way to Fistral Beach. The long sandy beach was almost deserted. No surprise there.

'Gordon Snell's wife told me he used to surf here,' Essy said.

'I used to have a go myself when I were a girl.'

'Really? Did Mum?'

'No.' Molly laughed. 'She weren't much for anything that messed up her hair or make-up. The surfers interested her though so she'd go along with her friends to sunbathe and flirt.'

'That figures.' All of these snippets of information helped fill in the picture she was forming in her head.

'They hold a lot of competitions here that attract the top surfers.' Molly pointed to the north end of the beach. 'Out there's the Cribbar. It's a reef and when the swell is high it makes the waves break sometimes up to thirty feet. It's a rare old sight to see.'

'But not today.'

'No, my 'andsome.' Her aunt shivered and tightened her raincoat around her. 'Why don't you get your bits and pieces done and we'll be off?'

Essy wasted no time collecting her sand and managed to take a few pictures, with some editing they should be useable. 'What's that place?' A massive, red-brick building overlooked the beach.

'That's the Headland Hotel. Proper posh it is.'

They couldn't eat their lunch on the beach and she didn't fancy picnicking at the bus station. 'Why don't we pop in there for a spot of lunch and eat our sandwiches at home later? It'll give us a chance to dry off for a while.'

'We're not dressed smart enough for that place.'

'Who cares? I feel bad for dragging you out in this. Maybe the rain will ease off before it's time to get the bus back.'

'I suppose we can but don't say I didn't warn you.'

They sneaked into the fancy loos first for a quick tidy up and then Essy slathered on her southern charm to secure them a table in the empty Terrace Restaurant. Any dress code the hotel had could clearly be ignored when they were desperate for business. She tried not to smile when her frugal aunt blanched at the menu prices. They both settled on the thick vegetable soup, which came with crusty bread and also asked for a bowl of chips to share. Essy discovered the thick, golden sticks of lusciousness were a world away from the French fries she was used to and almost ordered another bowl.

'The Pascows were off to see Ruan's uncle, do you know him?' The idle question took her aunt by surprise and a rush of colour bloomed in Molly's cheeks.

'Oh yes, I know Dick Menear.' Her trembling fingers fiddled with the white linen napkin turning it into a tight ball. 'Haven't seen him for years though.'

Wouldn't it be curious if he was the man who almost tempted her aunt into marriage? And if so what prevented it from happening? Her natural inquisitiveness ran rampant but one look at her aunt's closed expression made her realise that the subject was a no-go.

The rain drummed a relentless beat on the massive windows stretching from the sumptuously carpeted floor to the ornate plaster ceiling. In good weather she guessed there would be a stunning view out over the beach, a prime spot from which to watch the surfers. Right now there could be a car park out there and no one would be any the wiser.

'If we get our skates on we might catch the twenty to two bus and be home by four o'clock.' Molly broke her silence. 'There's no point hanging around in this weather. You'll have to come again on a nicer day.'

'Okay.' Essy reluctantly slipped the cold, clammy raincoat back on. At least she'd ticked the first beach off Gordon Snell's birthday list.

Her heart did a disappointed swoop towards her toes when there was no sight of Ruan and Vera at the bus station. Neither of them spoke much on the way home and almost as soon as they walked in the door Molly announced her intention of taking a nap. That left Essy to her thoughts. Thoughts she shouldn't be having.

'I'm off out for a walk.' Ruan pushed away the remains of his beans on toast and jumped up.

'In this weather? Didn't you get wet enough in Newquay?'

If he stayed he would be tempted to ask his mother about things she didn't want to discuss. Like his uncle for one. Vera had brushed off his concern and made little of the obvious downturn in Dick's health.

'It's at least ten years since you've been to see him and he's aged like everyone else,' she had told him. 'He's there on his own by choice. Last winter I asked him to move in here with me but he bit my head off. Said he'd had his fill of Herring Bay and didn't even plan to come back in a box when his time came.'

When they were with his uncle, Ruan happened to mention that they travelled to Newquay on the bus with Molly and Essy. That made Dick's jaw tighten and he dug his bony hands into the arms of the chair. His mother swiftly put an end to that conversation by chattering on about the terrible price of meat. The whole exchange puzzled him.

'I need some fresh air.'

'You'll be blown off the quay if you aren't careful. No one would think it's June. If it doesn't improve soon it'll be a miserable summer for the visitors.'

'I won't be long.' He wriggled on his red rubber boots and slipped on a matching waterproof coat. Ruan yanked up the hood before he stepped outside and reached the harbour without meeting anyone.

'Should've guessed you wouldn't own any boring rain clothes, Little Red Riding Hood.' Essy's lilting voice came out of nowhere.

'Snap. I like the hat.' He touched its white wide brim, unable to help smiling at the scarlet strawberries dotting the whole thing. The teasing scent of Essy's evocative perfume drifted through the rain and he suppressed a groan when she ran her tongue across her glossy red mouth. Ruan forced himself to step away. 'You didn't get wet enough in Newquay either? Did you just go there for a look around?'

'It was work really.'

'For your finding things business?' He felt his cheeks heat. 'Molly mentioned it.'

'Sand.'

'Sand?'

'Yeah, that's what I was looking for and, before you bother with any smart-ass remarks, I know Cornwall's got plenty of the stuff layin' around.' Essy's eyes sparkled and she launched into a quirky story about putting together an unusual birthday present for an ex-pat Cornishman.

'Do you do many overseas assignments?'

'No this is my first but... I was curious to come here and discover more about my mom's family.' A shadow flitted across her face. 'How was your uncle?'

The sudden about turn in the conversation surprised him because he'd expected a slew of probing questions relating to her chat with Sue Masters. 'Older. Grumpy.' Ruan almost mentioned Dick's odd reaction when her aunt's name came up but something held him back.

'What do you do when you're not ruining people's perfectly good kitchens?'

'Hey, that's not my fault. Blame your aunt,' he protested. 'What makes you think that's not my regular job anyway?' It was hardly a secret so he didn't understand his reluctance to tell her at least the partial truth.

'I don't see why it's such a big deal but you can forget it... for now.'

Ruan felt like a criminal given a stay of execution. 'Will you come out with me tomorrow evening?'

'I guess I could.'

'Will it work if I pick you up at seven?'

'No.' Essy sounded fierce. 'No way. We'll meet somewhere otherwise Molly will stick her nose into something that's none of her business.'

It reinforced his nagging certainty that she wasn't aware of the family troubles between them. Sue Masters must have been careful what she said.

'I'll be outside The Smugglers' at seven but for heaven's sake don't plan to spend the evening there. Too many ears and eyes. Pick somewhere quiet so we can eat first, then talk.' Her smile had a forced edge to it. 'Otherwise you'll ruin our appetites.'

'Fair enough.' Ruan nodded. They slogged back together in silence before going their separate ways. He wasn't looking forward to their next conversation.

Chapter Eight

If she didn't fill the day Essy would go stir crazy. Yesterday's bad weather had abated leaving behind a washed out baby blue sky. Perfect for another beach outing.

'I'm heading down to St Ives and Porthmeor Beach, Aunt Molly. Would you like to come along for the ride? I've decided not to be a wimp and take Annabelle.' She laughed at her aunt's puzzled expression. 'That's my cute car.' The explanation for her rental car's nickname made Molly chuckle.

'No thanks, dear. I've only now dried out from our trip to Newquay and I've an account to finish up before tomorrow. Do you want me to make you a sandwich?'

'No, thanks, I'll get something while I'm out and I promise I'll be careful if I decide to buy a pasty.'

'You'm making fun of me?'

'Not at all.' Essy couldn't help grinning. 'I'd better hurry and be off.'

The journey looked to be straightforward enough, if Annabelle behaved. She planned to take the most straightforward route and get on what should be a fairly major road the other side of St Austell. From there it should be pretty much a straight shot to St Ives and the Park and Ride service above the town. She could leave the car and ride a bus down into the town, avoiding the problem of finding somewhere to park. Porthmeor Beach was only a short walk from the centre of town and the beach was next to the famous Tate Gallery, which she didn't intend to miss.

'Do you fancy a bit of crab salad for your tea?' Molly offered.

She'd been debating when to break the news about her date tonight but now there wasn't any choice and a deep frown creased her aunt's face.

'You're having dinner with Ruan? You'm a silly girl.'

'Why? I thought you liked him?'

'That's nothing to do with it.'

'No one will tell me what the beef is between our families but it's nothing to do with Ruan and me so you'll have to get over it.'

'Get over it?' Molly's voice rose. 'Our Paula wrecked Vera's marriage and then ran off to America. Tree Pascow disappeared a few days after and no one's heard from him since. Put two and two together, Essy.'

A wave of nausea swept through her and she clapped her hand over her mouth. 'My mother and Ruan's father had an affair?' Sue Masters' reluctance to name names made sense now. 'When were you going to tell me?' Essy asked Aunt Molly.

'I'm some sorry. I didn't know what to do for the best and anyway it might not be true.' Her aunt hesitated. 'When I tackled Paula back in the day she denied anything was going on between them. She said they were simply good friends and we were all narrow-minded people who didn't see further than the end of our own noses.'

'You didn't believe her?'

'Not really and neither did anyone else.' Her aunt sounded weary. 'Tree had a bit of a reputation with women. They all liked him see and he returned the favour. It peeved Vera that he didn't do anything to discourage it after they got married and they were always arguing.'

'Tree? That's an odd name.'

'His full name was Tremayne but it got shortened when he was little.' A faint smile lightened Molly's face. 'Of course he grew up to be a gardener so it fitted him.'

Everything shifted into place and she did a few brisk calculations in her head. 'How old was he when this happened?'

'Tree was the same age as me so he'd have been about twenty-six.'

'But why does everyone blame Mom? He was a married man with a small son and took advantage of a teenage girl.'

'You've a lot to learn about the world.' Her aunt's eyes misted over. 'Back then the girl still got most of the blame. I'm not sure it's so different now, more's the pity. People said Paula were no better than she should be and tempted a good man.' Molly scoffed. 'They ignored the fact Tree would flirt with any woman who had a pulse.'

Essy sunk down on the sofa and covered her face with her hands.

'Do you see now why your mum didn't want to admit why she left?'

No way could she face Ruan tonight because she had to assume he knew the full story. The only choice was to detach herself and treat this like another job for Eureka! Finding things out was what she did and tracking down what happened to Ruan's father must be her number one priority.

'I suppose so.' She treated Molly to a conciliatory smile. 'Crab salad and a night in sounds perfect to me.'

Why did no one phone any more? Ruan found it easier to pick up nuances in a voice than any possible underlying message contained in Essy's terse text.

Can't meet tonight. Sorry.

Presumably she had discovered that her mother left Cornwall because of his father's appalling behaviour. That sucked, but if she cared anything for Ruan couldn't they at least talk things through? They weren't their parents.

Was he supposed to contact her and try to talk her around or draw a line under the undeniable attraction between them and move on? His mother would rip him to shreds if he asked her opinion, in fact he could already hear Vera's scathing response in his head.

'How many reasons do you want for staying away from that Essy creature? Paula Barnecutt destroyed my marriage and made you grow up fatherless.'

That was the one subject they clashed on more than any

other. He could never wrap his head around why she had stayed in the marriage. Or why after thirty years Vera still hadn't divorced her husband or sought proof as to whether he was alive or dead. She still wore her wedding ring.

He'd grown up hearing the constant arguments between his parents about his father's friendships with other women when they thought he was asleep and then the sight of his mother's sad, tear-stained face the next day. He could remember the overwhelming sense of relief when his father left a week before his sixth birthday and never came back. As he got older he picked up rumours about his father's liking for a pretty face, he supposed they thought that sounded better than calling him an out and out womaniser. Still to this day most people only said good things about Tree Pascow to Ruan's face. Out of respect for his mother? It didn't make sense. His deep-rooted dislike of his father's behaviour had shaped his life and led to him landing back in Cornwall, jobless and frustrated.

Life in London had been pretty good, if professionally somewhat unrewarding when he'd tired of churning out the same cookie cutter oversized houses, but overall he hadn't had too many complaints. He got on well with his work colleagues and when Helena Carter took over from his old boss she fitted right in. They clicked professionally and she was an attractive intelligent woman. One Friday evening at the usual end of the week office get-together in the local pub they ended up on their own halfway through the evening when all the people with families went home. Helena suggested they grabbed a curry and took a bottle of wine back to her flat where the inevitable happened. When he woke up in her bed the next morning they drank coffee and laughed over their slight hangovers. They stayed there together until Sunday evening when he finally returned to his own flat. He went into work that Monday morning in a good mood, all set to ask Helena if she was free for dinner that evening but was shocked to overhear a conversation between two of his co-workers.

'You think she took Ruan the boy wonder home with her Friday night?' Penny said. 'They were so wrapped around each other when I left the pub they didn't notice me leave.'

'Absolutely. Want to place a bet that it lasts a month at most before she tires of him? That's about her usual timeframe.' Johnny Bates had chuckled. 'Unless Toby comes home from Dubai and catches them at it. Poor sod.'

Ruan had slunk into his office and kept his head down, pretending to be hard at work. Of course he couldn't avoid Helena for ever and at lunchtime she called him into her office and closed the door, giving him a suggestive smile.

'Come here, darling.'

He reluctantly went to stand in front of her.

'I always find a little pick-me-up helps to get through a dreary workday. Do you agree?' She undid her blouse to expose her generous breasts, barely contained in a plunging black lace bra.

'For heaven's sake, Helena. Someone might come in.'

'Don't worry. They all know better than to do that when my door's closed.'

It sickened him that she made a regular habit of this. 'You didn't tell me you were married.'

'Is that what all this is about?' Her rich throaty laughter filled the room. 'I assumed you knew and didn't care. It doesn't need to make any difference to us. I'm sure Toby has friends with benefits too.' Helena gave a sly smile before she casually reached down and fondled him through his trousers.

Ruan shoved her away and bolted from the room, barely making it to the loo before throwing up until there was nothing left inside him. After brooding for several days he decided that no matter how humiliating it might be for him the HR director should be made aware of Helena's behaviour.

The woman had given him a pitying look. 'Are you sure you want to pursue this? You do understand that Helena will find out who made the complaint? She is the managing director's niece.' She suggested he might be happier working elsewhere and promised he'd leave with a decent reference, then sent him away to think it over.

When he refused to back down the HR director's prediction came true. Helena spread lies about Ruan's sexual preferences and his performance in the bedroom until he became the subject of muttered innuendoes and conversations stopped when he entered a room. He sensed sympathy from a few of his co-workers but no one openly backed him up because they were too concerned about their end of year appraisals and promotion prospects. At that point Ruan lost heart and withdrew the complaint.

With the same instinct as a homing pigeon he'd fled to Cornwall to lick his wounds but nothing was working out as expected.

I'll be outside the Smugglers at 7 if you change your mind.

Ruan fired off the quick message then stood in front of his overstuffed wardrobe. He slipped a new pale pink seersucker suit off the hanger and laid it on the bed along with a V-neck white T-shirt before going to shower. If Essy didn't turn up he could head over to Newquay and blow off some steam in one of the nightclubs. Anything to get away from Herring Bay.

On his way down to the quay he lingered outside the old chapel before cautiously picking his way around the outside. He didn't want his smart grey shoes smeared in smelly dog mess left behind by careless owners. Ruan peered over the high brick wall and studied the roof. A blue tarp covered one corner but apart from that it seemed in decent shape. The flimsy padlock holding the gates together wouldn't take much to spring apart but breaking and entering wasn't part of his agenda. If he asked too many questions around the village it would get back to Jackie, so he wrangled in his mind how else he could find out what he wanted to know? Ruan couldn't suppress a sly smile when it clicked. The other day his mother had mentioned taking a cake to Conan Worthington, the long retired minister from the chapel, who lived in a cottage on the road between Herring Bay and Penwarren. He should pay the old man a visit.

Ruan whistled as he strode off down the road.

'Hey, mate, watch where you're going.'

He barely stopped short of crashing into someone standing outside the pub.

'Well, bugger me. My dad said he'd seen you around.'

'Kit?' He struggled to reconcile his memories of a skinny, spotty teenager with this heavyset man sporting an unflattering black beard and attempting to cover up a receding hairline with a denim baseball cap.

'I can't believe you're back living in this dump.'

'You're here.'

'Yeah but only for a week to see the old man and let the kiddies play on the beach. Then it'll be back to civilisation. East Sussex. Brighton. What've you been up to all these years? I can't believe we've never bumped into each other in forever.'

Ruan's hesitation doomed him.

'If you don't have a hot date lined up let's have a drink and catch up?'

'I guess we could.'

'Are you working as an ice-cream salesman?' Kit tugged at his sleeve. 'I tried to describe you once to my Debbie. Told her about the time you turned up at the school dance in a skirt but she didn't fuckin' believe me.'

'It was a sarong.'

'Call it what you like. Looked like a skirt to everyone there.' Kit chuckled and grabbed Ruan's arm, steering him towards the door. 'God I've missed you.'

He wished he could say the same.

Chapter Nine

Essy flung open the bedroom window and savoured the fresh, salty air hoping a few deep steady breaths would settle her jangling insides.

Yesterday she went through the motions of carrying out her scheduled plans but with the sensation of watching everything from the outside. She almost felt Cornwall challenging her to pay attention to it by turning on a burst of amazing weather. The problem was that the questions racing around her head deteriorated from bad to worse. One particularly horrifying idea lodged there and refused to loosen its grip. So appalling she couldn't imagine speaking it out loud.

On the plus side Annabelle hadn't let her down. They'd tootled along, sticking carefully to the speed limit and survived several of the terrifying roundabouts before their welcome stop in St Ives. Porthmeor Beach was as gorgeous as she'd expected and she'd chatted to a few people enjoying the early summer sun in an effort to distract herself from thinking about Ruan. When she entered the Tate Gallery that resolution fell apart. The punch of colour created by the stunning contemporary art on display, startling against the stark white walls, reminded her so acutely of him that she'd stumbled outside struggling to breathe and barely managed to hold onto her lunch.

Molly hadn't said much when she returned and in the evening Essy drank far too much of the bottle of crisp Pinot Grigio she'd bought to go with their crab salad. At seven o'clock she couldn't help picturing Ruan waiting for her outside the dingy Smugglers' Arms. Did he go inside for a drink when she didn't turn up and flirt with another woman for the hell of it? Quite honestly she doubted it, but the idea made her feel a tad better.

'You fancy going out, my 'andsome?' Her aunt popped her head around the bedroom door. 'I'm heading over towards

Penwarren to see an old friend. It's a couple of miles the other side of Herring Bay but a gentle walk and it'll be pretty today.'

'I don't want to intrude.'

'Don't be daft. Conan loves visitors.' The corners of her mouth tightened. 'He were the Methodist minister back in the day and knew your mother well.'

'Do you think he'll talk to me about her?'

'Maybe. He can't get out much now and his eyesight and hearing aren't what they were.'

'I guess I could.'

'You'll want something sturdier than those flimsy things on your feet.'

Molly's disparaging headshake made it clear what she thought of her tangerine and silver thong sandals. They complimented the bright tangerine off the shoulder ruffled top and white capris she'd chosen this morning perfectly. Ruan would understand that diluting the outfit with sensible trainers would be a sacrilege but to appease her aunt she'd grit her teeth and obey orders.

'I'll change.' Essy slipped on the most practical shoes she'd brought with her, a pair of tan leather ankle boots, and rejoined her aunt downstairs.

'Even with his poor eyesight Reverend Worthington should see you coming.'

'I hate being drab.'

'No wonder you and Ruan get on.'

'Maybe it's in the genes. We could be related for all we know.' She blurted out the awful possibility, so much for keeping the idea to herself. It had erupted before she had a chance to clamp a lid on it.

'I'm sure you're not—'

'You can't be sure,' Essy snapped. 'The more I've thought about it the more likely it seems. There aren't any wedding pictures of Mom and Tony Havers. Who knows when they married or if they actually did?' She watched her aunt's eyes flare with shock as her words sunk in. 'Tree Pascow could've gone to America for all anyone knows.'

'If it is true better you find out now than later.'

Oh yeah, that makes me feel a ton better. Essy hadn't thought she could feel any worse. Another mistake.

Molly hitched her sensible black handbag on her shoulder. 'I told Conan I'd be there for his coffee time and I've packed a few of the buns he likes. We won't stay long because he has Meals on Wheels delivered for lunch around one o'clock, then takes a nap.'

No more was said and by the time they reached their destination Essy's mood had lifted. It was hard to stay miserable in these surroundings and she could have happily kept walking along the coastal path until her energy gave out. The picture postcard scenery, gentle breeze cooling her face and profusion of colourful wildflowers took her breath away. Tonight she'd search for a book on Cornish birds and try to identify some of the unrecognisable species swooping and squawking in the clear blue sky.

'It's not like this in winter.'

Her aunt's veiled warning came as she'd drifted into wistful musing about what sort of life she could have here.

'Too many folks from up country think it's all sunshine and ice creams. Reality hits them when it rains for days on end and the wind blows hard enough to knock you off your feet.'

'Most places are more appealing in good weather.' The non-committal response made her aunt scoff.

'Here we are.' Molly stopped outside a plain, whitewashed cottage and unlatched the gate.

'Oh wow, what a gorgeous spot.'

'Imagine when there's an easterly wind blowing!'

Of course her aunt was right because even today her hair whipped around her face as if trying to slap some sense back into her.

'He sure keeps it neat. How does he manage to do all this?'

Essy admired the beautiful display of what in her mind's eye were real English cottage garden flowers. Hollyhocks, delphiniums, dahlias and roses all vied for supremacy combining to fill the air with a heavenly scent she would love to capture in a bottle.

'He doesn't. The older villagers who remember all he did for them now take care of him. They see to the garden and any house repairs he needs.' Her aunt knocked loudly. 'He might not hear.'

'Oh, hello…'

'What are you doing here?' Her sharp question made Ruan's face turn the same vivid shade as his scarlet Nehru shirt. All she wanted to do was turn and run.

'Conan didn't say he was expecting anyone.' He fought to take his eyes off Essy but failed miserably. She looked bloody stunning in the fashionable shade of tangerine few people could carry off.

'Are you Reverend Worthington's bodyguard now?' Molly's piercing eyes bored through him and he couldn't think what he'd done to rile her up. Their family connection was surely old news to her?

'Not at all. I'll pop back in and say goodbye, then leave you to it. If I don't get back to work and finish a certain lady's kitchen soon she won't be pleased with me.' Even that didn't drag a smile out of her while Essy's expression still resembled the granite cliffs.

'Where are you all?' The minister's reedy voice rose over their conversation. 'Ruan, bring the ladies in if you wouldn't mind and we can all have coffee together.'

His chance to make a quick escape evaporated. 'I'll put the kettle on.'

'I'll make our coffee.' Molly held up a paper bag. 'I've brought seed buns to have with it.'

It took all his self-control not to groan out loud. On top of being persona non grata with both women, he'd be forced to at least pretend to eat one of the few foods he hated. Ruan gave in and led the way through to the living room. 'Here we are, Reverend Worthington, this is—'

'Don't spoil the surprise,' the old man interrupted and beckoned to Essy. 'My eyesight is poor, you'll have to come closer.' He peered at her through his thick lenses and a smile crept over his deeply-lined face. 'Well, well, if this isn't a day for surprises. First this interesting young man comes to pay me a visit and now you must be Paula Barnecutt's daughter.'

'Must I?' Essy's lilting drawl made the minister smile. 'I never thought Mom and I were that much alike but everyone here seems to think so.'

'There's no doubt about it. Sit down by me.'

'I'll help Molly with the coffee.' Ruan made a beeline towards the kitchen but almost bumped into her, already on her way out and carrying a loaded tray.

'Careful, I don't want this lot down over me.'

Essy was talking nineteen to the dozen about America but he picked up on her thoughtfulness in facing Conan, raising her voice without shouting and slowing down her normal rapid speech. Once Molly shared the coffee and buns around the conversation veered back to the weather and village gossip. Ruan nibbled at the outside edge of the bun then hid the rest in a napkin. He caught the dismay on Essy's face as she took a large bite of hers.

'Oh… that's… unusual.'

'They'm seed buns. They're yeast buns but made with caraway seeds instead of currants. It's an old Cornish recipe,' Molly explained. 'Lovely aren't they, Reverend Worthington?'

'You know they're my favourite and you've got a light touch with them, my dear lady.'

Ruan took a risk and winked at Essy. It surprised him when she smiled back and his heart did a flip.

'This young man tells me the old chapel is in poor condition.'

'It's been going downhill for years, I'm afraid,' Molly conceded. 'Why were you interested anyway?' She aimed the question his way but before he had the chance to respond she twitched a knowing smile. 'Oh I forgot.'

'Forgot what?' Essy frowned at them both.

'Ruan's an architect. His mother were some proud when he got his degree. We all were.'

'You never said.' Her complaint came across as petulant and he struggled not to laugh.

'That's not important now.' A thread of steel ran through the old man's weak voice. 'What does matter is what we're going to do about it? I physically can't do much... make that nothing, but my mind's not gone yet.' His faded blue eyes sparkled. 'I'm still in touch with a lot of people although I don't normally see as many as today in one go.'

'He's not going to get involved, Reverend. He'll be gone as soon as he gets another proper job, won't you, Ruan?' Molly tried to pin him down.

At this moment he couldn't rationalise his interest in the old chapel to himself let alone anyone else.

'The boy's reasons aren't important.' Worthington's firm tone put a stop to the conversation. 'I never asked *why* people came to chapel... of course, if they chose to tell me later I was happy to listen.'

When the two women arrived Ruan was on the verge of mentioning his father. The resentment was eating at him, and had been for years. Finding out the truth about what happened to Tree Pascow was the only way to move on.

'The first thing to find out is if Mr Webb has any plans for the chapel.' The minister shook his head. 'He won't talk to me, I'm sure.'

'I'm willing to give it a try.' Essy flashed her beguiling smile around. 'He'll assume I'm nothing more than an empty-headed guileless American interested in old buildings. I bet my last dollar I can winkle it out of him.'

Empty-headed? On Mars, maybe. He would love to question her motive for wanting to get involved but it wasn't any of his business.

'My lunch will be here soon.' Worthington slumped back in the chair and briefly closed his eyes. 'I know we didn't finish our chat, young man. Come again on Friday. Six o'clock sharp.'

'Uh, okay.'

'And you be here at the same time too, young lady.'

Before either of them could protest he shut them down with a warning headshake.

'I'll wash up our things.' Molly started to gather their dirty mugs on the tray.

'Leave it.' Worthington waved her away. 'The lunch woman can do them. Go. I need to think.'

Next thing the three of them ended up on the doorstep looking awkwardly at each other.

'I'll come up to your place ready to work after I've had my lunch, Molly.'

'Why don't you come back now and have a bite to eat with us? I made a nice quiche yesterday.'

'Do real men eat that?' Essy scoffed at him.

'Yes, and they sometimes bake it too.'

'You can cook?'

'You've got a problem with that too?'

'Too?'

'Along with whatever made you both bring the knives out today.' He caught Molly's flare of panic.

'Oh that.' Essy's eyes narrowed on him. 'You mean that little ole thing I found out.'

'Careful, dear,' Molly warned. 'We don't know—'

'What do you *think* you know?' Ruan's challenge made them blanch.

Chapter Ten

The accusation stuck in Essy's throat. Could she be wrong? A tiny nugget of hope flickered back to life.

'Betty's here with the reverend's lunch.' Molly pointed to the small white van parked outside the gate. 'If she hears our business it'll be all around Herring Bay before teatime. Wipe the sour looks off your faces.'

She tried her best and saw Ruan's mouth twitch in either amusement or annoyance as he obeyed too. Anyone with half a brain would see beneath their fixed smiles.

'Hello, Betty.' Her aunt bustled down the path to greet a woman who looked old enough to be receiving the meals instead of delivering them. 'I think we've worn the poor reverend out but I wanted him to meet Essy here, she's our Paula's girl.'

'Oh, I can see the likeness. I taught her in primary school you know.'

'Really?' Essy snatched on the admission like a starving bird on a breadcrumb.

'Bright little thing she was too.' Betty's eyes twinkled. 'Always chattering away and getting into trouble for it.'

'She still loves to talk.' Essy laughed. 'It works to her advantage now because she is a realtor and her gift of the gab helps to sell houses.'

'It's a pity she didn't come with you, I'd love to have seen her again.'

'Maybe she will another time.' A lame response but she couldn't tell the truth, her mother returning to Cornwall was less likely than the whole flying pink pig scenario.

'We ought to go.' Molly came to her rescue. 'Conan's waiting for his meal and my kitchen won't get painted if I don't feed this growing lad.' She poked Ruan's arm.

'Oh that wouldn't do. I'd love to pop in and see what he's done to it when it's finished.'

'I'll let you know and we'll have a cup of tea together so I can show it off.' Molly grabbed Essy's arm and whisked them all away.

The accusations she intended making were better off kept between the four walls of her aunt's house. They were a silent trio on the walk back and Ruan peeled off to make a quick stop at his own house to collect his painting clothes and work gear.

Molly pre-empted her urge to blurt everything out the moment he arrived to rejoin them.

'Lunch first. Lay the table, Essy. I'll cut the quiche and do a bit of salad to go with it.' Her aunt nodded at Ruan. 'Make us a pot of tea.'

Essy had zero appetite but kept that to herself. There was no mention of heating up the quiche and eating it cold sounded worse than disgusting. Also she harboured deep suspicions that she'd float away if forced to drink another cup of tea. Describing it as tolerable if taken without milk was still a generous evaluation in her book. Her aunt kept up a stream of innocuous conversation while they ate but as soon as they were all done she succumbed to a weary sigh.

'I suppose we'd better sort out this mess. Why don't you answer Ruan's question now, lovey?'

'Sure.' She glared at him. 'You knew that your father was the reason my mother left Herring Bay.'

'Yes, and I'm sorry.'

'Sorry? Sorry? That's all you can say?'

The anguish etched into his grim features deepened. 'What do you want me to say?' he pleaded. 'I was a five-year-old kid when he left. I'm sorry my mother still holds a candle for him but that's not my—'

'Yeah, *that's* not your fault but flirting with me when you knew we could be related? That's sick,' she yelled in his face.

'Related?' The colour leeched out of him. 'You think... I could never... Oh, Essy.' He turned to Molly. 'Tell her that's nonsense.'

'Is it?' her aunt's sad whisper tore through her.

I had good reasons to leave and better ones for never going back. Sometimes it's wise to let things be.

She should have been smart and listened to her mother's warning.

'Of course it is,' Ruan insisted, gripping the table so hard that his hands turned white.

'Paula disappeared on New Year's Day and your dad did a runner around the same time. We didn't hear a thing from her until the following Christmas.' Molly's eyes clouded as though it pained her to remember. 'She told us she was living in Tennessee and had a baby girl called Scarlett Caroline.'

'But I've always heard she was married by then to Essy's dad?'

'She never mentioned Tony Havers until the following year.' Molly let the implication hang.

'There are no wedding pictures of them and she's always been evasive when I ask for any details. Why can't you see what's staring you in the face?' Essy said.

Ruan wanted to brush away the tears spilling out of Essy's eyes but she'd chop his hand off if he was stupid enough to touch her. He made a concerted effort to lower his voice. 'Because it can't be true.'

'Prove it.'

His mother would be horrified to hear what he was about to say. Washing the family's dirty linen in public was an anathema to Vera but that was the least of his worries right now. Any remaining hope of a relationship with Essy, even simple friendship, depended on what he said in the next few minutes. Ruan's heart thudded. 'Molly, you were good friends with my mum. Didn't you ever ask her why she didn't have any more children?'

'It weren't my business.' Molly's face softened. 'I knew she wanted a big family because we used to talk about it when we were girls. We were going to find good men, marry them and raise our children in Herring Bay.' A flicker of sorrow dulled her eyes. 'She married and had you but—'

'My dad wasn't a good man.'

'I don't know about that. He were a hard worker and made good money doing people's gardens, several of the big houses around here wouldn't use no one else but Tree. He was always willing to help out anyone who needed a hand but he always got on better with the women than he did with men. They'd talk to him. Tell him stuff. That didn't go down well with a few of the husbands who suspected there was more to it than talk.' She shook her head sadly. 'Your mum and dad were good friends growing up and as far as I know neither of them ever went out with anyone else. They got engaged on her nineteenth birthday and married soon after.'

'I can't see what any of this has to do with Ruan's "claim",' Essy jumped into the conversation. 'Get to the point, please.'

'Mum had a rough time giving birth to me and nearly died,' he explained. 'Afterwards she was petrified to let my dad anywhere near her. She begged him to make sure there wouldn't be any more babies so he had a vasectomy. Sadly that wasn't enough for her and they slept in separate rooms for the rest of their marriage.'

Molly looked horrified. 'Poor Vera… I know she didn't have an easy delivery but I'd no idea about all the rest. It's hard not to feel sorry for your father as well now.'

Ruan hated to agree but for the first time he too felt his own sliver of pity for Tree Pascow.

'That still doesn't make it right for him to ruin my mother's life,' Essy protested. 'I don't care if she was a flirt or whatever, she was only seventeen. If she came onto Tree he knew the word no right enough and should've used it.'

'I totally agree. Don't think I'm trying to make excuses for him. I only heard the full story just before I left for uni. Mum and I had a set-to one day and she blurted it all out. If I'm stupid enough to bring the subject up again now she flies off the handle.'

'I'm sorry.' Her voice turned husky.

'Me too.' He fiddled with his shirt collar. 'I should have been more honest with you at the start.'

'Maybe.'

'You'm a good lad.' Molly's smile flickered back to life. 'Vera said once she should've been a better wife but I thought that was her way of trying to make his desertion more... palatable. Could've been a nugget of truth there after all.'

He heaved a sigh. 'I'd better get on with that painting.' He'd been honest and now it would be a waiting game. The ball was firmly in Essy's court.

Chapter Eleven

Essy joined her aunt in the kitchen for Ruan's grand reveal. She kept her eyes fixed on the amazing transformation he'd achieved since yesterday because she couldn't look directly at the man who'd churned her upside down and inside out. Ever since their soul-baring conversation she'd avoided him because her feelings surrounding the uneasy connection between their families were still massively conflicted.

'Wow, that's awesome. You sure know what you're doing.' The room had the calm, restful sense of being by the sea without being in any way kitschy with its soft grey and white paint brightened by splashes of dark blue.

'You have such a distinctive sense of style it must carry over in your own house,' Ruan replied.

His subtle compliment meant she couldn't hold back any longer and their eyes locked. Heat bloomed in her cheeks as his dark, searching gaze bored into her.

'I sure hope so. I bought a loft apartment over one of the stores in downtown Franklin and I've spent the last couple of years renovating it.'

'Well, I think this is 'andsome.' Molly beamed at Ruan. 'The only problem now is it shows up the rest of the house. When I've got a bit more money to spare you can do the living room next.'

He couldn't hide his awkwardness. Shifting his weight from one foot to the other. Clearing his throat. Shoving a hand through his hair until it stuck up. Far too kind to hurt her aunt's feelings he couldn't say outright that he'd no interest in becoming the local odd-job man.

'Do you have anything planned for the next hour or so only I'd sure love to take a look at this chapel y'all were goin' on about before I face the demon landlord?'

The relief flickering across his face told her she'd scored a home run. She hoped he got the hint that her gesture was more than a simple case of rescuing him.

'No I'm free. I'm happy to stroll down and check it out. Off you go to get changed.'

'What's wrong with what she's wearing now?' Molly asked.

Essy stifled a giggle under her aunt's puzzled scrutiny of the old jeans and baggy T-shirt she'd thrown on earlier. 'He knows I won't go outside the door in this.' A touch of satisfaction sneaked into Molly's expression. 'He'll do the same.' No way would Ruan walk around Herring Bay wearing his work overalls. Paint stains weren't in fashion this year.

'She's right.' A broad grin spread over his face.

'You'm a funny old pair. I'm off to the post office. Jane Moody won't care what I'm wearing.' Her aunt tugged at her leggings. 'These will do me.' She breezed out laughing and leaving them to stare at each other.

'Think she's right about us?'

Ruan's question startled her. 'Funny? Probably. Old? Hell no. A pair...' Her hesitation made his thick eyebrows shoot up. 'Probably more unlikely than—'

'Jackie Webb offering the village the old chapel as a community centre?'

'Yeah, exactly.' Essy appreciated him turning the awkward conversation around. 'Five minutes.'

'You'll never be ready.'

'Wanna bet?'

'No, I'd never bet against you doing a damn thing.' His warm laughter rumbled right through her.

'Quite right too.' She hustled out before he could think up another smart response.

Four minutes and thirty-five seconds later Essy glanced at her reflection in the mirror and gave herself a high-five. The man didn't know her as well as he thought. A paisley print mini dress reminiscent of the nineteen-seventies in varying shades of green and yellow. Chunky white wedge shoes. A leather choker

69

necklace. Her hair caught up with a wide yellow scarf. A hint of perfume. All finished off with a quick slash of scarlet lipstick.

Essy hurried down and posed, hand on hip on the bottom step.

'Twenty seconds left.' He flashed his phone in her face. 'Impressive.'

'Not bad yourself.'

'These old things?'

'Does anyone else in Cornwall appreciate that printed Cuban shirts and flared trousers are in for men this year?' He rocked anything she'd seen him wearing and this was no exception. Trust him to bring it all with him when he came to paint.

'Do I look like I care?'

'How long did it take you to get to that point?' The intensely personal question pulled the shutters down on his amusement. 'Really? That's out of bounds too?'

'Too?'

'Once we exhaust the subject of fashion there's not a whole lot you're willin' to talk about.'

'It's complicated.' He glanced at the floor instead of her.

'Usually is. I'll let you get away with it for now although I'm not sure you deserve it.' She slipped on her cross-body handbag, a circular bright green designer knock-off she'd found especially to wear with her new dress. Shallow? Essy brushed the thought away and headed for the door.

They didn't talk much on the walk down from Molly's and emerged at the harbour in bright sunshine.

'I don't know about you but I skipped breakfast and I'm starving. Do you fancy getting something from the bakery?' Ruan's question made Essy smile.

'Sure. I suppose it's too much to hope that they sell decent coffee too?'

'Sorry. John's got a self-serve machine but I risked it once and bitterly regretted it.'

She shook her head. 'Y'all don't seem to get it around here. You whine about the lack of visitors but don't go out of your way to give them a reason to come.'

'This isn't reason enough?' Ruan bristled, gesturing at the beautiful scenery around them.

'Hey, don't get me wrong,' Essy protested. 'It's awesome here but after people have done the whole coastal walk thing they want a damn good cup of tea or coffee and somewhere decent to grab a bite to eat. A lot of folks would poke around a good bookshop or buy some local crafts to take back home.' She told him about her foray into Tina Cloke's shop. 'She's incredibly talented but she's struggling to keep going. The visitors you do get probably don't even realise she's up there. I only stumbled across it because I happened to wander along that street.'

'Let's head for Wakeham's while we talk.' He led the way across the road. 'You're right, of course. I've heard about Tina but haven't had a chance to stop by there yet.' It galled him to admit that what she said made sense because her attack on Herring Bay felt deeply personal.

'Molly took me into y'all's little shop and I met Jane Moody. Her place isn't doing well either.'

'I know and if she loses the post office that could be the final straw. They're being closed down all over the country because they're "uneconomical" but they're the lifeblood of so many small villages.'

'She also mentioned a local garage that's closing down.'

'Hicks's is going out of business?' Ruan was shocked. 'I hadn't heard that. I remember Tommy Hicks from when I was a boy. I'm guessing he's well into his sixties by now. I suppose he's ready to retire.'

'Maybe.' Essy sniffed the air. 'Oh wow that smell is divine. Lead me to it.'

'Hot pasties and fresh bread. Nothing quite like it.' He stopped speaking as they prepared to walk by the war memorial. Faded poppy wreaths sat around the base of the

71

granite Celtic cross and he stared at the names etched on the shiny black slate plaque. 'The bakery's been in this same spot since before all of these poor men went off to the First and Second World Wars. Pascows, Menears, Hawkeys and Masters. They're all old Herring Bay families and plenty more besides those.' It touched him every time, this was one case where familiarity didn't breed contempt.

She rested her warm fingers on his bare forearm, setting the hairs on edge.

'Right, let's see what John has to offer this morning.' He plunged across the narrow street and into the bakery leaving Essy to follow along behind.

'Hello there, boy. What's up?' The tall wiry man always looked more like a marathon runner to him than a baker.

'Not much, Mr Wakeham. Do you want to tell my American friend here what's on offer?'

'You're Paula's girl.'

'I sure am.' Essy dragged her gaze away from the glass display cabinet. 'I'm in the mood for somethin' sweet.'

'I've got iced buns, custard tarts, Chelsea buns, jam doughnuts, congress tarts—'

'Oh Lord, I'll never decide.' She flashed the hapless baker her brightest smile and Ruan watched him fall under her spell. 'You pick for me.'

'You look like a vanilla custard slice lady.' John selected one of the iced cakes and slipped it in a white paper bag. 'Don't tell me – your usual custard tart?' He grinned at Ruan.

'You come here a lot?' Essy asked.

'The lad's in here most days.'

'What am I going to do if you retire?'

'Lose weight?' The baker roared with laughter. 'I'm not ready to give up yet. Someone's got to keep this place going.'

'Pleased to hear it.' He paid and they wandered back outside.

'This is… interesting.' Essy studied her layered pastry and took a tentative bite. 'Oh wow. I thought it looked stodgy but the pastry is light as air and this creamy filling is awesome. What is yours like?'

'Taste it.'

She nibbled a bite and wrinkled up her nose. 'It doesn't have much flavour.'

The simple tart filled with custard and sprinkled with nutmeg was a favourite from his childhood. They were his father's weakness too and Ruan clearly remembered watching for Tree to come home from work, hoping he'd be carrying a paper bag from Wakeham's. His dad would buy two custard tarts for them and a chocolate éclair for Vera. 'Let's go. We can eat while we walk this time.'

They headed back down Lemon Street to the harbour, past The Smugglers' Arms and around the corner into Wesley Street.

They stood in front of the wall surrounding the chapel not speaking and a ball of frustration twisted at his gut. He'd grown up with his father's disappearance and the reason behind it playing as the soundtrack of his life. That led him to be deeply wary of revealing too much of his true feelings to anyone. Of course his mother resembled a clam when it came to her emotions too but he'd no idea whether Vera's was part of her DNA or something she learned during her difficult marriage. Essy's dig about his love of fashion stung. She wasn't the first to call him out for being a lightweight. An emotional vacuum was the more pertinent description used by one old girlfriend. Nobody understood the effort it took to appear unconcerned and unmoved.

'Is the building solid?' She rubbed her hand over the surface of the bricks.

'It appears to be but it's hard to tell for certain without getting access to the inside.'

She examined the padlock holding the rusty iron gates together and tossed him a mischievous smile.

'Don't even think about it.' It was impossible not to laugh.

'A community centre. That wasn't a joke, was it?'

'Not really. The only meeting hall of any size was part of the chapel and once that closed all the local community groups dwindled away. Jackie Webb puts on a few things in the pub but it's not the same.'

'I hate to say this because Herring Bay is growing on me in an odd sort of way but I get why my mom wanted to leave.' As the words left her mouth she blushed, turning almost as red as her scarlet lips. They both knew a lack of shops or Zumba classes had little to do with Paula Barnecutt's decision.

'Even when I was young Herring Bay didn't have a lot going for it.' He shrugged. 'Big supermarkets. People being more mobile. The lack of employment opportunities. They've all taken their toll.' Ruan shoved his hands in his pockets. 'Sorry to be a miserable so and so.'

'You are a bit like Eeyore sometimes. I guess it's up to me to be Winnie the Pooh.'

That dragged a smile out of him. Staying gloomy around her was almost impossible.

'I'm goin' to tackle good ole Mr Webb.' Essy threw him a challenging smile. 'Are you willing to give that evening out of ours another try tonight?'

'If you want.'

Hints of deep moss green blossomed in her cool grey eyes. 'I'm not my mother and you aren't your father.'

'But they're part of us.'

'So what? That doesn't amount to a hill of beans unless we let it.'

'An evocative turn of phrase.'

'Pick me up at seven o'clock tonight.'

'Won't Molly mind?' He wasn't convinced the woman, or many other people come to that, would be happy to see the two of them together in any sense of the word.

'I'm not my aunt either.'

Ruan stared after her with a smile on his face as she marched off down the road.

Essy slowed down as soon as she turned the corner to catch her breath. Maybe she should follow Ruan's example and be more cautious. It wasn't in her nature but surely she could learn?

She pushed him to the back of her mind and braced herself to concentrate on the task at hand. Her earlier overflowing confidence in her ability to win over Jackie Webb started to wobble.

'You going in, love?'

A balding, heavily bearded man she hadn't seen before was holding open the pub door. 'I sure am.' She treated him to one of her broadest smiles.

'Hey, cool, you're an American. I love it over there. Took the wife and kiddies to Disney at Christmas.'

She smothered her distaste. Equating the whole of the United States with Disneyland was as criminal as comparing the widely varied United Kingdom with London. 'Awesome. Are you a local here? I haven't seen you around.'

'I was. I grew up in Herring Bay but got out fast as I could.'

'So did my mom.'

'You must be Molly Barnecutt's niece.' His sharp blue eyes narrowed. 'Ruan told me all about you.'

'You two are old friends?'

'Yep, sorry I should've said.' He grabbed her hand and pumped it like a flat tyre. 'Kitto Hawkey but everyone calls me Kit. I bumped into Ruan on Monday night. We caught up on nearly twenty years of news over a few drinks.'

'I'd sure love to chat some more but I've someone to see.' She'd love nothing better than to winkle a few stories out of him.

Kit waved towards a petite, bleached blonde sitting near the fireplace. 'That's my wife. Better be off.'

Essy spotted her quarry leaning on the bar with a half-drunk pint in one hand.

'Hello, my 'andsome.' Jackie Webb straightened up and attempted to suck in his ample gut. 'What are you drinking today?'

She ordered a small glass of rosé and when he set the wine down in front of her Essy dredged up a warm smile. 'Can you spare me a few minutes for a chat?'

'Anytime, my lover.' He bared his yellowing teeth in a wolfish smile then yelled to a scrawny young man who was playing darts to come and take over. Webb hoisted himself onto a stool and fixed his attention on her.

'Everyone around the village says that you're the expert to talk to about local history.' *Oh Lord, if he were a peacock his tail feathers would be fanned out.* 'Old buildings are a passion of mine and particularly old churches. A little birdy told me you own that cute ole Methodist Chapel on Wesley Street.'

'Well, yes, in a manner of speaking.'

'Could I have a peek inside? I sure would love to take a few pictures.'

'I s'ppose so.'

Grudging, but positive so Essy went for the Oscar and gazed admiringly around the pub. 'I imagine you're planning to expand your business over there soon? Maybe open a high-end restaurant to attract more visitors to this gorgeous part of the world?'

'I haven't decided yet but that's a possibility. You can't rush into these things.'

Yeah right. You've never rushed into anything your whole life.

'I could take you over now for a look around if you like?'

The offer caught her by surprise. 'That's generous but you're a busy man and I couldn't possibly trouble you. Perhaps I could borrow the keys until tomorrow morning and poke around on my own? I promise I'll be real careful.'

Jackie looked dubious but drew a bunch of keys from his pocket and prised off two.

'This one's for the gate, the other is the front door.' He dangled them in front of her. 'I expect we might be able to come to an agreement.'

Essy's flesh crawled.

'We need another barrel from the cellar, love.' A wispy-haired woman with an anxious expression scuttled in from the back of the pub.

'Now?'

'Yes, dear. We're out of bitter.'

'I'll be there when I'm good and ready.' He shooed her away. 'That's the wife. Ruby's bloody useless. I've got to see to everything.'

'The keys?' Essy sensed him hesitate. 'Please. Tomorrow morning.' Webb grunted and thrust the keys at her. She could hardly wait to see Ruan's face later.

Chapter Twelve

'Where are we going?' Ruan didn't sound pleased. 'I called in a big favour to snag us a table at eight o'clock. In the summer The Drifters is fully booked and it's a ten-minute drive from here.'

'We've got a few minutes to spare. Don't be a grouch. Here we are.' She stopped outside the chapel. 'You didn't ask how I got on with Jackie Webb.'

'I assumed if you'd found out anything significant you would've bragged about it by now.'

'Oh ye of little faith. Reverend Worthington would be disappointed in you.' She fumbled around in her fashionable silver tote bag, large enough to pack for a fortnight's holiday instead of a simple dinner date. 'Y'all didn't appreciate the wiles of a smart woman.' Essy dangled a rusty key in front of him.

'That's not for here?'

'Sure is.'

He watched her wriggle one of the keys into the padlock and next thing the gate swung open.

'Are you comin' or not, slowpoke?'

'I won't ask how you worked this miracle.'

They picked their way through the piles of rubbish littering the ground and then Essy worked a similar miracle on the rickety wood doors. She stood aside to let him go first and as soon as he did the breath caught in Ruan's throat. He appreciated her staying silent and began to wander around. Underneath the layer of dust and neglect the bones of the old building were strong. When the last congregation left had they refused to admit that they wouldn't return the next Sunday? The hymn numbers remained up on the board and a faded Union Jack flag hung by the altar. Ruan picked up a baby's pink shoe off the back row of chairs. Had it slipped unnoticed off a little girl's foot as her mother brushed away tears at the loss of their precious space?

'Wow. This is seriously awesome.'

'Yes, it is.'

'You could bring this back to life.' Essy's mid-Atlantic drawl jolted him back to reality.

'No, I couldn't.'

'Couldn't or won't?'

He made a deliberate play of looking at his watch. 'We need to be going.' The light left her eyes. 'We'll talk over dinner.'

'Don't throw me a bone to get rid of me like a hungry dog.'

'I'd never do that.' He rested his fingers against the curve of her smooth soft cheek and again her evocative scent surrounded him, making Ruan in danger of forgetting his common sense.

'I'm not givin' up on this... or you.'

'You probably should.' The twitch of a smile he'd come to recognise as a signal of her deep-rooted determination re-emerged. Maybe the Pascow family weren't the most stubborn people on planet Earth after all.

'I've got the key until tomorrow morning so we can come back again later if you want.'

'We'll see.'

She gave up haranguing him but Ruan guessed it was only a temporary reprieve. They locked up and strolled across the road to his car. His appetite had gone the way of the dodo.

'I'm not hungry either.' Essy shrugged her shoulders. 'Not for a fancy place where we've got to be polite.'

'How about a pasty and impolite behaviour on the beach?'

'You Cornishmen sure get to the point.'

'Was that a yes?'

'What do you think? Call and tell them we're sick or something.'

Cancelling this late in the day might blow his friendship with the head chef out of the water but he'd take that chance. Brian

Martin swore at him for a minute before accepting Ruan's apology.

'The beach isn't far. We'll walk and leave the car here.'

'Will Suzy Sunshine be okay?'

'Who?'

'I told you my rental's name is Annabelle.' Essy's eyes glittered as she pointed at his bright yellow Prius. 'How can you call this little beauty anything other than Suzy Sunshine?'

Her bizarre logic made him laugh and he'd no choice but to agree how brilliant she was.

'Stay here and I'll go to the shop for supplies.' Five minutes later he returned with two dried up ham rolls, a multi-pack of assorted crisps and a screw top bottle of cheap red wine. 'That's the best I could do. They didn't have any glasses but we can share.'

'You old smoothie.'

'Less of the old, thank you very much.' He linked his arm through hers. 'Come on. Let's relive my misspent youth.'

Herring Bay Beach wasn't hugely popular in the daytime because the sandy cove had no café or public toilets for families but it came to life in the evenings. Then it was the go-to destination for local teenagers, most of them up to no good.

'My equivalent was Percy Priest Lake outside of Nashville. A gang of us would pile into someone's pickup truck with a case of beer and drive out there on a hot summer's night. Crank up the music. Strip down and skinny-dip in the lake. Freeze our asses off.' Her eyes glazed over. 'Life was simple then.'

'Do we complicate it ourselves?'

'Maybe.'

'Be careful on the steps. Several are broken away.' Ruan held out his hand to help her down onto the sand.

'You've been here recently?'

'I've come down a few times when I needed... space.' With sunset fast approaching the light was rubbed soft around the edges throwing Essy's striking features into sharp relief.

'Don't you dare!' A shrieking teenage girl, her dark hair streaming behind her in the wind almost stumbled into them and would've fallen if a shirtless young man hadn't grabbed her arm.

'Time for a swim.' He grinned and scooped her off her feet then raced across the sand, heading for the sea.

'Should we—'

'Stop them?' Ruan shook his head. 'No way. She'll be disappointed. That's why she's wearing a bikini and is barefoot. Don't worry. If I thought for one moment she was being coerced I'd speak up.' He fought to hold his voice steady. 'I know what it's like to be on the receiving end of unwelcome… attention.' The shock on Essy's face made him wish he'd kept his mouth shut, it was too late now.

Her heart raced. 'From a woman?'

'Yes, Helena Carter. My boss. Make that ex-boss. She's the main reason I'm back here.' Ruan grasped her arm tighter. 'Let's find somewhere quiet to sit away from this lot.' He threw an indulgent smile towards the group of noisy, laughing youngsters gathered around a fire they'd created from driftwood.

They kept walking along the damp sand until finally all they heard was the gentle lapping of the waves on the beach and the squawk of an occasional seagull searching for food.

'It'll be more sheltered back by the wall.' He eyed her up. 'I hate to get your clothes messed up but bringing a blanket wasn't part of my plans for tonight.'

'Clothes aren't important. You are.' Essy swallowed hard. 'We are.' It took nerve to add those last two words because the 'we' was a potential red flag. All he did was pull her down beside him. 'Open the bottle and keep talking.'

'You like ordering me around, don't you?'

'A polite southern man would say, "Yes, ma'am", and do what he was told.' Had she gone too far? The newness between them reared its head.

'This well-mannered Cornishman will you let you take a drink first, how's that?'

'It'll have to do.' Essy grabbed the bottle and took a long swallow. 'God, that's awful.' She glugged another mouthful then passed it back. It amused her to see his contorted face when the bitter tannins in the wine hit home.

'You're right, it's disgusting. Here you finish it.'

'Thanks a bunch.'

'Generous to a fault, that's me.' Ruan ran his fingers through the sand like a small child.

'How about one confession each to start with? You pick first. Choose whichever would help you most right now.'

'I should've bought another bloody bottle of that rubbish.' He looked beaten down. 'I suppose the business with Helena bugs me the most. I feel less of a man for letting it happen.'

Exasperation coursed through her. 'But you were the victim.'

Ruan snorted. 'I dress weird. I'm "artistic". Do you seriously think people will believe me? They'd say it was fucking wishful thinking on my part. Even the bloody HR person brushed off my complaint when I reported it.'

'They did nothing?'

'Helena's uncle owns the company. Figure it out for yourself and guess who was quietly shunted out?'

'You could sue.'

He threw her a disbelieving look. 'Seriously? That would kill my mum. She's been through enough over the years. Mum's consistently had my back and I'm sure she would this time but...'

'You haven't given her the chance,' Essy ventured a guess. 'She doesn't know?'

'I used a cover story about being tired of London and needing to recharge my batteries.' Ruan's expression softened. 'That wasn't a complete lie. Work wasn't satisfying me any longer and I was tired of my supposedly carefree lifestyle.' He stroked her hand. 'Your turn, I think.'

She longed to know every single detail but a warning bell chimed in her head. This man had the guts to share something with her that he hadn't confessed to anyone else. The last thing he needed was her berating him.

'Fair enough.' Now she wished they hadn't finished the wine. Lousy or not it would've been better than nothing. 'I realise you weren't very old when he left but did you ever pick up anything about your father and any other women?'

'I remember plenty of arguments. He always claimed they were simply good friends of his but Mum never believed him.' Ruan shrugged. 'It's hard to credit his side of the story, especially knowing the physical side of their marriage was over so I tend to think she was right to be suspicious.'

'But why is Vera so hard on my mom if she knew your dad was...' She struggled to come up with a vaguely polite description for Tree Pascow.

'A womaniser?' He dropped his head in his hands, unable to look at her. 'Say it like it is.'

'Okay, but why blame Paula for everything?'

'Because for whatever reason that affair was different. It was serious enough to make him leave the marriage.' Ruan's voice roughened. 'I'm guessing it hurt her pride that your mum was so much younger and her best friend's sister. From her point of view Dad had been humiliating her for years and that was the final straw.'

'That makes sense.' An unwelcome trickle of understanding sneaked in. 'And you really don't know where your father is now?'

'No!'

'Your mom doesn't either?' Essy persisted.

'If she does she's never said.'

'Wouldn't you like to know what happened to him?'

'Not really.' Ruan shrugged. 'He's screwed up my life enough one way and another.'

'But if we tracked him down—'

'My father isn't one of your Eureka! projects.' He scrambled to his feet. 'He hasn't been in touch for over thirty years so that tells me he doesn't give a shit about us. Any of us. Including your mother.'

Ruan's pain ran far too deep for her to reason with him. 'I think it's best if I go.' Essy stood up and brushed the sand off her clothes. 'We were crazy to think any sort of relationship between us could work.' She hesitated for a few precious seconds, praying he would argue her out of it but his stony demeanour didn't alter, so Essy steeled herself to walk away and not look back.

Chapter Thirteen

Ruan barely noticed the beautiful weather as he slogged along the road. Maybe there would be a Christmas miracle in early July and Essy wouldn't turn up. After their confrontation on the beach he felt sure she wouldn't be keen to meet him either.

Reverend Worthington had chosen to see them together today on purpose. The shrewd old man was almost ninety-five but his mind was still razor-sharp.

He knocked and pushed the door open. Last time Ruan got scoffed at for daring to suggest it wasn't wise to leave it unlocked. 'I can't be getting up and down every time someone comes to visit,' the reverend had told him.

'You're early. Be a good boy and put my dinner dishes in the kitchen otherwise that nice girl will think she's got to help out.'

Nice girl?

'Oh dear, did you put your big feet in it?' Conan chuckled. 'What happened?'

'I came here to talk about my father not Essy Havers.'

'Rubbish. It's all of a one and you know it.'

'Maybe.'

'Is it all right to come on in?' Essy leaned in around the door, her vivid smile giving Ruan a Muhammad Ali strength punch in the gut.

'Of course, my dear. This lad was about to put the kettle on. You'll join us in a cup of tea.'

'Sure. I'll help.' She nodded at the tray he'd loaded with the remains of Conan's meal. 'You can carry that.'

Bossy woman. Their eyes met and his cheeks weren't the only ones burning as memories struck them both like a bolt of lightning. From the corner of his vision he caught the old man smirking.

The second they stepped into the tiny kitchen she kicked the door shut.

'For a man who's hard of hearing and half-blind he doesn't miss a darn thing. Has he had a go at you already?'

'Yes but—'

'I interrupted.' The glossy smile matched her shiny magenta sling-back ballet flats. 'Like them?' Essy turned one ankle around to show off the shoe to better advantage.

Her behaviour bewildered him.

'This is my way of apologising.' Her low raspy voice pulled at him. 'Molly told me I was being... daft.' A flicker of amusement curved the corners of her mouth. 'I've never been called that before.'

He couldn't hide his surprise.

'She pointed out the pretty obvious fact you aren't responsible for your mom's opinion and that it clearly bothered you. Molly said I must decide which mattered most and be more understanding of your feelings.'

'Is the kettle boiling yet?' Conan shouted in, sounding crotchety.

'Sure is, I'm fixin' to make it now,' Essy yelled back.

'I'd better do it. He's fussy.'

'Yeah we both know I'll mess up because Americans are only fit for tossing tea in harbours.'

'You said it.' Ruan busied himself making the drinks. It was a struggle to ignore the teasing scent radiating off her and tormenting him in the confined space.

'We're not done,' Essy lowered her voice to a husky whisper.

'I didn't suppose we were.' His obvious resignation widened her smile. Only by picking up the tray and disappearing back to the other room could he put a stop to her satisfaction, or at least the challenge of facing it.

'I believe you two want to hear the same story. Am I right?' Conan's bony hands clasped around the mug.

'I *know* the story,' Ruan gently corrected him. 'What I need is help to... cope with it better.'

'I understand that, but first you need to make certain what

you've heard is the truth. No story has a single point of view. As you young people say everyone involved had their own agenda. It's human nature.' His sympathetic smile landed on Essy. 'What did Paula tell you?'

A childish resentment bubbled up in Ruan.

'Don't worry, you shall have your turn.'

Worthington's conciliatory remark embarrassed him. 'Of course.' He slumped in the chair and shifted his expression to at least appear sympathetic.

Essy wished she could reassure him that she would be more than happy to let him go first.

'My dear?'

'Oh yeah, sorry. She never told me much beyond the basics about growing up here. I get the impression she clashed with her parents over what she wanted from life. Mom was obviously fond of Molly but the eight-year age gap stopped them being really close.' She took a few steadying breaths. 'Mom closes down if I ask too many questions. When I first raised the possibility of coming here she blew her top and warned me that she had good reasons for leaving and better ones for not coming back. Mom pleaded with me to leave it alone.'

'Do you wish you'd listened?'

The question made her think but not for long. 'No. I prefer facing things head on. It's got me in trouble more than a few times.'

'I can believe that.' Ruan angled her a rueful smile.

'My business wouldn't be as successful if I was a shrinking violet.'

'No one with any sense would use either word to describe you.'

'I sure hope not!' Essy's appalled response made both men smile.

'How much have you discovered already?' The minister's gentle question brought her back on track.

She explained everything she'd found out. 'What I really need to know was what prompted my mom to leave when she did and what happened to... Ruan's father?'

'It might help to hear about the part I played.' The worried crease between his eyes deepened. 'Tree was a decent man. He was always willing to help out his friends and neighbours and was a regular chapel-goer.'

'He was a womaniser.' Ruan sprang to his feet. 'I grew up hearing my parents arguing all the time about him and other women.'

'And how would he react?'

'He'd deny it, of course.'

'Maybe he was telling the truth as he saw it.'

'The truth?' Ruan's explosive reply made Conan wince.

'Every time there were rumours floating around the village he'd insist to me there was nothing more to it than friendship. Of course your mother found that hard to believe and I can't condemn her for that.' Conan's naturally moderate voice faded to nothingness. 'I can't tell you for certain who was right although naturally I have my ideas.'

'Come off it, it's crazy to say my mother left because he simply flirted with her.' Essy found this incredulous. 'I'm damn sure it went a whole lot farther but I still don't get why Vera is so down on my mother? Who is most at fault here? A married man with a child or a teenage girl flattered by attention he'd no right to give her?'

Memories darkened his pale eyes. 'I can't break the confidences Vera and Tree shared with me, separately I hasten to add, but it's no secret among those who knew them well that the marriage had its struggles.'

It was on the tip of her tongue to mention the story Ruan had shared about the private side of his parents' marriage but his fierce glare warned her off.

'I've heard enough.' Ruan sounded profoundly sad. 'Nothing you've said has changed my mind. My father couldn't keep away from other women and didn't give a damn for his family. That's what I've got to live with.' He stalked out and slammed the door behind him hard enough to make the windows rattle.

'You'll find a bottle of whisky and some glasses over there, my dear. I think a small one each wouldn't go amiss.' Worthington managed a watery smile and pointed to a cupboard in the corner. 'Then come sit by me.'

She'd asked for this. There was no going back now.

Chapter Fourteen

He could've sworn he got rid of the stars painted on his bedroom ceiling but they were still there. The wave of nausea swirling around Ruan's head eased when he closed his eyes. He tried to lie perfectly still but couldn't get comfortable.

'You back to life?'

He risked opening one eye. 'Kit?'

'Yep, it was my turn to rescue you.'

Ruan cautiously propped up on his elbows and glanced around. Now the dampness and lumps underneath his back made sense. Herring Bay Beach was no five star hotel bed.

'Been here before, haven't we?' Kit held out a bottle of beer. 'Hair of the dog?'

A rush of acid filled his throat. 'Er, no thanks. Why are we here?'

'Drunk on the beach at three in the morning? I found you drowning your sorrows in The Smugglers' last night and persuaded my long suffering wife I needed to take care of you.'

Snippets of memory trickled back in. 'Shit. What did I say?'

'You kept ranting on about your father and said Conan Worthington was an interfering old devil.' Kit took a jab at his arm. 'That was before you got all sad and tearful and droned on about your hot American babe.'

'Oh God.' A groan slipped out as he asked his friend, 'Was this all still in the pub?' This performance would all be around the village by now.

'Don't worry, mate. I dragged you out of there quick as I could.'

'Cheers.' A drift of music came on the wind and he spotted a group of teenagers, probably the same ones he saw the other night with Essy, gathered around a dying fire.

'That used to be us. Think we should warn them?'

'They wouldn't listen any more than we did.'

'You want to talk about it?' Kit asked.

'No.'

'Fine. I'd better be getting on back or Debbie will string me up.' He struggled to his feet and brushed the sand off his clothes. 'You going to walk back with me?'

'No, thanks. I'm good.'

'I meant what I said, that's if you even remember.' Kit grinned down at him. 'Come and see us in Sussex.'

'Will do.' They both knew it wouldn't happen but he played along anyway. 'The next time you're back down this way again there's a good chance I'll still be here.'

'Seriously?' Kit grimaced. 'Don't get me wrong, I love my old man and this place is great for a holiday but live here again? No way. Aren't you after another job back in London?'

'I'm not sure yet.' Even after more than a few drinks he'd thankfully kept a tight lid on his work troubles. 'I didn't realise how much I'd missed this.' He patted the sand. 'Don't you ever think it'd be an awesome place to bring up your kids?'

'Sometimes, but what's here for them when they're older? They'll bugger off same as we did.' His old friend gave him a searching look. 'What're you plotting? You were always full of bright ideas.'

That emerged as almost an accusation. He'd considered floating his half-formed plans regarding the old chapel but Kit's negative attitude towards Herring Bay and everything it stood for held him back.

'Not sure yet. We'll see.' The conversation wasn't going anywhere so what was the point in keeping on? He stumbled back up on his feet. 'I appreciate you... well, you know.' Before he could suppress the urge he gave Kit a tight hug before holding him at arm's length. 'Sorry. Didn't mean to embarrass you.'

'It's all right. No one saw us.'

'We don't want anyone thinking you've crossed over to the weird side.'

'You're not weird.' The instant protest made him smile. 'You've got the guts to be yourself. Not many of us have the courage to do that.'

In the moonlight Ruan could swear there were tears shimmering in Kit's eyes. Were there depths to his old friend he knew nothing about? Stupid question. Everyone had them if you looked hard enough.

'You'd better get off home to your family.' An unexpected pang of jealousy stabbed through him. Would his jumbled up life ever include the things other people appeared to take for granted? Essy flashed through his mind and a heavy sigh escaped. What chance did they stand of forging anything long-term? About zero. Before Kit could argue he waved him away. Ruan ambled towards the water, peeling off his shirt as he went.

I prefer to face things head on.

He stripped down to his boxers and walked into the sea up to his ankles. The frigid water stung his skin but he took a couple of deep breaths and plunged right in.

'You idiot. It's not worth it,' Essy yelled and made a grab for Ruan's arms.

Talk about luck. She'd been tossing and turning in bed and sneaked out of her aunt's house with the crazy notion that a walk on the beach might help.

The frigid water almost took her breath away and he struggled to fight her off. They wrangled for a while but she'd been a lifeguard at their neighbourhood pool one summer and knew a few tricks. Despite Ruan's size she soon dragged him back onto the beach out of danger.

'What the hell are you doing?' He sat up and glared at her.

'Saving your life? Just maybe I didn't want you to die, you idiot.'

'Die?' Ruan burst out laughing. 'You thought I was...' His smile faded. 'Oh, you silly woman.'

'If that's all the thanks I'm gonna get I'll toss you back in there.'

He struggled to his feet. 'Strange though it might seem to someone who lives hundreds of miles from the nearest beach, I was doing something pretty common here in Cornwall. We call it swimming.'

'At three in the morning?'

'Hey, you told me you used to go skinny-dipping. At least I kept a few clothes on. It was pretty damn good until you did your *Baywatch* bit.' Ruan flashed her a grin. 'Next time can you wear a sexy red swimsuit like Pamela Anderson?'

'Next time?' Essy shouted at him. 'Don't you ever...' She swiped at the tears seeping out of her eyes. All she could think when she saw him striding into the water was how angry and distraught he was yesterday.

'Oh, sweetheart, I'm sorry.' He cupped her face with his cold hands and stroked a kiss over her mouth.

Part of her ached to punish Ruan for scaring her that way but when he slipped his strong arms around her waist and pulled her against his hard, slick body all her senses sprang to life. The tang of salt on his skin. A wisp of smoke in the air from the teenagers' fire nearby. His dark eyes burning through her and the loud thump of their racing hearts echoing in her ears.

'Yeah, me too.' She sniffed his stale whisky-scented breath. 'I'm takin' a guess you have a hangover.'

'Not sure if it's been long enough since I stopped drinking to call it that. If it wasn't for my old friend Kit I'd be lying in the gutter outside the pub by now.' Ruan looked shamefaced.

'You were lucky. He introduced himself to me when I bumped into him the other day. Strikes me he's a good guy.'

'He is. Essy, this isn't who I am. Not really.'

'I know.' They were both struggling to define who they were right now. 'Come back to Molly's with me and I'll fix us some food. You can call it either a very late supper or an early breakfast.'

'I suppose that's the best offer I'm going to get?' The teasing lilt in his voice made her smile.

'Today it is.'

'I suppose bacon and eggs are a reasonable substitute.'

'You sure know how to flatter a lady.' Her fake pout made him chuckle but he suddenly clasped at his head and groaned.

'Oh God, I was wrong. It isn't too early for a hangover.' He rested his forehead against hers. 'Can I take you up on the offer after I've crashed for a while? A bottle of paracetamol, a gallon of water and a few hours' sleep might make me half-human again.'

'Does that usually do the trick?'

'There is no "usually". I meant what I said.' His fingers tangled in her hair and drew her closer. 'You were the one who insisted I'm not my father. I don't lie and I don't mess women around. Ever.'

'I know.' She could say so much more but he wasn't up to hearing it. Ruan jerked against her as a huge, juddering shiver ran through him. 'You'll catch pneumonia if you don't hurry up and get dressed.' Essy made a grab for his clothes. 'Now.' She thrust his shirt at him and ignored his muttered complaints about her being bossy and pushy. By the time he managed to drag his clothes on a touch of colour had seeped back into his skin.

'You must be freezing too. I'm not the only one who got wet. My home is closer. Come with me and get dried off.'

She put the blame for his stupidity on alcohol poisoning. Vera would have a heart attack on the spot if she discovered Essy in her kitchen.

'Okay that was a stupid suggestion. I'll shut up.'

She linked her arm through his. 'Come on. We'll walk back as far as the quay together then go our separate ways.'

'Only until later. We need to talk through yesterday.' A faint smile lifted his mouth. 'Notice I said need... not want.'

'Oh, I noticed. I wish we could've met in a regular sort of

way. We could even have enjoyed a brief romance like regular people do on vacation.'

'I warned you I don't do ordinary.' He tugged at his red jeans. 'This is nothing. It's the outside stuff.' Ruan took her hand and pressed it against his chest. 'You get that I'm not run-of-the-mill here either.' His voice turned gruff. 'Neither are you.'

'Is that so terrible?'

'Terrible? No, but it doesn't make for an easy life.'

Too many of the men she came across were content with 'easy' and 'normal'. She'd always chafed against those labels.

'Pleased to hear it. "Easy" bores me.'

'I'm pretty sure boredom isn't ever going to be our problem.' His rueful tone made her laugh. 'Come on, beautiful lady. If I don't fall into bed soon I'll fall at your feet. Not in a good way either.'

They wrapped their arms around each other and started to walk. Quiet in their own thoughts but together. Essy rather liked that.

Chapter Fifteen

'Where on earth have you been? Your bed hasn't been slept in and you weren't answering your mobile.'

Ruan faced his mother's accusatory stare. Something about her tight, grey expression stopped him from pointing out the fact that he was nearly forty years old and didn't need to account for his whereabouts to anyone.

'What are you doing up at this hour?' he asked, suddenly clicking that she was fully dressed. A lightweight cream jacket over her blouse and skirt. Brown shoes. Handbag on her shoulder.

'Your uncle is poorly. I need you to drive me to Newquay.'

'I'm really sorry but I'm not sure that's a great idea unless you want me to get done for drunk driving. We'll get a taxi.' Although her mouth tightened she didn't make any comment. 'Uncle Dick rang you?'

'No, of course he didn't,' Vera scoffed. 'Luckily Les Wilkes, his neighbour, works at a local farm and was sneaking a quick cigarette in his back garden before he headed off to help with the milking. He saw Dick lying on the ground and popped around to check on him.'

'Did he call for the ambulance?'

'No because my stubborn brother wouldn't let him. Les managed to help him up and move him indoors.'

Through the remains of his thumping headache Ruan struggled to make sense of the rambling story but finally cottoned on that Wilkes put his foot down and insisted that if Dick wouldn't let him call for the doctor he must get someone in to help out.

'It was me or social services and he decided I was the lesser of the evils.' Vera raked him with her sharp eyes. 'I don't want to know what you've been up to just go and get changed.'

'Give me ten minutes. I need a hot shower.'

'I'll have some tea and toast ready when you're done.'

Not exactly up to Essy's offer but best not to mention that. 'Black coffee, please, and skip the toast.' He gave his mother credit for only silently raising her eyebrows at him.

An hour later the taxi driver had dropped them off in Newquay with instructions to return in half an hour and they were having a stand-off with his truculent uncle.

'I'm not going back with you.' Dick's voice was remarkably loud and strong for a man who had been lying outside overnight with a badly sprained ankle.

'It'll only be for a few days, you silly old duffer.' Vera was losing her patience. 'You can't manage on your own here. If you won't come I'm calling your doctor now.'

Ruan crouched down in front of his uncle and worked on sounding sympathetic. In reality he wanted to haul his stubborn uncle out to the taxi, get back to Herring Bay and crawl into his own bed, all within the shortest amount of time. 'You know she means it.' One advantage to having Dick under their roof was the opportunity it presented to find out what surrounded his uncle's violent dislike of the village where he was born and raised.

'You'm a bossy old soul, Vera Pascow. Didn't matter that I was five years older, you ordered me around when we were little 'uns and you're no different now.'

'And you've always been an argumentative old so and so,' she snapped back at him. 'The boy will pack a few things from your bedroom and we'll be off.'

'I s'pose I've got no choice.' Dick jabbed his finger at Ruan. 'Don't you go nosing around mind!'

'I wouldn't dream of it. I won't be long.'

At the top of the steep stairs he tried the first door but that turned out to be the spare bedroom. Cold and unused. Next to it his uncle's room was equally cold and almost as sparsely furnished. On a straight back chair a pair of trousers was folded up neatly on the seat and the twin bed only boasted a single pillow and a threadbare blue quilt. When Ruan opened the narrow wardrobe the overwhelming smell of mothballs made him recoil. He lifted down a small suitcase from the top shelf and opened it up on the bed. With the trousers laid in the bottom he pulled underwear, a couple of shirts and several pairs of socks from the rickety chest of drawers. Everything was frayed and faded from repeated washing. He added a pair of reading glasses from the bedside table and a well-thumbed bible. After a quick scout around the bathroom he picked up his uncle's toothbrush with a wry smile. If his mother saw the bristles splayed out from years of use she'd toss it in the bin.

The barrenness of everything made him shiver and he snapped the case shut before going back downstairs.

'I'll put this in the taxi. Wait here and I'll be back in a minute to help him out.'

'Vera can manage.' Dick's insistence made his mother smile. 'We'll be all right, won't we?'

'Mum?'

'Off you go.' She shooed him away. 'We'll be there in a minute.'

Arguing was pointless so he hurried on out and stowed the suitcase in the boot. Nobody said much as they got settled in for the short drive but then his mother kept up a one-sided conversation about the weather until they neared Herring Bay, then even she fell silent.

When they made it inside the house his uncle sunk down on the sofa and gazed around.

'I never thought I'd come back here again.' He sounded bewildered.

Ruan opened his mouth to ask why the hell not but his mother jumped in with an offer of tea. Little to do with hospitality but a whole lot to do with shutting him up.

'No, thanks, Vera, I'm ready for bed.' His uncle's frown deepened. 'I expect the boy's got my old room?'

'I'll bring your case up, Uncle Dick. The spare bedroom is on the right.'

'Thanks.'

With his uncle out of hearing he thought he'd better attempt to reassure his mother. 'It's only for a few days. You did the right thing.'

'Did I? We'll see.'

'I'm going to take a nap.' Ruan grasped her arm. 'We'll do this together.'

She gave a brief shrug as if his presence wouldn't work miracles.

Molly didn't verbally ask any questions when she saw Essy loading sopping wet, sandy clothes into the washing machine but her raised eyebrows did the talking on her behalf. She chose the simplest option and stuck to a version of the truth, while omitting the part about her unnecessary rescue attempt.

'I sure won't do that again. The water was freezing. How y'all stand it I don't know!' She fetched the mop out of the cupboard under the stairs and tackled the damp floor.

'I saw Ruan down The Smugglers' last night. He was two sheets to the wind. The boy's not a happy drunk.'

If she tried to explain it might make matters worse so Essy went with a sympathetic nod and hoped that would do the trick.

'Are you going to tell him everything Reverend Worthington shared with you?'

'I think he deserves to know.' Molly's tight flickering smile wasn't encouraging. 'Don't you agree?'

'You must do what you think is best.'

'I will.'

'I'm sure.' Molly didn't need to roll her eyes to get her point across. 'I've got work to do. One of my clients is a hairdresser and he's worse than useless at keeping his accounts straight.'

Putting things off wasn't her way but she wondered if not quite noon counted as 'later' in Ruan's vocabulary. She could hardly walk around to knock on his door so pulled out her phone to send a brief message. While she finished cleaning up and returned the mop to its assigned spot Essy listened for the short ping indicating he'd sent a reply. After ten silent minutes

99

he did, saying could he take a rain check till tomorrow as he was still feeling rough. So, as she had the afternoon to kill, she rethought her plan for the day. The sun was shining and the closest beach on Gordon Snell's list was just outside St Austell. She ran upstairs and pulled out her laptop to check the tide table, having established she wouldn't get her feet wet (at least not involuntarily) if she didn't waste too much time, the next question was how best to get there. Parking appeared to be limited so Annabelle could stay here and she'd get there by bus and walking. Essy enacted a quick change into a strappy white linen top and lime green capris to co-ordinate perfectly with her new lime and white trainers. Herring Bay's steep hills and the Cornish landscape in general had forced her to make adjustments to her usual footwear choices or risk broken ankles.

'I'm off to check out Porthpean Beach.' She popped her head around the dining room door, appropriated by her aunt years ago as an office. 'I can't be bothered to take the car but if I hurry I'll catch the half past twelve bus. It looks as though I can pick up another bus when I reach St Austell out as far as the Penrice Hospital and I'll walk from there.'

'You'll like it. It's a pretty little place. We often went there as children. I remember your mother getting a wicked sunburn once. Silly girl were old enough to know better but she plastered olive oil all over her.' Her aunt shook her head. 'Laid up with sunstroke she were for days but said it was worth it. Brown as a berry she was.' A tired sigh escaped her. 'Off you go or you'll miss the bus.'

She ran down the hill to the bus stop and made it by the skin of her teeth. Automatically she plumped down in one of the front seats as if her aunt was with her. Essy stared out of the window and tried to make the most of the ever-changing scenery as they drove along the narrow lanes. Sometimes a flash of blue sea popped into view around a sharp corner before they hit another long stretch between towering hedges bursting with wildflowers.

You must do what you think is best.

Best for whom was the million-dollar question? If Ruan didn't make the first move and contact her she'd plant herself on his doorstep if necessary, whether it pissed his mother off or not. The decision lifted her spirits and she jumped off the bus in St Austell bubbling over with unspent energy. To burn it off she abandoned the second bus and walked, almost bouncing along in the new shoes. She'd never walked two miles that fast before and soon stood at the top of the gentle slipway leading down to the beach.

The far more secluded spot had none of the size or drama of Fistral and couldn't claim to be as picturesque as Porthmeor but something about the sheltered, sandy cove appealed to Essy. This was a real family beach where jet skis were banned and there were no serious surfers to be seen. No doubt this was why it stuck in Gordon Snell's mind all these decades. She pulled out her phone to take a few pictures and then made her way down onto the sand.

The first order of play was to remove her shoes. It had nothing to do with spoiling her new shoes but rather the need to experience the sand with her bare feet. The sun-warmed grittiness between her toes felt wonderful in comparison with the damp cold of Herring Bay Beach early this morning. Essy tipped her head up to the sun before remembering Aunt Molly's horror story. Luckily the Tennessee girl still lurked inside her and she'd stuffed a baseball cap in her bag. She didn't plan on returning to Herring Bay with scarlet skin to match her name. For a moment the gentle waves breaking on the beach tempted her but it only took dipping one foot in to remember this wasn't Florida. Around her children ran screaming and laughing into the water and she could only assume they were used to its sub-zero temperature. She watched as a skinny little boy wriggled out of the towel his mother had wrapped around him and raced back into the sea. The woman watched him with an indulgent smile apparently unfazed by his mottled purple skin.

Soon she had her vial of sand safely tucked away and eyed up the small café and shop overlooking the beach. It took a few minutes to navigate her way up there and one of the people she passed was a woman carrying away a tray of tea. Why would anyone want such a thing on the beach? Ruan popped back into her mind – no surprise there – and she could imagine him saying that he would've been extremely grateful for a hot drink after her ignominious rescue.

Ice cream struck her as the perfect lunch and Essy studied the varied selection written in chalk on the display board. When she asked the man behind the counter for advice several other people in the queue picked up on her accent and offered their opinions. British reticence clearly went by the board when they were near the sea.

'I'll guess I'll decide on one of the ninety-nine things y'all are talkin' about.' Her popular choice earned her more friendly smiles. 'With cream.'

'Keep it away from the seagulls. They're greedy buggers.' The ruddy-faced man handed over an enormous whipped vanilla ice cream with a stick of chocolate poking out of the top finished with a dollop of clotted cream. Paula would have a fit. Essy's mother was incredibly figure conscious and forever dropping hints that if her daughter wasn't careful age and gravity would catch up with her.

People were sitting along the wall so she picked an empty spot and joined them. She set down her bag and was careful to shield her ice cream from the predatory gull eyeing her up from his spot on top of a nearby light pole.

'Fancy seeing you here.' Kit Hawkey loomed over her. 'Bloody hot, isn't it?' He flicked off his cap and wiped ineffectually at the sweat sticking his thin hair to his scalp and trickling down his red shiny face. 'I'm being a typical Brit, aren't I?' He scrambled down to join her.

'Yeah.' He wouldn't survive a Tennessee summer with its seemingly endless stretches of thirty plus degree days, made hotter and even less bearable because of the high humidity. 'I know Ruan appreciated your help last night... although I guess calling it this morning is more accurate.'

He shaded his eyes with his hand. 'And you know this because?'

For the second time that day she explained.

'I remember his dad.' Kitto scratched at his beard. 'Mr Pascow was a nice enough old chap. Listen to me calling him old! He must've only been in his mid-twenties back then. If he wasn't working he'd usually be happy to kick a ball around with us. Not that Ruan was much for sports but he tried... to please his dad.'

'What about my mom?' The question dangled there for a moment.

'Remember we were only boys and she was a lot older.'

That wasn't much of an answer.

'Once Ruan asked me to come home with him for my tea but when we went in the house Mrs Pascow wasn't there. His dad came out of the kitchen and quickly closed the door behind him. I can see his face now. Eyes out on stalks. Scared stiff he was when he saw us standing there. He told me to go on home and when I ran around the corner into Duke Street I bumped head first into a woman creeping out of the Pascow's back gate.' Kit's face grew redder. 'It was your mum. I'm not saying...'

'It's okay. We both know what was goin' on.'

He struggled back up. 'I'd better be off or Debbie will wonder where I've got to. We'll be off back to Sussex tomorrow.' A slight frown creased his brow. 'Keep an eye on Ruan. He's not as tough as he makes out. All that "I-don't-give-a-damn-about-any-of-them" thing is an act.'

'I worked that out by day two of knowing him.'

'Good. You're exactly what he needs.'

If Kit was right, the other side of the coin was whether Ruan was what *she* needed?

Chapter Sixteen

'I'm going out. Anything you want?' Ruan combed his hair in the hall mirror.

'You're off to see that woman.'

Nothing remained a secret in Herring Bay for long. His mother's accusatory statement made it clear she knew he'd seen Essy behind her back. At eighteen he accepted an offer from Sheffield University to study architecture not only because of their exceptional programme but because it was over three hundred miles away from Cornwall. He was tired of living life under a microscope and being known as Tree Pascow's boy.

'Will you be home for your dinner? I'll have a nice bit of roast beef ready about one o'clock.' Vera huffed out a sigh. 'Dick hasn't been eating proper on his own. He needs feeding.'

That made her brother sound like a prize pig being fattened up for market.

'No. We're eating out.' He slung a bright blue cotton sweater around his shoulders.

'Be careful.'

Ruan headed outside to his car without answering. Hopefully their second attempt to eat at The Drifters would have more success than the first. Brian Martin hadn't made anything of it when he begged for another reservation. Back in their school days Brian, Ruan and Kit were close friends but they drifted apart over the years. It hadn't been hard to keep track of Brian because he'd become a wildly successful chef with top-rated television shows, best-selling cookbooks and a Michelin starred restaurant in Bath. Five years ago he gave it all up and returned to Cornwall.

If I hadn't I'd be dead by now.

Brian's blunt assessment when they reconnected over a beer at The Smugglers' had shocked the life out of him. The pressure of his demanding work commitments alongside making time for his wife and new baby son had driven him to the edge, but he'd regained much-needed balance with his new restaurant. The Drifters only had room for thirty diners but in less than two years it had become the most sought after place to eat in the southwest. Brian refused to enlarge it or open more than four days a week.

My staff need a life too.

Ruan parked outside Molly's and sat in the car for a few moments before deciding he was being an idiot. The only person's approval he needed to date Essy Havers was the lady herself. But until they had the conversation they'd been steadfastly avoiding that was a moot point. He got out of the car and headed up the path.

'Hey, handsome.' Essy opened the door with a broad smile. 'Awesome colour.'

The melon linen suit shouted summer, his mother would say far too loudly. In his view he'd toned it down by wearing it with a simple white T-shirt and tan loafers with no socks. 'Thanks.' He struggled to stop staring at her. Every time her flat out beauty caught him off guard. It was her zest for life that drew him in not her fashionable clothes, although he naturally appreciated those. The laser focus of her elusive grey-green eyes on him shot a pulse of desire straight to his core.

'I hope I'm gettin' fed properly this time?'

'I promise. No dried up sandwiches and the wine definitely won't taste like aircraft fuel. Do you need to tell Molly you're off?'

'No she…' Essy glanced over her shoulder and laughed because her aunt appeared like a genie out of a bottle.

'I hope you've got a pile of money in the bank. I hear they charge forty pounds for a bit of roast dinner at that fancy place.'

There was no point trying to explain they were paying for Brian's skill rather than the actual food itself. Essy told him that Molly had balked at paying almost eight pounds for a bowl of soup at a posh hotel in Newquay and compared it unfavourably with the huge saucepan she could make at home for the same price.

'Off you go and enjoy yourselves.' She clearly thought the idea unlikely.

'Oh we will.' Before they were subjected to any more warnings he whisked Essy away. They burst out laughing once they were in the car and driving out of Herring Bay. 'Nobody would describe your aunt as adventurous, would they?'

'Really? What makes you say that?' She giggled. 'Would my mother have been like that if she stayed here?' Every trace of good humour fell away.

He'd been stupid to hope they could make it all the way through lunch without at least one contentious subject raising its ugly head.

'Sorry.'

'Don't apologise. How about we save the heavy conversation for after we've eaten, so we don't get indigestion?'

'Yeah that sounds perfect.'

If he wasn't driving Ruan would've kissed her.

'Wow, that was incredible.' Essy reached for Ruan's hand across the table. 'Thank you.' That was probably the most delicious meal she'd ever tasted and eaten in the company of her favourite man. What wasn't there to like about that? 'I don't suppose there's any chance your friend might come out of the kitchen to say hi?'

'Every chance in the world.' A tall, raw-boned man with the face of a Norse god, a mane of white-blond hair and piercing blue eyes loomed over her. 'If nothing else I needed to see if you rival my old friend in the fashion department.'

Ruan's skin turned puce, deeply unflattering because it clashed with his suit.

'He knows I'm kidding. We're okay, aren't we, pal?'

'Of course we are, you overgrown beanpole. I see you still haven't learned any manners.'

'I turned into a real smoothie for a while but I'm over all that malarkey.'

On the way she'd discovered the bare bones of Brian Masters' story but had the suspicion some of his troubles remained private between the two men. Essy found it interesting that Kit Hawkey was the link between them. Maybe the deeply ordinary man, on the surface anyway, had wanted to break out of his mould but never had the nerve?

'That was awesome. I'm not a fan of fancied up food but yours was more like regular stuff but on another level.' Her review amused both men. 'Hey, I say it like it is. I don't do pretentious in anything.' Essy laughed. 'Well, a bit in my clothes I guess. I like to be on trend but I'm not obsessed.'

'Amen.' Brian's face split in a wide grin. 'I wish I could join you for coffee but duty calls. We've got several secluded areas in the garden for customers to enjoy and I've reserved the wildflower garden for you but can swap it to the rose arbour if you prefer?' He gave her a sideways glance.

'Not pretentious remember?'

'Pete will show you the way.' He beckoned over a cheerful red-headed waiter. 'He'll bring out whatever you want.' The public face shifted and she glimpsed the small, worried boy behind the celebrity chef mask. 'You'd better take good care of this one.' He tapped Ruan's arm.

The second person to make the same request in twenty-four hours. Did Ruan have any clue how many people cared for him?

'I'll do my best.'

The waiter reappeared with a tray of coffee so they followed him outside. Whoever designed the outside space was a genius. The series of themed 'rooms' were framed with trellis on three sides while remaining wide open to the staggering coastal views. The simple wicker furniture in the wildflower 'room' was softened by plump moss-green cushions. It all blended seamlessly with the glorious profusion of scented wildflowers surrounding them.

'Wow, this is somethin' else.'

'Shall we go and sit down before you get blown away?'

Despite the warm sunshine a stiff breeze blew in from the sea, catching her hair and tossing it around her face but she still giggled. 'Spoilsport.'

'Not really, I'm just rather fond of you.'

His precise, oh so English way of expressing how much he cared for her touched Essy's heart.

'Well, I'm rather fond of you too. La di da.' Her attempt to mimic him made them both laugh and raised her hopes that they could survive this with their relationship intact. One of them had to push open the door neither really wished to open. 'So who's going first?'

'You,' Ruan pleaded. 'I need to know—'

'Everything Conan told me after you left.' The minister's grey, taut face was etched in her mind. 'He wasn't blind to your dad's failings but they were still good friends.' She pressed a finger to Ruan's lips when he opened his mouth to protest. 'Shush, let me speak.'

'Sorry.'

A flare of anger surged through her. If she could get her hands on Tremayne Pascow she'd give him a piece of her mind for creating this turmoil in his son.

'I know. I guess he saw the good in your father. Someone he could rely on to help with any maintenance problems in the chapel. A man who would always lend a hand when a neighbour was in trouble. He purposely grew more vegetables than your family could eat and shared the extra with anyone who needed it.'

Ruan pushed her away. 'That might be true but I saw Mum struggle to make ends meet after Dad left us and cleaning other people's houses was the only thing she could fit in around taking care of me.' He struggled to be fair. 'Mum would tell me off if she heard me saying that because she still works for a few favoured people by choice. I tried to persuade her to stop a few years ago because I had the means to help her out but she laughed and said she didn't like being idle and got a lot of satisfaction from her job.' Sadness thickened his voice. 'Surely you haven't forgotten the way he treated your mother?'

'No, but Conan helped me to see that from a different perspective as well. He said that Mom's family never understood her burning desire for a different sort of life and it caused massive arguments at their home. Tree was a good listener and Conan thinks she desperately needed a friend.'

'That almost makes it worse. He took advantage of a vulnerable teenager because he wasn't getting any sex at home.' Ruan's voice rose.

'The reverend skirted around whether the relationship was a physical one. He hinted that things aren't always what they seem. Conan did admit he sent your father away.' Before she started Essy meant to phrase that more tactfully but it was too late now.

'He sent Dad away?' Ruan's jaw dropped.

'Well, not exactly.'

'What exactly *do* you mean?'

She reached for his hands and tightened her grasp when he half-heartedly attempted to pull away. 'When they were in the middle of all this mess my aunt went to see Conan.'

'Molly was mixed up in this too?' His voice rose. 'Did no one consider being honest with me about what happened once I was old enough to understand?'

'Stop it. Just stop it,' Essy snapped. 'Don't make this all about you. You're not the only one affected. There's me. Vera and Paula. Molly. Then there's an old man who's questioned his actions for the last thirty plus years.'

He folded in on himself like a deflated balloon. 'Sorry.'

She recited the story as she'd heard it word for word. Molly had been worried about her sister and pleaded with the minister to intervene. 'Conan had a quiet chat with your father on the Christmas Eve. Tree insisted nothing was going on before finally admitting he might have been friendlier with Paula than he should have. The reverend urged him to do the right thing and break off the relationship before he did any more damage.

'Paula disappeared from her home in the early hours of New Year's Day after leaving a note to tell her family not to come after her. The news spread around the village, your folks argued about it and your dad returned to see Conan.' She lowered her voice. 'He still remembers word for word what Tree said. I never set out to hurt anyone. I was only trying to help her but I've ruined that girl's life. Vera has had enough and the boy hates me too, I've seen it in his eyes. I don't blame either of them. In my own way I've always loved my wife and I worship little Ruan but they'll be better off without me. I've got friends in France, fishermen I can get work with.'

'Didn't he realise what conclusion people would jump to?'

'I guess not.'

Ruan's dark brows knitted together. 'I need to process this.'

'Do you want to talk some more?'

'No.' His empty stare frightened her. 'Not today. Let's go.'

'Now?'

'Yes, now.' It took him a huge effort to stand back up. 'I'll take you home.'

'We can help each other through this.'

'I'm not sure we can.' Ruan's voice broke. 'This turns things upside down. Give me time.'

'I'll do anything you want if you promise you won't give up on us.'

'Oh, Essy, some things aren't meant to be.' He stroked her cheek, then his arm dropped away. 'Perhaps we're one of them. There's a lot of history to get past.'

'We'll see.' The vow she'd made to tread softly hammered in her head. By his puzzled expression her lover hadn't expected such a restrained response. He'd forgotten how stubborn she could be.

Chapter Seventeen

'Why won't you tell me where you're going?'

Ruan adjusted the straps and settled his backpack on his shoulders. Ever since he stormed back into the house after the disastrous date with Essy his mother had plagued him. Three days later she still hadn't given up.

'What about your uncle? You promised to help me out with taking care of him but I should've known that was all talk. Turns out you're a Pascow man through and through after all.' She turned chalk-white. 'Oh, my love, I'm some sorry. I shouldn't have said that. You're a good boy and always have been. Our Dick being here has got me all flummoxed.'

He managed a brief nod, being any more conciliatory was beyond him right now. 'Uncle Dick doesn't seem too bad. I could run him home before I leave.'

'Run him home? He's not going back to that cold, miserable place anytime soon if I have my way.'

'We can't force him to stay.' He mentally closed the door on his escape route. It had been a ridiculous idea to pack a bag and imagine he could pop over to France to search for his father. Had he seriously planned to wander around every Breton fishing village asking about a man who might or might not have gone to that area three decades ago? White-hot anger had stopped him thinking straight.

'The boy's right.' Dick limped into the kitchen. 'I'm getting around all right and I don't intend to clutter up the place any longer.'

'Don't be daft.' Vera dismissed her brother like she was swatting an annoying fly. 'You can barely put any weight on that ankle. The doctor's coming about ten this morning to take a look at it.'

'What doctor? You should've asked me first.'

'You would've said no.'

'Women,' Dick grumbled. 'Don't get mixed up with any of them, my lad. They're nothing but bloody trouble.'

For once he agreed with his uncle. If a certain inquisitive American hadn't turned up his life would be trundling along nicely. *Rubbish*. His life hadn't been 'nice' for a long time.

'You're right but they've usually got good intentions.' Underneath Essy's bluster lay a heart of gold, which he carelessly stomped on when she opened up to him. 'You might as well give in.' Ruan let his bag drop to the floor. 'I am.'

His mother looked like a cat let loose in a cream factory.

'For now.' The warning he tossed in made no difference to her satisfied smile. He hadn't honestly expected it to but it seemed feeble to give in without some sort of gesture. 'How about I cook breakfast?' Anything to delay the inevitable. Vera would guess something was eating at him and the real question was how much to tell her? When she swore that his father hadn't left to be with Paula he'd assumed that was the loyal wife talking but perhaps she'd known all along where he went? In the past she had flown off the handle when he asked why she never went through legal channels to get a divorce or have Tremayne Pascow declared dead. Vera insisted he was still her husband and she would keep her wedding vows.

'I'm not going to like cooking for myself after this. You're both spoiling me.' Dick patted his stomach.

'I'd be happy to have you stay for good,' Vera persisted. 'Ruan will be off again when he gets himself sorted out. I could do with the company, it's not much fun here on my own.'

'Can't resist, can you? I knew you'd start nagging because it's what you do. You've never been content to leave things be. No wonder Tree looked for a bit of sympathy elsewhere. Wasn't right what he did mind, but sometimes people are driven to things. You know what I'm talking about.' Deep frown lines creased his uncle's face. 'I'm not hungry. I'm going back to bed and you can tell the doc to clear off when he gets here.' He hobbled out of the room.

'Oh, Mum. Why couldn't you let him be?'

'As he said it's not my way.' She sounded unmoved but Ruan found that hard to believe. 'Your father often said I drove him to… forget it, that's all in the past now.'

'No, we're not forgetting it.' Finally his insistent tone had an effect and she exhaled a resigned sigh. 'I'll make a pot of tea and we're going to talk.'

'You'll regret it.'

Ruan crossed the fingers on one hand and reached for the kettle with the other.

Giving in wasn't her style. After Ruan, silent and grim-faced, dropped her off on Sunday she was swept by an overwhelming desire to crawl under the duvet and weep but she plastered on a smile and raved to her aunt about what a great time they had at The Drifters. She doubted it threw Molly off the scent and expected the questions would come soon enough.

First thing Monday morning she reworked her to-do list. At the top was finishing the job she was being paid for by visiting Gordon Snell's last three favourite beaches. Once that was done she would focus on tracking down Tree Pascow. A distant third, but equally important in ways she couldn't put into words, was the old Methodist Chapel. That was lodged in the distant corner of her brain reserved for things that needed mulling over before she took any action. Ruan would say that's where the possibility of finding his father should be tucked away.

Holywell Beach, on the north coast near Newquay, was her destination on Monday afternoon and, despite all her worries, she'd soaked up the sun on a golden expanse of sand that rivalled anything California could offer. Being Cornwall the weather naturally changed yesterday and she experienced Perranporth and Godrevy through a bank of heavy mist and fog. It made sense now that so many visitors returned to Cornwall year after year, it must be the only way to ensure that over time they'd catch all the different holiday spots at their best.

In the early days of Eureka! she made the decision to stick with finding inanimate objects. Missing persons' cases were a whole other ball game and frequently took an emotional toll on the searchers. Now she'd take the risk. Essy rationalised that many of the same techniques she used to find an elusive piece of china would work on people.

She briefly considered contacting Ruan to suggest they work on this together but he'd pleaded for time so that's what he'd get even if it half-killed her to wait. The next move must come from him. Although her aunt had decent internet access, the urge to get out of Herring Bay wouldn't leave her alone.

'What are you up to today, my 'andsome.' Molly's sharp gaze landed on Essy's notebook.

'I'm heading into St Austell on the bus.' After staring at Annabelle day in and day out sitting around unused she'd reluctantly returned her to the rental office, the poor thing deserved someone who'd appreciate her better. 'I need to go to the library and do some research connected with this beach project.' That wasn't strictly a lie because she had genuinely considered digging up more of the history behind Gordon Snell's favourite beaches.

'I might join you. I could do with a few bits and pieces in the Poundshop.'

'Great.' She struggled to hide her dismay.

'I doubt I'll hang around as long as you. I get my books from the mobile van that comes here once a fortnight. Saves carrying them on the bus.' Her aunt slid her a sly smile. 'Of course if you're meeting anyone I wouldn't want to poke my nose in? Ruan's always been a keen reader.'

'I've no idea what he's up to today.' Or what he'd done the past few days. Not that it didn't cross her mind. Multiple times.

'You told me all about the fancy food you ate but never did say what happened when you told him all that stuff about his dad. I bet he got on his high horse?'

'Well, yeah, but do you blame him?' Her anger on Ruan's

behalf bubbled up. 'Seems y'all never took him to account. I get it when he was a little kid but not now.'

'His mum did what she thought was for the best.' Molly shrugged. 'I had my say to Reverend Worthington that one time because I was worried about Paula and our parents were on the verge of giving up on her.' Her expression darkened. 'Are you sticking your nose in the Pascows' business?'

'It's my business too.' Essy held her ground.

'Finding Tree Pascow won't do anyone any good.'

'You can't know that.'

'You're a silly girl sometimes.' Molly sounded exasperated.

'Like my mom?'

'You said it not me.'

'Don't you think closure is a good thing?'

'Bah! Load of rubbish.' Tears welled up in her aunt's eyes. 'If you'd ever lost anyone important to you I doubt you'd think so either.'

There was probably a lot of truth in that. How could she know? Her father didn't count because he was alive and well in Canada. A long-distance parent who had little impact on her life. Every year she received a Christmas card from Tony Havers, normally adorned with a glossy picture of his new family. Clearly he didn't consider it tactless to brag about his glamorous second wife and their three daughters. Essy's half-sisters were all blonde-haired, blue-eyed and a glowing testimonial of North American orthodontics.

'What does Paula think about you dragging all this up?'

Essy glanced away and pretended to be busy sorting out her handbag.

'I thought so. You haven't told her.'

'Are *you* going to?' That challenge pulled the rug out from under the conversation and stopped it dead.

'I still say you don't have the right to go poking around if Vera and Paula don't want you to. Promise me you'll give them both a ring and ask them first before you do anything rash.'

Years ago she would've blown off the advice and ploughed on her own course. 'How about I forget going to St Austell and pop over to see Vera now?' Her aunt's face turned the colour of sour milk.

'To the house?'

'Oh Lord, I can't win. What's the difference between that and phoning? Pussyfooting around isn't in my nature. It definitely wasn't in yours when you tackled Conan about my mom, even though I bet your folks weren't thrilled.' The sly dig, or praise depending how it was taken, made the corners of Molly's mouth twitch.

'Have your breakfast first.'

A slice of toast and a cup of coffee wouldn't change her mind but one small concession wouldn't hurt. 'Fine.' Essy watched the frying pan come out. She wouldn't get out of here until she'd consumed enough in the way of saturated fats and carbohydrates to make her mother blanch. She plastered on a smile and offered to help. Softly, softly.

Chapter Eighteen

They sat across the kitchen table from each other like two stone statues.

'I'll give that interfering Conan Worthington a piece of my mind when I see him.' The threat burst out of his mother.

'For telling the truth?'

'Truth? Don't you think he should have had the decency to tell me first before that woman?'

Ruan's head spun. 'You didn't know that he encouraged Dad to go?'

'Of course I didn't.' Her head drooped to rest on her folded arms. 'I would never have asked Tree to leave.'

The blind loyalty she clung onto for his father bewildered him. 'Maybe Dad finally realised that you deserved better?'

'Better?' Vera scoffed. 'Left to raise you on my own with very little money in the face of all the gossip going around?' She picked at a loose thread on the tablecloth. 'Everyone took it for granted he'd gone off with that girl although we heard later that she married someone else. We still don't know that for certain one way or the other.'

'Would you seriously have taken him back?'

'You don't understand what it's like to truly love someone. I know I'm to blame for some of our problems.' His mother's face turned bright red. 'A lot of things are more important than... sex from my way of looking at things, but I suppose it's different for men.'

There wasn't any point in arguing that particular assumption with her.

'I don't need or want your pity. Or that American woman's.'

'She's not "that American woman". Her name is Essy. She deserves to know the truth. We all do.' The knowledge hit Ruan like a bolt of lightning. She had been right all along. Wouldn't she just love hearing that? 'There are agencies that help to find missing people.'

'No!'

'Wouldn't you prefer to know... one way or the other?'

'If he's alive or dead?'

Despite everything Ruan wasn't certain how he'd feel if they proved there was no chance of ever reconnecting with his father. His mother's stoicism crumbled and she wiped a hand over her moist eyes.

'If you don't want to find out that's fine, but I do.' His raised voice shocked her. 'I'm going to take Essy up on her offer to work together on this.'

'That's not fair. You're forcing my hand.'

'Not at all.' He needed to make his intentions clear. 'I can't promise to keep the result quiet. All my life I've been dogged by speculation and I'm sick and tired of it.'

'I'm sorry, love. I'm selfish. Always have been.' Vera's face sunk into deep, ageing furrows. 'Ask Dick.'

'Ask me what?' His uncle hobbled in from the hall.

'Tell him I was a selfish little girl and I'm no different now.'

'If I say that you might keep me prisoner here until Christmas.' Dick's eyes twinkled. 'You've always liked to get your own way and it never crosses your mind you might be wrong.'

Somehow Ruan didn't think they were talking solely about his father. There could be more family secrets than he realised and perhaps where his father had disappeared was the least of them.

'Was I wrong about you and Molly?'

'Shush, Vera.' Dick sounded angry, and sad. 'There's no point digging all that up again.'

'Digging what up? What's Molly got to do with anything?'

'Nothing for you to worry about.' His mother chided him. 'Do what you have to do with... Essy, but don't blame me if you don't like what you find out.' She turned to Dick. 'The boy's determined to discover what happened to Tree.'

'About bloody time.'

That shocked him. He'd assumed that Dick would toe his mother's line. Interesting.

'That's another subject she overruled me on.' His voice turned gruff. 'I wanted to approach the Salvation Army and ask for their help but she wouldn't have anything to do with it. She should've divorced Tree or at least been a proper widow. Found a decent man to make a life with.'

'I made my choices. You made yours. You could've ignored my advice but you didn't. Now I'm going to stick the kettle on and we'll say no more about it all. The boy will do what he wants and we'll survive it... one way or another.'

Dragging this all out in plain sight had only opened the way for more questions. Ruan's mind raced wondering what the innuendo-laden conversation between the siblings meant. He'd asked for this.

The doorbell jangled and Essy almost turned tail and ran. Talk about a déjà vu moment. If Ruan hadn't practically dragged her into Molly's that first day would she have gone in or climbed back in her car and hightailed it back to London?

'Oh! It's you.'

'Yeah, is that a problem?' She didn't give Ruan time to reply. 'I know I promised to give you time but you've had enough and this needs sorting out.' Not exactly how she meant to phrase it but his fixed stare unnerved her. 'Uh, I'm sorry to be so...'

'Blunt? Forthright?' Laughter lines fanned around his eyes and she felt a giggle coming on. 'So Essy.'

Was that a good or bad thing?

'Have you been looking into your crystal ball?'

And they called southerners hard to understand? In her opinion the Cornish had them beat by a mile.

'We've just been talking about you.'

'Really?' She'd bet her last dollar that Vera Pascow hadn't said anything flattering.

'I told my mum about your chat with Worthington.'

'Oh. I bet that didn't go down well?'

'Don't keep the girl out there,' his mother yelled from inside the house somewhere.

'I suppose we'd better get it over with.' Ruan's grimace made the decision for her.

'She can wait a minute.' Shock flared in his dark eyes when she cradled his face with her fingers and brushed her mouth against his warm lips in a soft kiss. Another day he'd enjoy the full treatment but for now the imprint and taste of her on his mouth should do the trick. She would be uppermost in his mind, a devious weapon against his mother's pervasive influence. Essy stroked the dark stubble she'd never seen him with before. He told her once that he drew the line at following fashion where facial hair was concerned, something which could be connected to the only picture she'd seen of Tree Pascow where he was sporting a bushy light brown beard.

'Later we're—'

'Oh yeah, there's a lot we're doing later.' She watched his skin flush.

'Not in Herring Bay. Too many prying eyes.'

They were definitely on the same page there. Essy grabbed his hand. 'Let's go, but remember that thought.'

'As if I could forget.'

His warm rumbling laughter snaked through her and pooled in the base of her stomach. 'That was the plan.'

'I guessed that.' Ruan gave her a lazy, sexy smile and shouted over his shoulder to tell his mother that they were coming.

Walking into the house Essy felt like a lamb off to be slaughtered.

'Hello, dear.'

Essy struggled to hide her surprise. This was the first time Vera had voluntarily spoken to her.

120

'Sit down and I'll pour you a cup of tea.'

'She prefers coffee.' Ruan's gentle correction brought a hint of colour to his mother's hollow cheeks.

'It doesn't matter.' She didn't want to rock the boat that his mother had tentatively pushed in her direction but he squeezed her hand as if to say, yes it does, I'm sticking up for you, it's in a small way but that's where these things start.

'Coffee it is.' The taut smile warned Essy she shouldn't read too much into the sudden overture. 'This is my brother, by the way, Dick Menear. He had a fall and hurt his ankle so he's staying with us until he's well enough to go home to Newquay.'

'Pleased to meet you.' She stuck out her hand towards the small man with iron-grey hair perched at the end of the table. 'I'm—'

'Paula's girl.'

God, by the time she left this place she'd have no identity left of her own.

'You knew my mother?'

'Oh yes.'

'Let's get one thing straight.' Vera plonked a steaming mug of coffee in front of her and gestured to a china bowl of sugar in the middle of the table. 'I've heard what Reverend Worthington had to say and I'm not happy about it. For a start it was the first I'd heard of it and also I've never had the desire to track my husband down... for reasons that are none of your business.'

'Mum!'

'I'm sure you'll tell her all this later anyway so I'm saving you the trouble.' Vera's keen eyes pinned Essy down. 'I learned when this one was a boy that he'd go his own way. Your mother was the same and I expect you are too.'

'Would you at least be willing to answer a few of my questions?'

'No.'

The blunt response took her aback.

'I won't stand in your way but I'm not helping you.' Vera calmly drank her tea and ignored everyone's shocked stares.

'Oh right. Fair enough. Well, I appreciate your honesty.' Essy pushed her chair away and stood back up. 'It was good to… talk with you.' Describing the virtually one-sided conversation that way was a stretch but clearly only Vera was allowed to be outspoken and rude.

'I'll see you out.'

By the sound of Ruan's clipped voice if he was hooked up to a blood pressure meter it would shoot through the roof. She managed her goodbyes with a level of dignity that would make her mother proud. It wasn't kind to experience a distinct frisson of satisfaction when Ruan draped his arm around her shoulder and bussed a fleeting kiss on her cheek.

They barely made it outside the door before he exploded.

'If Mum didn't need help with my uncle I'd move out tonight. The doc took a look at it this morning, against Dick's wishes but she overruled him as usual. It's badly sprained and if he doesn't stop walking on it he's asking for trouble. Dick's being stubborn about using the crutches, which means Mum needs me here so it's two against one.'

He shoved a hand through his hair and messed up the style in a charming way. Essy held her tongue because he wasn't in the mood to find the observation amusing. Along with the unaccustomed stubble Ruan was dressed in old grey sweatpants and a ragged white T-shirt. The peek into this different side of him was endearing.

'Stubborn? Someone in your family? Never!' She slipped her arms around his waist and nestled into his chest, inhaling the intoxicating scent of his air-dried clothes. 'Hey, it's okay. We're good again and that's more important than anything.' Essy glanced up. 'We are, aren't we?'

'Yes, it's all good. You're absolutely right about what really matters.' His eyes brightened. 'Bet you like hearing that?'

'Maybe.'

'When I get you somewhere on our own I'm going to let this down, and...' He stroked his fingers through her ponytail. 'Sorry, I shouldn't take it for granted that's what you want too.'

Essy could swat Helena Carter from here to John O'Groats for making this wonderful man doubt himself. 'Hey, stop that. It is. Very much so.' Now her fingers did the wandering and lingered on the knot holding his sweatpants up. 'I promise I won't leave you in any doubt.'

'Good.'

The deep huskiness to his voice almost undid her. If Vera Pascow wasn't lurking on the other side of the door...

'I'll start making enquiries about your father. Why don't we meet in The Smugglers' tomorrow at seven?'

'I don't deserve you.'

'Yeah, you absolutely do.' Essy chuckled. 'You did something bad in a previous life and I'm your punishment. It's karma.'

'I'm happy to keep on being punished. That's all I'm saying.' He popped a kiss on her nose and gave her backside a pat. 'Off you go before I lose the will to send you away.'

'Until tomorrow.' Despite all the dampers Vera had tried to lay on them she trotted off, lighter in spirits than she'd been in a very long time.

Chapter Nineteen

In Ruan's mind anyone who claimed they enjoyed running was a sadist. He slumped against the rough granite wall backing up to the beach and took a long swig from his water bottle. In London he kept fit by working out in an upscale gym at least four times a week. Those were the days. Now his exercise routine, a loose description if ever he heard it, consisted of walking around the village and the occasional venture along the cliff path. He'd needed something to burn off the simmering anger lingering inside him. When he tried to press his mother she'd refused to discuss the subject of finding his father any further.

A petite blonde sauntered across the road and stopped in front of him. 'Well, if it isn't you, Ruan Pascow. Long time no see.'

Dark roots. Tired brown eyes. One uneven tooth crossed over another on the bottom. Flickers of memory tugged at him but nothing clicked until she took tiny licks of her ice cream.

'Julia North?'

The first girl he ever kissed. Unconsciously he glanced down at the beach where they'd done the deed.

'I'm flattered you remember.'

'Are you still living here?'

'I never moved away. I married Guy Masters but we split up a couple of years ago.'

'That's a shame. The divorce, I mean.'

'I heard you were back but no one's saying why.' She raked him with a searching look but he kept his expression bland and unrevealing. 'I thought you were too flash for Cornwall these days? Weren't you a fancy architect in London?'

'Yes but I fancied a change of pace. I wanted to reconnect with my roots.' The well- worn lie tripped out. Interestingly enough with each day that passed a touch more truth seeped into the words. 'I'd better be off before my legs seize up.'

'Maybe I'll see you around. I'll be in The Smugglers' tonight with some of the old gang from school. You should join us.'

Julia's suggestion made him wince. A drink together for old times' sake might have been interesting but he'd no desire to cross paths again with certain people from the past.

'I'm sure we'll bump into each other. Herring Bay is a small place.'

With his water bottle clipped back on his shorts he said a quick goodbye and sprinted off. He slackened his pace when he reached Wesley Street and stood there mooning over the old chapel again, he was getting as bad as his mother. The day he and Essy went inside was a revelation and it was totally his fault they didn't return the next morning. While he mused he idly fiddled with the lock on the gate and it sprung open.

There was no one in sight and none of the ubiquitous security cameras the rest of the country was swamped with, probably because Jackie Webb was too mean. Without stopping to think he slipped in through the gate and carefully draped the lock back on the chain so it would look intact to a casual observer. All he intended doing was wander around the outside again to get a better idea of the condition of the building but when he rattled the iron handle on one of the wooden entrance doors it came off in his hand. A responsible person would report the problem to Jackie. He would too. After he had another quick look inside.

Ruan crept in and made his way to the centre aisle and slowly turned all the way around to better get the full effect of the space. Thirty years of neglect hadn't improved the late Victorian building, which would never have won any architecture awards in the first place. A gaping spot drew his eye to where the organ once stood and he wouldn't be stupid enough to risk venturing up the stairs to the choir loft. He wandered further back and pushed open a creaking door leading to the vestry and the minister's old office. At the peak of its congregation in the early twentieth century an extension was built onto the back of the building and that's where he headed for next.

He picked his way around piles of old mouldy hymn books lining the narrow wooden passage and as soon as he entered the bare, rectangular room more long-buried memories resurfaced. As a boy it was where he attended Sunday school and fading, peeling posters of bible stories still clung to the walls. The straight-backed chairs remained in the familiar semi-circles facing a lectern where the teacher would stand. Ruan wandered into the narrow kitchen and ran his fingers over the rickety old oven. The deep butler's style sink was stained with rust from taps that had long ago stopped dripping. He could still taste the watered down orange squash and cheap biscuits they were given as a treat when class was over.

An unfamiliar stirring of excitement kicked off a raft of ideas and a thrill that his work hadn't kicked off in a long time ran through him. A stage could be built at one end to use for various local productions. Volunteers could perhaps run a café in the main part of the room. The community needed a meeting place. He'd seen examples of renovations for similar buildings where they included spaces rented out to local artisans. That could attract more visitors to Herring Bay and provide valuable income.

He enjoyed the fantasy for a few minutes before spotting a damp patch in one corner of the ceiling. Even if by some miracle Jackie Webb was persuaded to donate the building or sell the chapel at below market value what then? Simply to weatherproof the listed building would cost a fortune and where would the money come from? Most people here could barely keep their own heads above water financially and had little in the way of spare cash to donate, no matter how worthy the cause.

'What the fuck are you doing poking around here?' Jackie Webb stood in the doorway glowering at him. 'Wasn't it enough to send your girlfriend to do your dirty work? Thought she could pull the wool over my eyes, did you?'

Pointing out that it had worked up to a certain extent would be unwise.

'Any reason I shouldn't call the police?' Jackie yanked out his mobile and waved it in the air.

'Yeah, because you'll look silly when I back up his story.' Essy locked eyes with Ruan in the faint hope she could work out what the hell he was playing at.

'Uh, I saw the lock was broken on the gate and came in as far as the front of the building. That's when I saw one of the handles was off the door. I thought you might have a burglar.'

The landlord laughed at the lame explanation.

'And you didn't come tell me straight away because...?' Jackie hitched his thumbs in his belt and scowled.

'He thought he might catch them in the act,' Essy blurted out the first idea that flitted into her frazzled brain. 'You might have copper pipes. Burglars are always stealing those.'

'That's bloody rubbish. I don't know why you pair want to stick your nose in my business but you can cut it out.'

'It's because we see the building's potential and think it's a crime to let it fall down. That's what is going to happen if you don't take action soon.'

If they hadn't been on the verge of getting reported to the police she would've thrown her arms around Ruan and kissed him. Finally he got it.

'You cheeky bugger.' The landlord's eyes narrowed. 'Have you been talking to my soft-hearted wife?'

'Your wife?' Essy had only seen the mousy woman a couple of times and certainly never spoken to her.

'She's always nagging me to do something about this dump. Seems to think she's got some say in it just because...' He stopped mid-sentence and threw them both a dirty look. 'I'll tell you the same thing I told her.' She smelled stale beer on his breath when Jackie stepped closer. 'Stick your nose out of my affairs. Now clear out so I can lock up and if I catch either of you here again I'll call in the old Bill. No questions asked.'

She didn't much fancy seeing the inside of a British police cell. 'That sure is understandin' of you. You're a sweet man. I promise it won't happen again. Let's go.' Essy tugged on Ruan's sleeve and he trudged over to the door alongside her.

They made their way out through the chapel in silence.

'You're a sweet man?' He parodied her words. 'Did you have to bloody wag your eyelashes at him?'

'Wag my eyelashes?' she hissed. Anyone who knew her well would recognise she was madder than hell. This man still had a lot to learn about her. 'That's all the thanks I get for rescuing your ass?'

'Hey, I'm sorry.'

'You're sorry?' *Do better than that or you won't get a kiss, let alone anything else, this side of Christmas.*

'Really, really sorry,' Ruan pleaded with her. 'Is that any better?'

'Perhaps.'

'How about I'm an utter idiot who doesn't deserve to be rescued from spending the rest of his life in prison?' His dark eyes sparkled in that unbearably sexy way.

'Oh yeah, like they're goin' to lock you up and throw away the key for jimmying a dodgy lock and *not* stealing anything from a derelict building.'

'I might be exaggerating slightly but you get the point.'

'If you're lucky I'll let the "slightly" part go for now.' Essy couldn't resist teasing him. 'Come back to Molly's with me and I'll treat you to the nearest thing to a decent cup of coffee you'll find around here. I bought supplies to save my sanity.'

'I'd love nothing better but I'm hot and sweaty.'

Now she waggled her eyelashes on purpose.

'You're a wicked woman. I've been running and I need a shower.' Ruan looked resigned. 'I'd better referee between

Mum and my uncle for a while but I'm still good to meet up later if you are?'

'Sure, if Jackie Webb doesn't ban us from the pub.'

'He needs our money too badly but we can always grab a bottle of cheap plonk and hit the beach again.'

'Wow, you sure know how to crawl back into my good books.'

'That's me. Always full of good ideas.' He could barely suppress his excitement. 'I got a bloody good look at the chapel before I was... interrupted and it could be...'

She watched his joy drain away.

'Mum would tell me to get my head out of the clouds. It's a waste of breath discussing it. For a start neither of us plans to stay here.' His voice turned to gravel. 'Do we?'

Essy stared at him in shock.

Whatever made him ask such a dumb question? Ruan asked himself. He needed a swift kick up the backside. 'Forget it.' He gestured around them. 'We're in a bubble right now. It's great but it's not real life. I'll get a job with another architecture firm soon, probably back in London. You'll go back to Tennessee in a week or two and that'll be it.'

'You sure about that?' Essy's husky drawl hit him like a punch in the gut.

'Absolutely.'

'I guess we'll see. Strikes me some things are meant to be.' The enigmatic response left him dangling. 'Why don't you run along and get cleaned up? I've got things to tell you later.'

'What sort of things?'

'Wait and see.' Essy smiled and sauntered away, leaving him to stare after her.

It took a huge effort to get his legs moving again and trail back home. He forced down enough cottage pie at dinner to stop his mother asking if he was all right and went upstairs to change. For the first time since he was about fourteen years old he couldn't work up any enthusiasm when he stood in front of the open wardrobe because his mind was too full of other stuff. Ruan threw on some faded black jeans and a loose fitting cream linen shirt before shoving his feet in a pair of tan loafers. Shave or not shave? He reached for his razor, then tossed it aside.

All he did before leaving was to rake a comb through his hair and slip his wallet and phone in his pocket.

The second he walked into the pub and saw Essy balanced on one of the bar stools he knew he was doomed. With no make-up and wearing a sky-blue sundress and white plastic flip-flops she was more beautiful than ever.

'Great minds think alike.' Her gaze travelled down over him. 'Are you prepared to admit now I might have a point with the whole destiny thing?' When he didn't reply she chuckled. 'What does a lady have to do around here to get a drink anyway?'

'Make friends with the landlord?'

'Oh she tried that.' Essy leaned in closer, surrounding him with her heat and intoxicating perfume. 'She thinks she stands a better chance with you.'

Better chance of what exactly he was afraid to ask.

Chapter Twenty

'I'll get these in. How about a whisky?' After the information Essy shared about his father another beer wasn't going to hack it.

'Sure.' She pushed her chair back. 'I'm off to the loo.' Her infectious grin re-emerged. 'Isn't that what y'all call the restroom?'

'You'll be mistaken for being English if you keep that up.'

'Not Cornish?'

When he leaned closer her lush scent distracted him from everything apart from the overwhelming need to get her on her own. 'You've got to live here for generations before it's even a remote possibility you'll be considered local.'

'Sounds like Tennessee. Mama gets mad when someone reminds her that despite living there for over thirty-five years it doesn't make her southern. Doesn't matter that she wears her hair big, never steps outside the door without full make-up and has taught herself to speak with a slow drawl. To real southerners she'll still always be that cute little English gal who sells houses.'

'It's hard to escape our pasts,' Ruan mused. 'Harder than *we* thought, that's for sure.'

'Get those drinks in.'

The cloud filtering her smile saddened him but he watched her go and made his way back to the bar.

'You came!' Julia North grinned at him as if she had won the lottery jackpot.

'Yes, but I'm—'

'I told you a few of the old gang would be here.' She pointed to a packed table by the window. 'Come and join us.' The perfume that drifted his way was heavy on the musk and light on subtlety.

'That's kind of you but I'm with someone.'

'Yeah, he's with me.'

He stifled a laugh when Essy draped her arm around his shoulder and flashed Julia a massively fake smile.

'Wow, I can't believe he didn't mention having an American girlfriend.' Julia clicked her fingers. 'Oh my God you're Molly's niece, aren't you? That means...' A rash of heat mottled her neck as the connection between them registered.

'I'm Essy Havers. And you are?'

'Julia North.' She dropped a proprietary hand on his other shoulder. 'Ruan and I go back a long way, don't we?'

He mumbled something non-committal.

'Everyone will be thrilled to see you both. Come on.'

'Thanks, I'd sure love to hear some of your stories.'

Surely Essy realised he didn't have a lot of fond memories from his childhood? Why would she do this?

'I'm guessing that's a yes from us then.' Ruan eked out a thin smile. 'We'll get our drinks and join you in a minute.' He fought to hold on to his temper when Julia bounced off, clearly unable to wait a second longer to spread the news.

'I get you're mad but she would've gone on and on and I didn't think you'd want that. Don't worry we'll keep it short then come up with a valid reason to leave.' Her eyes bored through him. 'How about you kiss me? Make it real good because I'm damn sure your ex is watching.'

'She's not my... we hung out together some when we were about fifteen and messed around a bit, you know the kind of thing.'

'Oh yeah, I know. Like me and Dippy Dwayne.'

'Dippy Dwayne?'

'I fancied him almost as much as he fancied himself.' Her eyes glittered. 'You gonna give me that kiss or do I have to...'

It wasn't hard to blot out their surroundings, linger on her red glossy mouth and taste the fruity red wine she'd been drinking. 'How's that?'

'Dangerous, Mr Pascow. Very dangerous.'

132

'That was the plan. Let's go.' He grabbed their drinks and his nerve held until he caught Paul Bonny's distinctive laugh, reminiscent of a braying donkey, and froze.

Essy winced when Ruan's fingers tightened around her hand. This was a monumental error. To start with they should have met somewhere quieter because it had been beyond stupid to update him on the search for his father here. She shouldn't have let the badly bleached blonde falling all over him bug her because he didn't show any interest whatsoever in perky Julia. What was up with her? Jealousy wasn't her style. She chose her relationships with care and when they ended she usually remained friends with her exes. The problem was, if she wanted to label it as such, that she cared deeply for this man. Perhaps more than she should?

'Leave the talkin' to me.' Most people here couldn't get enough of listening to her accent so for his sake she'd slather it on like butter on a hot biscuit. Essy pushed in front of him and swanned up to the table. 'This sure is awesome. I want to hear all about y'all.' She tugged Ruan in closer. 'You'll have to tell me everything about this awesome guy too.' The ruddy-faced, balding man next to Julia was openly sneering. It only took about five minutes to wheedle out the story of Paul Bonny's amazing achievements, his words not hers, that mainly consisted of school sporting triumphs when he was a teenager. Judging by the gut hanging over the waist of his tight jeans he couldn't run to the end of the quay these days. She knocked back a swig of whisky.

'So what did you do after university, Paul? A guy like you must've made a real impression out there.'

'Paul stayed here and took over his father's insurance business,' Julia jumped in. 'Too many people think they have to leave Cornwall in order to be successful.' She tilted her head in Ruan's direction.

Much as it pained her to admire the other woman she was

forced to give her credit. Julia stuck up for her friends. Her mother always taught her if she couldn't say something kind about another person then don't say anything at all.

'You're absolutely right.'

'Julia says you're Molly Barnecutt's niece. We've all heard of your mother.' A dark-haired woman at the far end of the table spoke up. 'What are *you* doing here out of the good old USA?'

She phrased her reply with great care. 'I'm combining business with pleasure. I needed to come here for a job I'm working on and wanted to see where my mother came from.'

'She's a typical American. They all want to find out where they're from, you know trace their family tree and all that stuff.' The conspiratorial wink Ruan shared around the table irritated her. 'You're hoping to find out you're descended from a highwayman or smuggler, aren't you, sweetheart?'

The brief flash of anger dissipated. He had rescued her from making a fool of herself. And him. It hadn't been uppermost in her mind that these people would have grown up hearing whispered stories about her mom and Tree Pascow.

'I sure am. That would be somethin' to tell the folks back home.' Essy turned the conversation to American holidays people had taken and what she thought about Cornwall.

'Looking a bit... ordinary tonight, aren't we?' Paul jabbed a finger towards Ruan and she sensed him stiffen up. 'You should've seen him at the school leaving dance. He wore a bloody skirt like the girls.' Stumbling to his feet he leaned across the table to send a wave of stale alcohol laden breath over Essy. 'Couldn't kick a football to save your life, could you, mate?'

Ruan grabbed Paul by the shirt collar.

'You're still the ignorant lout you were in school but I don't have to put up with it now.'

'Keep the noise down, gents, or get out.'

For the first time in her life she was pleased to see Jackie Webb.

'Don't worry we're out of here.' Ruan thrust Paul away and if Julia hadn't put out her arm to steady him the idiot would have fallen on the floor. 'Great idea this was.' He glared at Julia. 'Did you think we were all going to have a quiet drink together and be best friends?'

'I'm sorry.' Julia's voice trembled and she threw Essy a pleading look. 'I never meant...'

'Yeah, I know.' For some reason she believed the woman. All of a sudden she became aware of the hush around them. Everyone was staring or whispering behind their hands and this was all her fault. 'I'm sorry too.' She steered Ruan out through the pub and only dared to exhale when they made it back out in the fresh air. 'Do you want to...'

'I'll walk you home.'

It sounded more like a threat than a generous offer but she didn't argue and they trudged away up the hill until they reached Molly's gate.

'I won't come in.'

'Don't be childish. You're bigger than that idiot who mouthed off at you.' She took a risk on throwing in a touch of humour. 'Not literally. You're definitely in better shape.' The edges of his mouth curled into a brief smile. 'He's a good example of what eating a pasty a day will do for a guy. Look at it from his point of view. You rose above your difficulties and became a successful architect in London.' She twirled around. 'Now you're back in Herring Bay with an extremely hot, classy American lady hanging on your arm. How do you think that makes him feel?' Essy touched his cheek. 'He's living on the fact when he was fourteen he was a decent football player. Whoop di do. Don't get me wrong, I'm not putting him down for staying here. There's nothing wrong with that if it's what he wanted but my guess is he didn't get to choose. His dad probably pulled the family business card and forced him into it.' She lowered her voice to a whisper. 'Bitterness can do funny things to people.'

'You're too smart for me.'

'Not at all.' She glanced towards the house. 'You gonna change your mind?'

'No, but not because I'm still mad. I'll apologise to Julia tomorrow, if you're okay with me talking to her?' The twinkle in his eyes made her giggle.

'She's no threat to us.'

A fleeting sadness tripped across his face. 'You really think…'

'Shush. Don't jinx it.'

'Okay. Look, I need time to process what you told me earlier about my dad.' His warm laughter rumbled through her. 'Time to process? I've been hanging out with you so long I'm starting to sound American myself.'

'I'll have you talkin' with a southern drawl soon, sweetie pie.' Essy had a bright idea. 'Why don't we have a day out tomorrow? Away from all this. We can pretend we're on vacation. You pick a place and surprise me.' He looked wary but finally managed a brief nod.

'Sounds good.' Her skin burned when he stroked his thumbs in teasing circles over her face with a deliberation that forced her to imagine how incredible it would feel to be touched that way all over. 'Thank you.'

'What for?'

'Being you. That's all. Simply being you.'

She'd received more flowery compliments before but the emotion thickening his voice got to her.

'I'll pick you up at nine tomorrow. Wear your walking shoes and bring your swimsuit.' A huge grin lit him up. 'You might need it, you might not. Wait and see.'

Essy's relief that they were back on a steady footing was muted by worry. The million-dollar question was what Ruan would choose to do with the information she had discovered about his father.

Chapter Twenty-One

Ruan stood with the back door propped open and sipped his tea while watching the sunrise. He spent the whole night brooding over what Essy shared with him yesterday without making up his mind whether or not to tell his mother.

'What's on your mind, love?' His mother sounded worried.

'Just wondering if the weather is going to hold out.'

'Oh, Ruan, you're a hopeless liar but I'm not complaining about that.'

His father had told enough lies for them all.

'I'm taking Essy out today.'

'I'll never be thrilled about you taking up with her but that isn't what's bothering you, is it?'

'No.' Her concern made the decision for him. 'Let's go inside.' Ruan joined her in the kitchen. 'There's plenty of tea in the pot I'll pour you a cup. Uncle Dick isn't up yet, is he?' It was funny how he'd become a fixture, hobbling around on his crutches and complaining at regular intervals. More out of habit he suspected than any real malice.

'He's never been an early riser. Not by choice.' Her eyes took on a far off look. 'Our poor mother had her hands full trying to shift him out of bed and off to school on time.'

'Essy found out something you might... or might not want to know.' He pulled out a chair and encouraged her to sit down.

'He's dead, isn't he?' Vera pressed her hands to her face and stumbled over her words.

'No, at least we're pretty sure he's not. There's no death registered in his name.' Ruan gave his mum an abbreviated version of Essy's search for Tree Pascow. She had spent hours trawling the internet using many of the same tricks as she did in her normal line of work.

'Is it legal to do all that?'

Accessing databases sounded dodgy to his mother but she had no clue how much ordinary people could find out if they knew how and where to look.

'Yes. She found a couple of possibilities then narrowed it down from there.'

'So where is he?'

'Possibly Wales.' Ruan gave her the details of a man living in a small town on the Gower Peninsula that matched his father. 'Essy suggested we go there to see him face to face but I wondered if it might be best to ask the Salvation Army to approach him.' Rejection might not come as harsh second-hand. 'What do you think?'

'You won't like my opinion.'

'Let's hear it anyway.' He tried for a smile.

'If Tree wanted to get back in touch he knows where we are. He's the one who left.' She held up her hand when he started to protest. 'You asked for my opinion and that's it.' Vera pushed her chair away. 'I'm going to take my tea back to bed.'

The thought of food made his stomach churn so he abandoned the idea of making any breakfast. Essy had ventured to suggest that the possibility of solving the mystery surrounding his father was one of his reasons for returning to Cornwall. If she was right did that mean she was a catalyst rather than the instigator he'd assumed her to be? Ruan tapped out a quick message and pressed send.

Pick you up at 7? Will feed you breakfast. Need to talk.

His mobile stayed silent while he rinsed out his mug and set it on the draining board, half-heartedly made his bed and dressed. He almost cut himself in the middle of shaving when it buzzed back to life.

You had me at breakfast. I'm ready now. Come and get me.

It would set the tongues wagging if they were seen leaving Herring Bay together this early in the morning but what the hell? The gossips must be kicking up a storm after his set-to with Paul Bonny in The Smugglers' yesterday, this would simply give them more ammunition.

She sneaked down the stairs barefoot and prised open the front door.

'Leaving some early, aren't you?' Molly appeared from the kitchen brandishing a mug of tea and grinning like the Cheshire Cat.

'Ruan's picking me up now so we can have breakfast and get on with our day out.'

'Enjoy yourselves and I'll see you later.'

'Don't I get a warning about hanging out with him? You're slipping, Aunt Molly.'

'And you're a cheeky little madam.' She shooed Essy out of the door. 'You don't listen to me anyway so I'm not wasting my breath.'

Yesterday's dressed-down look wasn't repeated this morning when Ruan rolled up in Suzy Sunshine. Another Cuban short-sleeved shirt, this one with neon pink flamingos, bright yellow pineapples and vivid green tropical leaves. He was clearly optimistic about the weather with his matching green Bermuda shorts and brown leather slide sandals. Essy loved this outward expression of his creativity but since he had admitted to using his fashionable clothes as a form of armour, she wished he didn't need to do that around her.

She slipped on her oversized Jackie O style sunglasses and ran her gaze over him. 'That's better. I might not burn my eyeballs now.'

'Too much?'

'Nah, you're never "too much" for my taste.' Now she was the one being eyed up. Without knowing the plan for the day she'd chosen pale grey jeans and a white T-shirt topped with a thin bubble gum pink cardigan for a pop of colour.

'Pleased to see you got the pink memo.' He swung her around and caught her in both arms before pulling her close for a long delicious kiss. 'Right, now we've assured Molly that I'm crazy as ever let's get going.'

They turned around and caught her aunt gawking out of the front window. When the curtain dropped with a sharp tug it was impossible not to burst out laughing.

'What's the breakfast plan?' Essy hopped in and buckled her seat belt.

'It's on the back seat.' He pointed to a couple of brown paper bags and a thermos. 'Let's get out of Herring Bay then we'll stop for a picnic.'

'Great.'

The early morning chill still lingered in the air when they spread out a blanket and sat on the grass overlooking Penwarren, but Essy soaked up the difference between an early July morning in Cornwall and one back home in Tennessee. She remembered being out of school for the summer and her mother dragging her out of bed at half past five in the morning to join her weeding the garden before Paula had to go to work. That was the coolest part of the day but they still retreated back into the house an hour later dripping with sweat.

She clasped her hands around her steaming mug of coffee and watched the picturesque village slumbering in the early morning sun. A few fishing boats were heading out to sea and she made out tiny stick figures of people starting to go about their business along the harbour.

'Fresh chocolate croissants.' Ruan passed over the warm paper bag and the sweet, tempting aroma seeping out almost made her swoon. 'I banged on John Wakeham's back door to get these before the bakery opened.'

'It will be a shame if he closes down.'

It didn't take long to polish off two pastries and drain her coffee before it struck her that he hadn't touched a thing. 'You aren't hungry? They're awesome.'

'I told my mum.' The words tumbled out and she reached over to squeeze his hand.

'And?' After he managed to spill out the whole story she shook her head. 'So we're on our own.' It didn't surprise her. A woman who had stuck her head in the sand for over thirty years wasn't likely to change now. 'I'm okay to do whatever you want.'

'Really?' Ruan glanced up from under his long dark lashes and the completely random thought flittered through her head how unfair it was that men were fortunate they didn't have to resort to industrial strength mascara for the same effect. 'So if I say we should leave well alone you're happy to go along with that?'

'Happy? Not sure I'd go that far. But at the end of the day he's your father and only connected to me in a… loose kind of way.' She picked her words with care and explained that for herself she'd appreciate closure but couldn't bear to hurt him or anyone else she cared for in the process.

'I'll think on it some more. We don't have to decide right now.' He seemed to pull himself back together. 'The other day you said you wished we could simply have fun together, so let's do it.'

'That's an awesome idea.' Neither of them were naïve enough to believe they could leave the past behind forever but that was okay. 'Where are we going?'

'First stop is Cape Cornwall. It's about four miles north of Land's End, near St Just. It'll take us the best part of an hour and a half or so to get there.'

'Let me guess, it's beautiful.'

'You're mocking me.' He wagged his finger at her. 'It truly is though. It's retained the wild, ruggedness Land's End used to have before they turned it into a bloody theme park.'

They climbed back in the car and by unspoken agreement they didn't talk much. Essy wasn't aware she'd dropped off to sleep until she startled awake and stared around her, completely disoriented for a few moments.

'Please tell me I didn't snore or drool?'

'Uh, no. Do you normally?'

'It has been known.'

'You'll be relieved to hear that didn't happen today.' He turned the car off the main road. 'This part's really narrow you might want to breathe in.'

'Very funny, I'm sure.'

When a bus rumbled towards them a few minutes later and there were only stone walls on either side Essy was forced to acknowledge the fairness of his warning. She screwed up her eyes when Ruan reversed the car and said a silent, but fervent prayer that no one was coming the other way. Somehow they survived and at the second attempt made it all the way to the car park.

'Lord have mercy.' She flopped back in the seat and gasped.

'I promised you an exciting time and this is only the start.'

'Not sure I'm gonna make it through a whole day of this.'

'Put your walking shoes on and I'll buy you an ice cream.' Ruan's promise made her smile.

'That sounds like bribery.'

'Whatever works.'

There must be a million ice cream vans in Cornwall because she hadn't seen a place yet without one, thankfully this remote spot was no exception. After studying the chalkboard until Ruan begged her to pick something or he'd choose for her, Essy selected a large scoop of white chocolate raspberry with the obligatory chocolate flake. In an effort to show some restraint she resisted the temptation to top it with cream.

After a gentle amble up to the top of the hill they dropped down on the grass in front of the stone monument he told her was dedicated to the Heinz family who bought the land and donated it to the National Trust.

'Britain only has two capes and this is one of them,' Ruan explained. 'The Atlantic currents divide here. Some of the water flows north into the Bristol Channel and the Irish Sea and the rest becomes the English Channel. See those rocks?' He pointed to two massive rock formations right in front of them. 'Those are the Brisons Rocks. They're supposed to resemble General de Gaulle in his bath although I think that's stretching the imagination.'

'What's that thing that looks like a chimney?' She pointed to a brick stack behind them.

'Uh, it is a chimney.' His eyes sparkled. 'That belonged to the old Cape Cornwall Mine. They used to get tin and copper from under the sea but it's all closed down now.' His forehead creased in a deep frown. 'Too much of Cornwall is nothing more than a museum these days. It brings the tourists in but... at a price.'

'A lot of places are the same way.'

'I know but maybe it's the architect in me.' He seemed to be talking to himself. 'I want to see places living and vibrant not fossilised in the past.'

'And people?'

Ruan tilted her a quizzical smile. 'Them too. We don't need to forget but learn from history rather than getting stuck there.' He sprang back up on his feet. 'Come on. I'll be a grumpy old man if I sit here any longer. Let's walk around and back down through the field to see St Helen's Oratory. It's the remains of an ancient chapel probably from Roman times.'

Every day she discovered more about him and the contradictions that made him who he was only made Ruan more interesting in her eyes. She grasped his outstretched hand and they set off again together.

Chapter Twenty-Two

Ruan's utterly shallow side decided it was worth coming out today if for no other reason than to see every inch of Essy's gorgeous curves displayed in a magnificent nineteen-fifties style scarlet polka dot bikini. His choice to bring her to the newly renovated Jubilee Pool in Penzance was spot on.

'Could you make your drooling a little less obvious?' The amused lilt to her voice told him not to take the question seriously.

'I could but where would be the fun in that?'

'This place is incredible. I've never seen anything like it before. Is it original Art Deco?'

'Yes, it opened in 1935, the year of King George V's Silver Jubilee. In its day it was the place to visit.'

'Did you come here growing up?'

'A few times but it was already deteriorating and closed by the time I was a teenager. Age and the weather took its toll on the seawater pool and after a bad storm about six years earlier there were doubts it could ever be brought back to life. But the local community wouldn't let it die and set up a charitable group to revive the pool and take over running it from the council.'

'We could do a similar thing with your old Methodist Chapel.'

Ruan wasn't sure which question to pose first – whether she was completely mad or exactly what she meant by the 'we' part.

'Don't nitpick my words. Think of it in an abstract sort of way... for now,' she said.

'We'll talk more about that another day.' He grabbed her hands. 'Our plan was to have fun without all the rest of it interfering.' She must hear the frustration in his voice. 'I put the damper on things over breakfast but I thought after that we were good to go?'

'We are.' Essy tilted a wry smile his way. 'I guess we aren't great at the dating thing.'

'Think of all the baggage we've got. The family stuff and everything else.'

'Yeah, what of it?'

'So we're not a couple of teenagers crushing on each other without a brain in our heads. There's no law says we can't combine fun with talking about more than... fluff.' The decision freed him. 'Let's get in the geothermal pool. It was all over the news when they opened it a couple of months ago and I've been wanting to come and test it out.'

'You sure getting hotter is a good plan?' A wicked smile tugged at her lush mouth. 'We might need to get a room tonight at this rate.'

'Might?' When their eyes locked it sent his heart into overdrive. Beads of sweat glistened on Essy's skin and the heat bloomed the scent of the tropical sun cream he'd slathered on her earlier.

'Yeah, might.' She trailed a finger down and teasingly rested it in the middle of his chest. 'Keeping our options open raises the stakes.'

'They aren't high enough already?'

'Play along, it'll be more fun and that's what we're supposed to be having today.' Her husky voice throbbed with the challenge.

'Pool. Now.' He tugged on her hand. 'You're dangerous.' The only answer he received was a peal of rich laughter as he half-dragged her towards the pool.

This was the essence of summer by the coast in her opinion, licking an ice cream while she dried off in the sunshine after a swim with her skin tacky to the touch from salt. Native Tennesseans only experienced that on vacation in Florida or along the Alabama Gulf Coast. The only thing missing today was sand and like most people Essy had a love/hate relationship with that anyway.

'I wish I could bottle this up and take it home with me.'

A pang of distress flooded Ruan's face and she wished she'd thought harder before speaking. In an effort to distract him Essy rattled on about her commission from Gordon Snell's wife and how she understood the old man's longing for his native land far better now. She sneaked another quick peek but his expression hadn't altered.

'I'll apologise if you want but—'

'You prefer to face up to things and I've got more than a touch of mother in me, right?' Ruan's amused description of their differences made her smile.

How could they be so in tune with each other after a few short weeks? She'd dated Pete Warner for nearly two years before they amicably went their separate ways but he never understood her half as well.

'Well, yeah,' Essy ploughed on. 'We both know I've a business and a home to go back to. I haven't bought my return ticket but it's got to come at some point.'

'Are we just a holiday romance?' His dark brows knitted together. 'My feelings for you are confusing. Is that simply weird old me or are you the same?' His lame attempt to smile failed.

'I'm the same. You said we weren't teenagers in the heat of a heavy duty crush but perhaps letting go of some of our adult, responsible behaviour isn't such a bad thing.' She stroked his leg, feeling his muscles tense and flex under her fingers. 'We're not sure where things are going between us but I can deal with that if you can too?' She was giving them both a free pass.

'Okay. Sounds fair to me.'

'You know an ice cream doesn't count as lunch, right? I assume you've made plans for feeding me and planned what we're going to do for the rest of the afternoon?'

Ruan decided to stick to being literal. If he was stupid enough to tell her all the plans and dreams lodged in his brain involving her she'd run a mile in the opposite direction.

'We're going to make a short drive over to Marazion, park the car and find somewhere to eat.' After checking the tide times yesterday he worked out they could wander around the small village until the causeway across to St Michael's Mount was walkable again about mid-afternoon. Once on the island they could explore the castle, the stunning gardens and the old village and harbour. 'Does that suit you?'

She wrinkled up her nose and pretended to think. 'It will do.'

Ruan tugged his shorts over his bathing trunks and shrugged on his shirt. 'Let's feed you before you faint from malnutrition.'

'You've got a nerve.' Essy jabbed a pointy finger in his stomach. 'Who asked for a second chocolate flake in his ice cream?'

'They're puny these days. Not like they used to be.'

'Are you going to turn into one of those grouchy old men who complain about everything?'

'Hang around long enough and you'll find out... I mean...'

Essy held up her hand in a clear warning for him to stop digging a bigger hole for himself. Without another word they gathered up their things and made their way out to the car.

'Tell me about this St Michael's whatever it's called on the way.'

Thank goodness she rescued him from his own stupidity. While he drove Ruan gave her the potted version of the Mount's history going all the way back to the first century. He included tales of the mythical giant Cormoran, the island's Bronze Age settlers, the capture of the mount by the French during the Norman Conquest and ended up with the generations of the St Aubyn family who had owned it and lived there since the middle of the fifteenth century.

'The family gave the Mount to the National Trust a while ago now, but with the condition they could still live in it on a long lease and operate the tourist business there.'

He tracked down an empty parking spot so they could join all the other visitors wandering around Marazion. With plenty of time to spare they found a table at a small restaurant with an outside terrace and a great view of the island and lingered over plates of delicious Cornish hake and scallops, washed down with a bottle of chilled white wine.

Essy shaded her eyes with her hand and gazed across the table at him. 'I'll have to let you plan days out more often. You're pretty damn good at it.'

The breath caught in his throat, the same as it did every time she hinted at something further down the road for them.

'I was lucky. The weather was on our side.'

'I'm sure you had a Plan B.'

'Perhaps.' It would be smart to keep some tricks up his sleeve for the next rainy day.

'Is it time to go?' The energy bouncing off her shot another surge of desire through him. 'We could always skip the island…' She trailed her tongue over her lower lip.

'No. Let's do it.' His voice turned gruff. 'Anticipation is a great aphrodisiac.' Ruan wasn't assuming too much because Essy couldn't have spelled out her intentions any clearer if she took out a full size ad in the newspaper.

'Not sure we need one but I'll go along with your thinkin' for now.'

For the next couple of hours they did the whole tourist thing. They walked over to the island over the cobblestone causeway and hiked up to see the ancient castle before heading back down to the small village and harbour. Naturally they ate more ice cream because she declared that if it wasn't enshrined in law as a compulsory activity at regular intervals then it should be. Shortly before six o'clock they joined all the other exhausted visitors walking back across the causeway before it closed for the next high tide.

'Now what?' Essy's cheeks were flushed. He supposed some of the pinkness could be put down to sunburn but perhaps a touch of awkwardness lingered there too?

He needed her to understand she wasn't the only uncertain

one. 'I used to have a decent amount of confidence around women. They were either attracted to me or they weren't and I was fine with that. But...'

'That Helena witch knocked it to the kerb?'

Ruan twitched a smile. 'You could put it that way.'

'You'll be fine.' She grabbed his hands. 'We'll be fine. I'm not her and you're with me now. It's all good.'

Sometimes he talked too much so today he kept his agreement to a brief nod.

'Let's track down a shop. I need a toothbrush and a few bits and pieces. Then we'll look for a cute B&B.'

He loved her calm matter of fact manner and in less than an hour Ruan found himself standing in a cramped, very pink and very floral bedroom overlooking the harbour.

'I don't know about you but all the salt has dried on my skin and I'm sweaty and sticky.' Essy's declaration came with a glorious smile. 'I reckon we need a shower.'

'We?' The tiny shower wedged into one corner was barely big enough for one person.

'Yeah. We.' She languidly peeled off her clothes, dropped them on the floor and beckoned him over. 'Come on, live dangerously.'

Ruan struggled not to gawk at her strong, beautiful body but eventually gave up the effort. He almost tripped over his feet while trying to get undressed and the more he tried to shush her giggles the harder Essy laughed. Any minute now the landlady would bang on the door and tell them to keep the noise down.

'I do nothing but live dangerously around you... and no, that's not a complaint.'

'It better not be.'

Chapter Twenty-Three

Essy smiled at her phone then set it back on the bedside table. Aunt Molly's reply to her text told her to enjoy herself. No warning. Seems as though her aunt had given up flogging that particular dead horse. Last night Ruan was reticent to broach the subject of contacting his mother in case she worried when he didn't come home but she'd assured him she planned to let Molly know. They had a good laugh, unable to decide if that made them responsible adults or sad. Eventually they landed on thoughtful.

'Hey, where's my lovely lady? You're too far away.' Ruan's searching fingers crept around her waist and yanked her back across the bed.

'Wow, you certainly wake up raring to go!' Next thing she was flipped on her back, kissed all over and straddled by her hot, gorgeous man.

Their first exploratory lovemaking session last night established that the Carter woman hadn't done Ruan any lasting damage, far from it.

'And you aren't?' He palmed her breast until she writhed under him.

Essy relished the delicious tug deep inside her as he sunk into her and blurred the line between them. She cried out his name and he seized her mouth in a fierce, possessive kiss then gripped her shoulders as the last shudders ran through him.

'That's better than any alarm clock,' he gasped and rolled off her, flopping back on the pillow.

'Wow, you're such a romantic.'

'Sorry. I'm not the hearts and flowers type.' Ruan's mischievous grin broke out. 'Maybe on my clothes if it's the fashion but if you want all that fancy stuff I'm afraid I'm not your man.'

'How did you get into fashion in such a huge way?'

'How did you?' A wide swathe of defensiveness ran through his voice.

'There's no need to turn into a cactus.' The gentle admonition hit home and he dredged up a tiny smile. 'My mom's always been a clothes nut and loved nothing better than having a little girl to dress up. Christmas, Easter, the Fourth of July, you name it I had a new outfit for the occasion. She would have loved to be a model and she's certainly got the looks for it but never got the chance.'

Essy caught his flicker of dismay.

'So my mom didn't get to fulfil her childhood dream. Very few folks do but she loves her job and she's awesome at it. She doesn't need anyone's pity.'

'Sorry.' He caressed her cheek. 'I just feel guilty for the way my father treated her.'

'Look I'm not saying he didn't behave badly but Mom would be the first to tell you that she wasn't the perfect kid. Far from it. She and Molly were chalk and cheese. My aunt always toed the line with their parents while Mom jumped over it in leaps and bounds. She would've left Herring Bay one way or another.'

'You're probably right.'

She'd take the grudging agreement for now. 'Back to the clothes thing. Mom always had fashion magazines lying around the house so while other kids learned to read with *Green Eggs and Ham* or *The Hardy Boys*, I soaked up *Vogue* and *Elle*.' When she didn't speak again his mouth settled into a straight line.

'As a little kid I spent hours drawing and painting pictures and I always used the brightest colours. If I wasn't doing that I usually had my head stuck in a book, I practically taught myself to read. I wasn't even six for Christ's sake but it used to irritate my dad no end. He was always dragging me outside to kick a football around or encouraging me to play with my toy cars.' His husky whisper was barely audible.

'What was *his* father like?'

'I never knew him. Why?'

'Just wondered. Perhaps he used to hassle Tree for similar stuff and it left a mark on him.'

'It's possible. Do you think I fell into a love of all things eye-catching to spite him?' Ruan's sad headshake upset her.

'Maybe, but your passion for anything artistic isn't fake.'

'No. I joined a drama club at school and loved putting on a costume to become someone else.' His expression cleared. 'Maybe that's what I've been doing with my clothes ever since? I've never put that into words before.'

Essy pressed her hands to his face. 'There's nothing wrong with enjoying fashion. I do too. But when it becomes a prop to hide behind... It's something to think about, that's all.'

'So is this.'

As he drew them into a deep, lingering kiss she sensed Ruan withdraw the emotional side of him that had opened up so freely in the aftermath of their lovemaking. Her body instantly responded and the conversation was over.

'What made you become an architect? I would've thought something connected with the theatre, perhaps a costume designer would be more up your alley?'

Ruan considered how to reply. The last thing he wanted was to make her sad or feel sorry for him. They were in the car on the way home, a captive audience where Essy was concerned.

'I'll take a guess and you can say if I'm right. You put up with so much crap from people in the village because you didn't always conform to their idea of normal but architecture was a "respectable" way to use your artistic skills that no one could argue with.' Her air quotes made him cringe. 'Plus if your dad bothered to check how you'd turned out it would be a see-I-did-fine-without-you moment.'

Ruan blinked away a rush of tears. The damn woman stirred

him like no one else before but he veered between loving and resenting her for that. After he checked his rear-view mirror he indicated and pulled over on the side of the road.

'Pick my moments, don't I?' The gentle pressure of her hand stroking his back settled him down.

'Seems to be your thing but don't take that the wrong way. It's good for me.'

'You sound like someone setting out to run in the rain. Determined to stick to their plan but hating every moment.'

'Rain or sunshine doesn't make a difference to me I still hate every minute when I'm out running,' he said. 'I'd rather knock out a good cardio and weights session in the gym any day. There's not one close enough to Herring Bay to ward off pasty-gut.' He tapped his stomach.

'I'm a Zumba girl myself. I'm too social for running. I love the loud thumping music and plenty of friends to chat to.' She bit her lip.

'Say it. Go on.'

'In our imaginary community centre we could hold exercise classes. Maybe even fit in a small gym?' Essy shrugged. 'Runnin' away with myself again.'

'I thought we were in agreement on running?'

'Smart mouth.'

'Yes, but it's only to avoid what we were really talking about.' Breaking old habits was hard. 'I'm a decent architect and I enjoy bringing my ideas to life but... I'll never be great because it's not my passion.' A heavy sigh escaped before he could pull it back. 'It's hard to consider throwing in all those years of training and a decent well-paying job for a whim.' He flinched under her silent scrutiny. 'It wouldn't be a whim exactly. It's still hard at nearly forty to consider starting over again.' Ruan played with a strand of her silky, dark hair that had worked loose from her thick braid and remembered what it looked like spread over the crisp white sheets last night... and over him. He struggled to refocus. 'I'm not sure I want to leave Cornwall, at least not anytime soon. A different direction within the architecture field might do the trick.'

'Something like—'

He kissed her into silence. 'Hold the idea.'

'Will do.'

A temporary reprieve was the best he could hope for. 'Let's get going.' He started the car back up and set off again.

'This might be another crazy idea of mine but how about we all get together for Sunday lunch tomorrow?' she asked.

'You mean with my mum and your aunt Molly?'

'Yeah.' Her smile turned rueful. 'Dumb, huh?'

'I'd never call you that.'

'Only because you want back in my bed.'

'A true statement.' The quick rejoinder made her laugh.

'If we're gonna be… together I want them to at least tolerate each other's company.'

'Have you forgotten my uncle? His ankle is still giving him trouble so Mum won't let him go back home anytime soon.'

'Oh yeah, that could be interesting. Molly was really weird when his name got mentioned. I think there's some history between them.' Essy sighed.

'I'm pretty sure you're right. I forgot to tell you that the other day I picked up a few hints that Dick and Molly were a couple at one point and Mum might've been involved in breaking them up. It wasn't spelled out as such and neither of them wanted to talk about it.'

'Interesting.'

'I thought so. Why don't you explore the idea of lunch with Molly and I'll sound out my mum? Perhaps leave it until next week. Give them time to mull over the idea.'

'Yeah, all right.'

They crested the hill from Penwarren and made their way through Herring Bay. Very few visitors were wandering around despite the perfect summer weather. Trying to be optimistic he supposed it might improve once the schools let out for the holidays, but somehow he doubted it.

'Here we are.' He stopped outside Molly's house. What should he say now? Thanking her for a great time was lame and grossly inadequate. Too effusive and she'd be frightened off.

'You're doin' it again.' Essy shook her head. 'I had an awesome time too and I want to do it again. As soon as possible. Don't over analyse everything.'

He'd grown up hyper-aware of the possible consequences of his actions and those of other people because he'd seen the effects of his father's choices on his life and the lives of those around him. Tree's disappearance had altered the path of his childhood and shaped the man he'd become. Ruan didn't regret spending the night with Essy but she couldn't deny it changed things.

The fire in her eyes softened to a flicker. 'I'm not belittling your feelings. They're valid and I respect them.'

'But they frustrate you sometimes?'

'Yeah, but I'm sure I do the same to you.'

'Maybe.' Ruan succumbed to a proper smile. 'Off you go, I'll ring later.'

'No kiss?' Essy nuzzled into his neck 'We've burned our boats now. A kiss isn't goin' to make any difference to prying eyes.'

'I suppose not.' He pretended to sound reluctant which worked until she stroked his thigh and inched closer to dangerous territory. 'Demanding woman.' A deep, satisfying kiss wiped out her triumphant laugh. He eased away but the sight of her slowly licking the taste of him from her mouth almost finished him off. 'Tomorrow?'

'Oh yeah.' She flung the car door open with a dramatic sigh. 'My bed's going to be mighty cold and empty tonight.'

'Torture me a bit more, why don't you?'

'See ya.' Essy sashayed off, swinging her hips as she walked up the path. Killing him all over again.

Ruan sung to himself all the way home and his good mood lasted until he strolled into the kitchen and faced down his mother's grim stare. The one thing he'd avoided telling Essy was his mother's reaction when he shot her a text last night. Vera's answer had arrived in the form of complete silence. Something she knew he would have no difficulty understanding.

Chapter Twenty-Four

'Pity you weren't back a bit earlier, I've been chatting to our Paula.' Molly hurried out of the kitchen wiping her hands on a tea towel. 'She were some sorry to miss you.'

Essy's good mood subsided like a punctured balloon.

'Don't worry I kept my mouth shut.'

'It doesn't bother me. Ruan and I are free agents and more than old enough to make our own choices.' That sounded like a teenage proclamation of independence. 'Anyway I'm goin' to tell her myself next time we talk.'

Molly was straightening her Toby jugs and there was something jittery about her demeanour.

'You can do it face to face tomorrow.'

'What on earth are you getting at?'

'I still can't believe it.' Molly's face shone. 'I'll see my baby sister again after all these years!'

Essy struggled to process the news that her mother had decided to come to Cornwall and was booked on a flight arriving in London first thing in the morning. No doubt the decision had something to do with the information she'd been getting, or more to the point not getting from her only child.

'I told her you'd be at Heathrow to meet her.'

'Me?' Her mind raced.

'I've already checked the trains. You'll have to leave this afternoon because there's no sleeper train on a Saturday. You don't want to be changing trains so the next straight through one leaves at quarter past five. Maybe Ruan can run you up to the station? It takes about four hours to get to Reading. It's cheaper to get a hotel there tonight then hop on the bus to Heathrow in the morning.'

It was a challenge to follow her aunt's rapid conversation. She had been here over a month now but still struggled to decipher the Cornish accent when it was spoken too quickly or by a group of locals all talking at once. Essy didn't need to understand every word to work out that by lunchtime tomorrow she would be on a train bringing her mother back to Herring Bay.

'You could look a bit more pleased.'

'Sorry, I guess I'm surprised, that's all. Yeah, it's great news.'

'I bet you haven't told her about stirring up all this business with Tree Pascow have you?'

There was no point lying. 'No.'

'You'll have plenty of time to talk on the train.'

That did nothing to lift her spirits.

'I've fixed us a bite of lunch.'

It would raise even more red flags if she admitted to having zero appetite. The word lunch reminded her of Ruan's suggestion of them all getting together. She wouldn't mention that now. 'Great. I'll go wash my hands and—'

'Phone that man of yours?'

She didn't bother denying it. Talking things through with him should help. Essy ran upstairs, closed the bedroom door behind her, flopped on the bed and kicked off her flip-flops.

'Hey, gorgeous hunk, have you got a few minutes to talk?' His brittle response set off alarm bells. *Too busy right now?* She attempted to sound understanding when he promised to call later. If he was surprised to find her speaking to him from the train to London Ruan only had himself to blame.

'I suppose that was *her* again? Can't she leave you alone for five minutes?'

'The phone call was from Essy if that's who you were referring to.' Ruan faced off with his mother. The moment he set foot in the house she had started in on him and hadn't let up yet. 'I'll ring her back when you've finished haranguing me.'

'You're a stubborn boy. Always were and always will be.'

'That's where you're wrong.' He glared at her. 'In case you hadn't bloody well noticed I'm a grown man, not a kid you can

158

boss around. No wonder Dad scarpered.' The colour leeched from her face. 'Sorry. I didn't mean—'

'Yes you did.' The only visible sign of distress she allowed was the tight line her mouth stretched into. 'I admit I made mistakes in my marriage but I didn't deserve the way he treated me.'

'No you didn't, but I don't need you playing the "after all I've done for you" card either,' Ruan snapped at her. 'You didn't have much to say when I took Essy out yesterday so why are you so bent out of shape because we stayed out the night? It's the twenty-first century, Mum, and we're two consenting adults. Please don't push your hang ups about sex onto me.' As soon as the words popped out he regretted them.

She smoothed her trembling hands down over her skirt. 'You need to leave. Now.'

'Can't we talk about this?' he pleaded.

'No. I should never have told you about that... business. I didn't expect you to throw it back in my face every time we had a disagreement.'

Disagreement? Ruan would call this a hell of a lot more than a 'disagreement' and wanted to rail against her unfairness but her voice throbbed with the same implacable tone he'd heard all his life. 'Fine I'll go. I'll be back for my stuff tomorrow.'

His mother opened her mouth to speak but immediately slammed it shut again. He'd stupidly thought she might apologise but that wasn't in her DNA. Ruan stormed out of the house and set off walking, with no clue where he was going. A few minutes later he glanced around the harbour and tossed up his options. Mary Warren probably had a room empty at her B&B but getting one at The Smugglers' would stir up far less questions, as long as Jackie Webb got his money he wouldn't care why Ruan was there. Those were his only choices unless he wanted to hike all the way across to Penwarren, but the surge of anger that propelled him this far had dissipated to leave behind a deep, sad weariness.

Five minutes later he was sitting in the pub and staring into a pint of beer he'd no desire to drink. Ruan toyed with his phone and debated ringing Essy back. He longed to vent his frustration to her but it might be wise to simmer down first.

'You look as cheerful as I feel.'

Julia North looked wary and he couldn't blame her after his rude behaviour the last time they met.

'If you aren't expecting company, do you mind if I join you?'

'Sure. Go ahead.' He tried to figure out how best to apologise while she settled down in the chair opposite.

'I'm sorry about the other day.' Julia beat him to it. 'That wasn't one of my smartest ideas. Guy would say that was typical. Act first. Think later.'

'I was an ass. I should've laughed off Paul's dumb remarks.' He shoved a hand through his straggly hair and sighed.

'Maybe.'

'I promised Essy I'd put things right with you but didn't follow through.'

'I liked her.'

'Oh right.' He struggled to hide his surprise.

'You two are good together.' Julia knocked back her wine and held out the empty glass. 'If you want to make amends you can fill this up. Chardonnay.'

He noticed her swaying slightly and wondered how many she'd drunk already. 'Happy to.' While he was at the bar he whipped his conscience into shape and apologised to Jackie Webb. 'I also need a room for tonight.'

'No probs. A single with breakfast is forty pounds. In advance. And don't worry about the other evening, mate. Paul can be a nuisance sometimes. He's got a loose mouth when he's had a few.' Jackie nodded towards Julia. 'I've had to cut them both off more than once and made sure they got home all right a few times as well.'

The unexpectedly considerate side to the landlord caught

him unawares. 'I'll keep an eye on her.' He paid for the wine and rejoined Julia.

'I thought you must be stomping the grapes yourself you were gone so long.' Julia seized the glass out of his hand.

'What do you do these days anyway? I never asked.'

A cloud shadowed her face and she took a large slug of wine. 'I've worked all sorts of jobs, anything to pay the bills really. There's never anything going here in the village so right now I'm temping at a solicitor's office in St Austell three days a week, but that's only until September. I pick up a few hours waitressing in The Drifters too when they're busy.'

'Did you and Guy have any kids?'

'One. A beautiful three-year-old daughter called Ava.'

'You share custody?'

Her harsh laughter conflicted with the sadness lingering around her pursed mouth.

'That's a joke. He's a building contractor and lives in Saudi Arabia with his latest bimbo. I spend half my bloody life chasing him for child support.'

'That's not right.'

'Tell me about it.'

'Where's Ava today?'

Julia's eyes narrowed. 'Why? Do you think I left her home alone to come out drinking?'

'No!'

'Sorry.' She sighed as though everything was too much. 'She's with Guy's mum. Sue is good to us. She gives me a break when she can. It's not her fault her son is a dick.'

'Are you and Paul an item?'

'Not really.' Julia picked up her glass before setting it down again. 'You wouldn't get it.'

'Try me.'

'We're both stuck like bloody hamsters on a wheel. He's divorced too but Paul's the complete opposite of Guy. He wants to spend more time with his little boy but his ex-partner moved

to Scotland and makes it hard as she can for him to see Kenny.'
Julia gestured to the wine. 'This blurs the edges.'

'How about a coffee? I could do with one and then I'll float an idea to see what you think.'

'I suppose we can. You were always full of crazy plans.'

Her indulgent smile took him back twenty-five years but when he stood up she suddenly jumped up too and flung her arms around him.

'You're one of the good ones, Ruan Pascow. I shouldn't have let you go.'

The way he remembered things he was the one who broke off their brief relationship but he let that pass. Out of nowhere she pressed a brief, hard kiss on his mouth and over her shoulder he spotted Essy. Frozen in the doorway of the pub and staring at him in disbelief. By the time he wriggled away from Julia she had disappeared.

There had to be a logical explanation. Essy should've given him the benefit of the doubt and strolled over to speak to them both, but her emotions were all churned up and she wasn't thinking straight. After the night they spent together and her mother's looming arrival she couldn't decide if she was on her head or her heels. It took less than five minutes the other evening to suss out that Julia North still carried a candle for Ruan. Essy couldn't blame her for that but it didn't mean she had to like it.

She hurried along the street and dived around the corner out of sight. With her face plastered against the wall to stifle her heavy breaths she heard Ruan calling her name. After their unsatisfying phone call she hadn't been able to leave for London without facing him and even took her life in her hands by knocking on Vera Pascow's door.

'What do you want now? Haven't you caused enough trouble? He's gone off somewhere. Don't ask me where I'm only his mother. I don't count for anything these days.'

Ruan's bright yellow Prius was parked outside the house so Essy gambled against the fact he could've caught the bus out of Herring Bay and wandered around the village. She'd already checked out the beach and the shop before poking her head inside the pub.

A quick glance at her watch told her she couldn't waste any more time. The taxi she'd ordered would arrive at her aunt's house in half an hour and she still needed to throw a few overnight things in a bag. Ruan could be riled up because of his mother, no doubt Vera said a few choice words about her precious son rolling back in this morning. In her gut she knew he would've stood up for them, which would've aggravated the woman even more. None of that explained why he was brazenly hugging and kissing Julia North a few minutes ago.

Essy dragged herself back to Tregrehan Road and managed to sneak in unnoticed because Molly was taking a bath. If she didn't make an effort with her appearance Paula would pick up on it immediately. No doubt her mother had enough questions without her fashion-conscious daughter arriving to meet her like something the cat dragged in. First she changed into red capris and an off the shoulder white blouse with flounced sleeves for the train up to London. Essy dragged out her shiny red backpack and started with a short-sleeved, uncrushable knit dress in bright purple and pink thin stripes that would do for tomorrow. A toilet bag packed with essentials and her make-up went in next.

When she stepped out onto the small landing to head downstairs the bathroom door opened and Molly bustled out wearing her faded pink dressing gown and with her hair wrapped up in a towel. A coincidence? Very doubtful.

'Did you find Ruan to talk to?'

Why was she stupid enough to think her disappearance would go unnoticed?

'No.' That wasn't a complete lie. 'I'll wait outside for the taxi and ring when I get to Reading.'

'Take care of yourself.' Her aunt's eyes glazed over. 'Bring my Paula back here safe mind.'

She should be more sympathetic. Something else to remember when she picked up her mother. Her turmoil paled when compared to what must be going through the sisters' minds.

'I sure will. It'll be all right.'

'Off you go. I don't want you missing that train.' Molly shooed her away.

For now she would push Ruan from her mind and concentrate on what to tell, or rather not tell, her mother tomorrow.

Chapter Twenty-Five

'Gone?' Ruan felt the blood drain from his face. 'Gone where? When's she coming back? Is she coming back? Please tell me she hasn't...'

'Come in, for goodness' sake, or you'll wake all the neighbours.' Molly hustled him inside.

Banging on her door at seven o'clock on a Sunday morning probably hadn't been very considerate. The poor woman was still in her dressing gown and her hair stuck up worse than his own.

'Sorry, but I was worried about Essy.'

'I guessed that.' Her mouth gaped in a loud yawn. 'Get in the kitchen and we'll put the kettle on.' A twinkle brightened her tired eyes. 'I enjoy showing it off to anyone now, especially the man who magically transformed it for me. I've had lots of compliments.'

He tried to show an interest when she chattered on about the various friends who had admired the renovations but his heart wasn't in it.

'Toast?'

'No, thanks.' He hadn't eaten since his substantial breakfast yesterday in Marazion with Essy. Ruan's appetite had disappeared along with the woman he loved. Yes, loved. He couldn't deny it any longer. It struck him like a bolt of lightning when she ran out of the pub. He didn't search for her as long or hard as he wanted, partly out of guilt for abandoning Julia, but also because he hadn't been certain she wanted to be caught.

'I'm doing you a slice. Starving won't help.' Molly retrieved the butter and marmalade from the fridge.

He almost complained that she wasn't his mother but it wouldn't be smart to mention Vera. So what did he do five minutes later? After polishing off the toast and tea she forced on him he dumped out all his worries like a burst piñata.

'You've heard Essy's side of the story so I suppose you agree I'm not to be trusted? I've no feelings for Julia other than friendship. Honestly. How could she even think that?' He slammed his fist on the table and Molly managed to rescue the sugar bowl before it bounced off the edge.

'Calm yourself, boy.' She topped up their tea. 'Essy didn't tell me anything.'

'Seriously? Why did you let me rant on like a complete idiot?'

Molly looked worried. 'There's something you need to hear.' A long, rambling story tumbled out of her and by the end he couldn't decide whether to laugh or cry.

'Paula's coming here?'

'Yes and the girl is all of a tizzy. When she rang you the poor soul really needed to talk but you were all flummoxed because your mum had a go at you.' Molly shook her head. 'Neither one of you was thinking straight and then she sees Julia throwing herself at you... and you weren't throwing her back either.'

'I did!' His voice rose. 'Not soon enough I suppose but she took me by surprise.' Ruan groaned. 'What the hell's wrong with me? That damn woman in London...' He bit his lip. 'Forget it.'

'Forget what? Tell me if it will help. I know how to keep things to myself,' Molly said, sympathy in her kind gaze.

He slumped back in the chair and a few minutes later he'd poured out everything. 'I didn't mean to tell you all that. You must be a witch.'

'You know that business with the other woman weren't your fault, don't you? She knew she were doing wrong. It's easier to blame someone else than face up to our own faults.' She folded a paper napkin over and over until it resembled a postage stamp. 'We've all done it, my 'andsome.'

'I'm a good listener too if you fancy talking... except when Essy needed me, but I'll put that right.'

'It's all water under the bridge now.'

He couldn't help wondering if this had anything to do with his uncle but pushing her wouldn't help.

'You ought to get on home and put things right with Vera.'

'Easier said than done.' His grouchy tone didn't impress her. 'Am I allowed to make a phone call to Essy? Even prisoners get that.'

'Wait until this evening. You don't want to be jabbering at her on the train. Off you go. I need to do something with this rat's nest.' Molly tugged at her hair.

His mother would be out of bed by now. Time to face the music again.

Ruan traipsed down the road and rather than take the short cut through the harbour up to Hewas Road he zigzagged along through the back streets. It didn't delay anywhere near long enough the time it took to arrive at the very door he stormed out of yesterday. Before he had the chance to pull his keys out Vera opened the door.

'I suppose you've come for your things?'

It could be all in his imagination but she almost sounded scared. There was no disguising the exhaustion etched into her pale tired face.

'Maybe... but first I want to apologise.'

'Oh.' Two spots of pink appeared on her gaunt cheeks. 'I reckon I'm the one who needs to do that.'

'Is it all right if I come in?'

'Of course.' Her voice wobbled. 'This is your home.'

They didn't speak again until they were in the kitchen and his mother finished making a pot of tea.

'Dick tore me off a strip when I told him about our set-to yesterday.' She heaved a weary sigh. 'He was right, of course, just like you were.'

'You know I had to say those things, don't you?'

Vera rolled her shoulders in a slight shrug. 'Yes, but that didn't make it any easier to hear.'

'I know.' He reached across the table and briefly squeezed her thin cold hands. 'I do appreciate everything you've done for me and I don't say so often enough.'

'It was no more than all decent parents do.'

'Yes, it was. Whether Dad leaving had anything to do with a certain three letter word beginning with s is irrelevant.' He couldn't resist a small smile. 'It doesn't alter the fact that he buggered off and left you to bring me up with no help.'

'Thank you. Did you stay up with Essy last night?' She slapped her hand over her mouth. 'See, there I go again. It's none of my business.'

'I'll let you off this time.' Ruan explained where he'd gone. 'So will you step in and rescue me from Jackie Webb's lumpy mattress and dubious bathroom?'

A wide smile inched across his mother's face.

'I suppose I could.'

'There's just one thing… well, a couple, I suppose.' He took a steadying breath. They needed a few ground rules before going forward. 'I won't flaunt my relationship with Essy, but you need to respect it and our right to a private life. We both know I'm not going to stay tucked up in my old bedroom here forever, but I need us to be good while I'm here.'

'I can live with that.'

'So we're okay now?'

Vera nodded. 'I hope so. I've only ever wanted the best for you.'

'I know.' Other people's ideas of the best thing for him rarely coincided with his own but his mother had apologised, something that was rarer than a blue moon in itself and promised to treat him as an adult. He would take what he could get and be grateful.

'Oh Lord, British train food is as bad as I remember.' Her mother tossed her largely uneaten chicken salad sandwich back in its cardboard sleeve. 'Everything's so dreary. Look at it!'

She pointed out of the dirty window at the jammed together red-brick houses with their narrow back gardens butting up to the railway tracks. An endless trail of rubbish, old cars and abandoned appliances followed them along.

Ever since she met Paula at the airport Essy had been bombarded with a litany of complaints about the bumpy, interminable flight across the Atlantic, the rude waiter in the café where they snatched a quick breakfast and the bus to Reading which was too hot and the internet slower than a snail.

'I know but once we get past all this the countryside is real pretty. Everything's so lush and green. I love seeing the sheep and cows in the fields and all the tiny villages dotted around the place. And Cornwall's out of this world... but then you know that.' Irritation at her mother's negative attitude made her reckless. 'You must have some fond memories of growing up there? What about favourite foods you've missed? Pasties? Cream teas? Ice cream with those yummy chocolate flake things?'

'For pity's sake, don't try so hard.' Paula exhaled a weary sigh.

'Why did you come if you're going to be this way?' She could be putting things right with her lover instead of dealing with her grouchy mother.

'Because you forced me to.'

'I did not!' Her raised voice made the people around them turn and stare. Essy barely managed to suppress a giggle when she remembered Ruan trying to politely tell her she was loud.

'Yeah, you did, honey, with all that talk about Molly and Herring Bay.' Paula looked miles away. 'For thirty-two damn years I've managed... not to forget it all, but put it largely out of my mind. You've ruined that.'

'But you always told me to face my fears. Stand up to them. Show them who's boss.' That dragged a faint smile out of her mother.

'You little madam.' There was no venom in the words but rather a touch of pride. 'Apart from your sand collecting nonsense, what've you been up to, or shouldn't I ask?'

Essy ignored the putdown.

'Well?'

Her stomach tightened. 'You would never say much to me about why you left—'

'So you thought you had the right to poke your nose in and ask questions?' Paula's slim hands gripped her water bottle. 'I bet Molly didn't like that? I hope you're happy with what you found out?'

'Happy isn't the right word.'

'That's the first damn sensible thing you've said today.'

'Would you rather I shut up?'

'Tell me the rest after we get there.' Deep creases settled in her mother's overly made-up face. 'I'm tired and all these folks are gonna think we're a couple of clichéd mouthy Americans if we keep on this way.'

They'd no doubt already established that fact but she nodded and Paula turned away, tucked a rolled up sweater behind her head and closed her eyes. Essy disobeyed her aunt's explicit instructions and didn't say a word when they crossed the Tamar Bridge into Cornwall.

'We're at Par.' She shook her mother awake. 'St Austell will be—'

'In about ten minutes. Time to get myself together.' The lipstick came out and the touch of bright pink helped her tired appearance. After that the bleached blonde hair was fluffed and sprayed. 'Right.'

When Paula tugged on a linen jacket Essy almost warned she wouldn't need it but to someone who'd come from the peak of a steamy Tennessee summer that wouldn't be the case.

'Oh Lord, tell me Molly's not meeting us at the station?'

'No, I told her we'd get a taxi. She's making pasties for our dinner.'

'Pasties?'

'She'll be offended if you don't eat one.'

Paula quirked a weary smile. 'Oh, don't worry, I'll eat one. I can taste it already.'

The same far off look returned. She couldn't imagine what was going through her mother's mind right now.

When they stepped onto the platform her mother ground to a halt and stared around her, taking everything in like an alien who just landed from Mars.

'They've sure spruced this old place up. It used to be really dingy and there never used to be an elevator. The day I left I remember dragging my suitcase up over the stairs and standing on the platform with the rain blowing in sideways. I wondered what the hell I was doing.' Their eyes locked. 'I made the right choice and I don't regret it for one moment.'

'None of it? What about Aunt Molly? She's missed you somethin' awful. And your parents? You didn't even go back when they passed away.' The torrent of accusations burst out before she could stop herself.

'You've no right to judge me. For years I couldn't afford the plane fare anyway and then things kept on falling apart in my personal life. I refused to come back as a failure. By the time things picked up I'd left it too long... or that's what I always tried to convince myself.'

'I'm sorry. Let's get a taxi.'

They barely spoke during the drive and Paula stubbornly turned away from the window. Their driver made the turning for Herring Bay and halfway down Pengolva Hill her mother sprang back to life and tapped his shoulder.

'Stop here.'

They pulled off the road exactly where Essy stopped to gaze out over the sea when she first arrived. Paula flung the car door open and jumped out, so she decided to follow suit.

'This is it. My favourite view in the whole world.' Her face was wreathed in a massive smile. 'I used to hike up when I'd had enough of all the hassle goin' on down there.' She pointed to the village. 'I'd stare out to sea, take a few deep breaths and imagine heading for the horizon.'

'And never comin' back?'

'Oh, honey.' The tears trickling down Paula's face snaked a trail of black mascara with them.

Next thing Essy was engulfed in her mother's arms and she blurted out the words she'd wanted to say since they met at the airport this morning.

'I'm glad you're here. Really glad.' They had differences, like any mother and daughter, but the tight bonds drawing them together were always there.

'Me too. Me too.'

'Oy, you'm running up some bill here,' the driver yelled out at them.

'Come on. Lead me to my first pasty in three decades.'

'Sounds like a plan.' The tight knot in her stomach loosened its grip.

As they pulled up outside her aunt's house she saw Molly hovering on the doorstep and glancing anxiously out to the street. Essy felt Paula stiffen next to her and heard her draw in a sharp breath.

'I was almost silly enough to say how old Molly is looking but I'm sure she'll think the same about me.'

Being an only child Essy was sketchy on the sibling dynamic but recalled going to her tenth high school reunion a few years ago and feeling the same about many of her old classmates. 'Are we getting out?'

That jolted her mother back to life and Paula leapt from the car and set off running, leaving her to pay the driver and grab their bags. By the time she joined them the two women were somehow managing to hug, laugh and talk at the same time.

'Pop those upstairs, lovey.' Molly waved Essy in and turned her fond gaze back on her long-lost sister. 'We've got a lot to catch up on, haven't we?'

'We sure have.' Paula sighed. 'Too much. I can't bear to think about all these years we've wasted.'

'Then don't. What's done is done. We can't turn the clock back.' Molly shook her head. 'We've all made mistakes. I wasn't a good sister when you needed one.' Big fat tears dripped down her face and it made Essy's throat constrict when her mother gently brushed them away.

'I wasn't either. I left you to bear the brunt of Mum and Dad's anger when your heart was already broken. We both know that was my fault too.'

Essy didn't dream of interrupting but itched to ask whether they were talking about Dick Menear.

'It wasn't meant to be.' Molly sounded more her usual pragmatic self. 'Come on. We're going to have a proper cream tea to welcome you home.' She squeezed Paula's arm. 'I bought in plenty of clotted cream. Mum used to tell you off for eating it by the spoonful when she wasn't looking.' Her aunt looked wistful. 'They weren't all bad times, were they?'

'No they weren't.' Her mother's voice was little more than a whisper. 'That's what I forgot... or didn't let myself remember.'

Now Essy brushed away her own tears. She was happy to be the catalyst for bringing Paula back to Cornwall and her hopes soared that they could deal with whatever arose as the family they were. Together.

Chapter Twenty-Six

Last night he bottled out of ringing Essy by convincing himself he would interrupt the family reunion going on in Tregrehan Road. Yesterday wasn't a complete bust though because after he reluctantly returned to Julia she seized on his idea of trying to find a way to save the old Methodist Chapel and turn it into some version of a community centre. They batted suggestions around and it turned out several of their old school friends were active in local affairs. Paul Bonny was on the council and Heather Bunt ran the constituency office for the local Member of Parliament.

'I'm sure they'll all be interested in getting involved. Most of us who stayed wish Herring Bay could be more like it used to be.'

When he said the dream was to make it better she gave him the same tilted smile that used to make his heart flip. It didn't have the same effect now but seeing the fresh sparkle in her eyes lifted his mood.

'We should see about getting the local shopkeepers on board because this affects them too. I'm sure John Wakeham and Jane Moody would be interested. You've got younger people like Tina Cloke as well. I'm sure she knows lots of local artists who would leap at an affordable space to promote their crafts. How would you feel about meeting us all again to talk some more about this?' When she made the suggestion Julia rushed to reassure him that she would make it clear to everyone they had to start fresh. 'That includes you.'

The burst of spunkiness had made him laugh. He supposed that meant he wouldn't be leaving Herring Bay anytime soon.

His mother came into the kitchen breaking his thoughts. 'Your uncle has to go for an X-ray up at Penrice Hospital this morning. Can you take him? Please.'

'I'd be happy to.' That was a first. His mother usually issued orders rather than making requests. Maybe the different footing he'd fought to establish yesterday might last.

Vera screwed the top back on the marmalade. 'What do you think to asking Molly and Essy over for a bit of dinner tonight?'

Because he'd been busy getting things straight he'd omitted to mention one crucial fact but now he couldn't avoid it.

'That's a kind thought but... there's something I didn't get around to telling you yesterday. A couple of things really.'

'Have you done something to upset the girl?'

Great, he was getting the blame before Vera even heard the full story. Before he could lose the nerve he blurted out the part about Essy catching him out in a clinch with Julia North.

'Well, of course she got upset. No one likes to think they're being made a fool of.'

They were on dangerous territory.

'I only wanted a chance to explain, Mum. Was that too much to ask?'

She sat down and gestured towards the teapot. Ruan poured her out a mug and slid it across the table.

'You don't want to hear this but you haven't known each other long. Trust is something you have to earn.' She exhaled a weary sigh. 'Your father always had an "explanation" for his friendships with other women but I couldn't rely on whether or not they were the truth.'

'But you still love him? Why?' He reached for her hand. 'You're worth more than the way he treated you.' A shimmer of sadness clouded his mother's eyes.

'I had my faults. You know some of them.' A tinge of pink coloured her cheeks.

He ached to say this didn't have to define her life. That she should slough off her marriage and move on. But he held his tongue. Deep down his mum knew all this and had made her choices. That was the same privilege she'd always encouraged in him as a boy, standing up for him when they didn't fit in with his peers. Only yesterday he begged her to give him that same freedom now.

'Let's not harp on about all that any longer. What else did you want to tell me?'

Want to tell her? Ruan almost burst out laughing. Paula's arrival in Herring Bay was the last news he *wanted* to break.

Essy watched the two sisters from the doorway, hunched over a photo album and alternately sharing a laugh before sinking into quiet contemplation as they flipped through the pages. Keeping up the façade of happiness was straining her acting skills. If she didn't hear from Ruan soon she would march over to his house, bang on the door and insist he talk to her.

'I'm gonna leave y'all for a while. I need a couple of things from the shop.' She didn't flinch when Molly and Paula gave her matching curious stares.

'You'll be back for your dinner at five?' Molly asked. 'I'm making a nice bit of stew. Your mum tells me she hasn't eaten a dumpling in all these years.' She poked her sister's well-toned arm. 'That's why she's like a rake and I'm—'

'A proper Barnecutt.' Paula grinned and finished the sentence for her sister. Her mother seemed younger here and more relaxed. Yes, she was wearing make-up but nowhere near as much as usual and she'd ditched her usual smart fashions for jeans and a simple pale blue shirt.

'I should be here. I'll let you know if I'll be... delayed.' She briefly considered sending Ruan a text but that would give him wiggle room. Turning up on his doorstep gave him no choice.

A distinctly un-summery breeze whipped in off the sea and the sky clung to the ominous grey clouds that were there when she woke up this morning, threatening rain but not following through yet. She noticed a few desultory visitors ambling around the harbour and by the look of their sturdy boots, loaded backpacks and waterproof coats tied around the waist of baggy hiking clothes, they were the typical serious walkers tackling the coastal path. One of the top things Herring Bay desperately needed was a decent café that would welcome customers with muddy boots and wet dogs. Next was a well-stocked outdoor shop with basic essentials like decent socks and blister plasters. The glory days of its fishing past couldn't be recreated but adapting was the key to survival.

She found herself knocking on Ruan's door with no clear plan of what to say.

'Hello, my dear.' Dick Menear leaned on his crutches and grimaced when he attempted to shift out of her way. 'Come in. You came to see the boy, I s'pose?'

'I hope she did.' Ruan leapt down the stairs two at a time and landed in front of her as his mother appeared from the kitchen. 'Do you fancy an ice cream?' He grabbed her arm and steered her back outside before she could formulate an answer.

Essy raked her gaze over his frayed blue jeans and plain black T-shirt. 'Sure you didn't want to change first?' That wiped the smile off his face. 'Sorry. You look great.' He grabbed her hand and tugged her towards the road. 'Where are we going?'

'Going?'

'Yeah.' A shiver rolled through her. 'The calendar says July but in case you hadn't noticed it's not a pleasant sunny day.'

'Walk fast and you'll soon warm up.' His dark eyes lost their sombre hue when he slipped an arm across her shoulders. 'This better?' A hint of wariness sneaked back into his expression. 'I know we need to talk. I came up to Molly's but you were gone and... I didn't think you would want me knocking on the door.'

'I'm here now.'

'Oh you are.' He stopped halfway down the hill and cupped her chin, tilting her to meet his kiss.

Essy lost herself to the taste of him and was barely aware of the first fat raindrops plopping down on her face. Not so a few minutes later when the skies well and truly opened up.

'You want to go back to my place or race to The Smugglers'?'

The options weren't thrilling. 'Yours, I guess.'

'My mum won't eat you.'

Essy wasn't so sure. 'I bet our night away didn't thrill her?'

'About as much as me "kissing" Julia North didn't thrill you?' The exaggerated air quotes made her blush. 'Let's go get dried off then I want to hear all about your mum.'

The idea of holding that conversation with Vera hovering within earshot was beyond depressing, but she allowed him to lead her back into the house like a lamb to the slaughter.

Ruan put a finger to his mouth and gestured towards the stairs. For once they might be in luck. He'd managed to creep into the kitchen and drag a couple of towels out of the airing cupboard without any sign of his family.

'You're not fifteen and trying to sneak that Julia North in under my nose.' A deep frown was etched into his mother's face. 'You should treat Essy better.'

Ruan wasn't certain which of them was more shocked. He was stunned into silence and Essy's mouth gaped wide enough to catch a family of flies.

'Come up with me, dear, and I'll find you something dry to put on.'

'That sure is kind of you, Mrs Pascow, but there's really no need.'

He caught the tinge of panic pulling at her voice but couldn't think up a way to get Essy out of accepting his mother's offer fast enough.

'Call me Vera.'

Ruan trudged up the stairs after them and dived into his own bedroom. After changing out of his own wet clothes he hovered on the landing. He could hear them chattering away through the walls and at least it sounded like a two-way conversation as opposed to one of his mother's lectures.

'I don't believe it.' Uncle Dick popped out of his room

sporting a wide grin. 'That's the second time in as many days that she's taken my advice.'

'What are you on about?'

'I told my stubborn sister she needed to stick her nose out of your private life and I also said if she was smart she'd be friendly to young Essy or she'd drive you away otherwise.' He shook his head. 'Your father had his faults but she weren't an easy woman to live with either.'

'She knows that.'

'Maybe she does now but she didn't back then. She could've won a gold medal in the nagging Olympics.'

Ruan struggled not to laugh. 'Fancy a cup of tea while we wait?'

'Why not.' Dick grimaced. 'You go first. It takes me an age.'

They found out at the hospital that the latest X-ray showed his ankle was healing slower than had been predicted. The doctor insisted he use the crutches for at least another week and warned him he'd need to take care for a good while longer after that.

With the tea made Ruan fetched the tin of chocolate biscuits. This might be a chance for them to have a chat without his mother interfering.

'It'll take more than this to make me talk.' Dick laughed and selected one of his favourite chocolate covered caramel crunch creams.

'Did you like my dad?'

'Like him? Most people *liked* your father. It was hard not to.' He looked thoughtful. 'Girls especially liked him and he returned the favour. Most men envied the knack he had for talking to women. Not awkward like the rest of us. He and Vera were close all through school but it surprised me a bit when I heard they were going out together.'

'Why?'

'I can't rightly say.' Dick scratched his beard. 'Could never put my finger on it except they always seemed more like best friends than—' His face coloured up. 'Most teenagers can't keep their hands off each other but they weren't like that. I assumed it would fizzle out but then Vera came home on her nineteenth birthday with an engagement ring on her finger. It wasn't like they were expecting you or anything. You came along pretty quick though. Proper little honeymoon baby you were.' His expression darkened. 'Your mum had a few, you know... female problems I think and next thing they're in separate bedrooms. Stayed that way too.'

'Doesn't excuse him having affairs all over the place.'

'No. If he was.' His uncle looked serious. 'Tree always denied it.'

'You believed him?'

'Don't know if I did or I didn't. Wasn't my opinion that was important though, was it? Vera was convinced and that's all that mattered in the long run.'

Ruan took a chance. 'You'll probably tell me to stick my nose out of your business but why do you dislike Herring Bay so much? Is it something to do with Molly Barnecutt?'

His uncle's face turned to stone.

Chapter Twenty-Seven

Essy felt like Peter Rabbit cornered in Mr McGregor's garden but without a handy gate through which to escape.

Vera's neat, plain bedroom reflected her personality. Nothing was out of place and no speck of dust dared to linger on the highly-polished furniture. Essy assumed the solid dark oak furniture had belonged to Ruan's grandparents. He told her once that his parents moved into the house when they got married with the older Pascows. Within a couple of years his grandparents surprised everyone by retiring to Spain and living there the rest of their lives. In their wills they divided up everything between the two children, leaving the house to Vera and all of their money to Dick.

Vera picked out a selection of clothes and laid them on top of the old-fashioned pink quilted bedspread. 'I hope granny pants are better than nothing.' She pointed to a pair of sensible white cotton underwear. 'It's all I wear. You'll have to go without a bra because I don't have anything to fit you. I never was well-endowed in that direction.' She wandered over to stare out of the window while Essy stripped off, rubbed some warmth back into her cold skin and tugged on the borrowed clothes.

The sweatpants were baggy at her waist and only reached halfway down her shins. Topped with a loose pale green cotton jumper the outfit looked tolerable but she didn't have a clue how she would explain her appearance to her mum and Molly.

'Thanks, that's much better.'

Vera managed something resembling a smile. 'Ruan will have a good laugh when he sees you. He's always trying to make me wear more up to date stuff but I'm fine the way I am.'

'It's a good thing we're all different.'

'My boy's different all right.' Her questioning gaze landed on Essy. 'Not everyone appreciates that.'

'I do.' Wow, that earned her another tight smile.

'If it wasn't for who you are I think I'd like you.'

'Yeah, I feel the same.' Her face burned under Vera's intense scrutiny. 'When I came here I sure didn't plan on hooking up with the son of the man who messed around with my mother.' This conversation was turning into a massive surprise. The idea of finding common ground with Ruan's mother had seemed more unlikely than Essy becoming an astronaut and going to Mars.

'You're Paula's daughter all right.'

She chose to take that as a compliment although it probably wasn't intended that way. 'She'll be happy to hear that but maybe you can tell her so yourself.'

'I'm not likely to run over to Tennessee and see her, now am I?' Vera scoffed.

'Oh didn't Ruan tell you...' She slammed her mouth shut. Talk about putting her foot in it big time. She should've guessed his mother wouldn't be acting so agreeably if she knew Paula was back in Herring Bay.

'Tell me what?'

Essy blurted out the whole story and watched the penny drop.

'I'd better go and see how Dick is. If I don't keep an eye on him he'll do too much and I'll never get rid of him.' The faint wobble in Vera's voice hinted at her inner turmoil.

'Can't we hash this out?'

'Hash this out?'

Vera's mock American accent stomped on the faint hope that they could find some level of common ground. Ruan was right in the first place. There could never be an 'us' for the two of them. She should have the sense to kick the dust of Cornwall off her feet and high tail it back to Tennessee as fast as her legs would carry her.

She scooped up her wet clothes. 'I'll make sure you get your things back. Don't worry I'm done here in Cornwall. I'll be off home again as soon as I can arrange it. '

'But Ruan will be—'

'You can tell him yourself that I've gone and why.' Essy evaded Vera's attempt to grab her arm and pushed out past her. A loose tread on the stairs almost tripped her up but she stumbled over the last couple of steps into the hall.

'Essy, do you want a coffee?'

Hot tears flooded her eyes as Ruan's rumbling voice drifted out from the kitchen but she flung open the front door and took off running.

If his uncle thought he could out-wait Ruan he would soon discover his mistake.

'You're a nosy bugger, like my flaming sister. I'm not talking about the Barnecutt woman or this godforsaken place.'

'What are you being pig-headed about now?' His mother bustled into the kitchen and glanced at them both.

He waited to see if his uncle would explain but Dick settled into a morose silence and glowered at the floor. Vera snatched a tea towel from the hook on the wall and started to dry the dishes. By some miracle the plate didn't shatter when she slammed it down on the counter but her severe expression warned him not to make any comment if he valued his life.

Ruan wondered where Essy had got to.

'I'm going to pack and get off home to Newquay.' His uncle shoved back his chair and heaved up on his feet. Dick shoved his crutches under his arms. 'I've managed on my own all these years without your help, apart from your turning up with a few buns to salve your conscience every now and then.'

His mother turned pale as his uncle hobbled away and Ruan couldn't help feeling sorry for her. Like the rest of the human race she wasn't perfect but she was intensely loyal to those she loved, sometimes to a fault, and had tried her best to care for her equally stubborn brother.

'Where's Essy? I thought I heard her come downstairs?'

'You did.' She avoided his eyes and reached for another plate to dry, giving it far more attention than necessary.

'Mum?'

'She's gone.' Vera's steady gaze bored through him. 'Probably to tell Molly and her precious *mother* that she's leaving and going back to America.'

'I did try to tell you about Paula.' He had bottled out in the end, convincing himself a few hours one way or the other wouldn't make any difference.

'Try harder another time.'

'It still doesn't explain why she ran out on me.'

'Oh grow up.' His mother sounded exasperated. 'That girl had the sense to see what you apparently won't. No good can come of you two... you know.'

'Sleeping together? Being in love?' Ruan watched as his words stabbed her like sharp needles. 'Why shouldn't I love a smart, funny, beautiful woman whose only fault, as far I can make out, and this is your opinion not mine, is being honest and speaking the truth?'

'You want my advice, boy?' Dick limped back in. 'Go after your American girl and take her well away from this damn place.' A spray of spit fanned out from his mouth. 'If I'd been more of a man I'd have me a good wife and perhaps a couple of kids by now. Instead I listened to your mother and now I'm a bitter old devil living out his days grumbling about everyone and everything.' His uncle's expression softened. 'I've rung for a taxi and it'll be here in a few minutes. Would you mind carrying my bag down, please?'

'Don't go, Dick, please,' Vera begged. 'I'm sorry. For everything. I'll be some worried if you leave now. You know what the doctor said.' She touched his uncle's arm. 'I could have a word with Molly...'

His uncle shook his head sadly. 'It's too late. She was a good woman and didn't deserve to be tarred with the same brush as her sister.'

'I know but Paula stuck her oar in first and then it all snowballed.' A tear rolled down his mother's face and she angrily brushed it away. 'I was jealous. You worshipped Molly and Tree and I weren't ever that way.'

Dick nodded. 'Let's forget it. We're all each other has now apart from your boy here. I'll hang on a bit longer and then we'll see how things go.' He plodded off upstairs again. The kitchen throbbed with the shadow of words that shouldn't have been said alongside others festering away in the miserable silence.

'You know I've got a million more questions now, don't you?' Ruan asked. 'Am I likely to get any answers?'

'What do you want me to say?'

Did she honestly not know? 'You could start by telling me what you did to split up Molly and Dick and why, but I'm guessing you won't do that. Let's concentrate on me and Essy instead. It's only been a matter of hours but you've already broken your promise to support me and let me live my own life. I'm not going to stop loving her because you're against it. If there's any way on earth I can convince her to give me – us – another chance, then I will.'

His mother remained silent and stoic.

The brief window of understanding between them had clearly slammed shut and that realisation made him want to scream.

'You're goin' back home to Tennessee? But I just got here!' Paula's protest was understandable but Essy couldn't see any other way to save her last threads of self-respect.

'Sorry, but I've done the job I came here to do and there's no real reason for me to hang on.'

'What about all the other stuff?' Slashes of heat made her mother's cheeks burn. 'You were determined to dig up all the dirt you imagined I was hiding and if you claim you've abandoned that garbage, I won't believe you.'

'Yeah, well, you can believe it or not but I'm done. I found out enough. Do you want to know what I think?' Both women stared at her. 'They treated you like dirt, Mom, everyone. Your family and the whole damn village and you were right to leave. Happy now?' Hands on hips she straightened to her full height. 'I'm goin' to pack and then I'm off.'

In the seclusion of her bedroom she didn't bother holding back her tears any longer as she started to pack. Essy flung her clothes in every which way and absentmindedly wondered why everything fitted perfectly coming over but now the suitcase and backpack were both filled to bursting point. Despite her anguish she dredged up a watery smile. One day Ruan teased her unmercifully when she complained about how small her closet was in Molly's spare bedroom.

You shopped remember? It's what we do. A new shirt here. A pair of shoes there. Maybe we should both consider therapy for our retail addictions?

She slumped on the bed and clasped her head in her hands. With more time could they have beaten the odds? By now his mother might have convinced him Ruan was better off without a woman who had caused nothing but trouble for their family. Essy grabbed a tissue to blow her snotty nose.

It took a massive effort to drag herself back up to standing but if she didn't hurry up he might come looking for her. Other people thought she was strong and resolute but if she saw Ruan's warm, sexy smile again and bathed in a level of understanding she'd never experienced with any other man, her resolve would turn to mush.

Hash this out?

Vera's derision slammed back into her. She refused to make him choose between them. Ruan would choose Essy but the estrangement would be a barrier between them and eat away at something that was once so magical. As she was trying to cram one more book into her overstuffed backpack a slip of paper fell out with the details of Tree Pascow's possible address in Wales. Should she get the train to London and the next flight back to Tennessee or do this one last thing for Ruan?

Essy combed her hair, hitched it into a messy ponytail and slicked on a layer of red glossy lipstick. She took a breath and headed back downstairs. What difference would one more lie make?

Chapter Twenty-Eight

Ruan grabbed his small overnight bag and sneaked out of the front door to his car, grateful that neither Vera nor Dick were up early this morning. He had considered letting his mother know where he was headed but she'd made it perfectly clear where she stood on the subject of finding his father. He stowed his luggage in the boot and turned the key in the ignition.

Dogged determination kept him going until he hit the outskirts of Swansea, when his lack of sleep and almost four hours of driving through persistent drizzle and heavy traffic caught up with him. He could be less than an hour from coming face to face with the man he'd last seen almost thirty years ago and needed to get his head together. Ruan pulled off at the next service area and slumped over the steering wheel. If he hadn't been such an ass Essy could've been here with him now but his stubbornness forced him to do it alone, or not at all.

But not at all was no longer an option. That was crystal clear now in a way it had never been before. He was convinced that the possibility of finding out the truth about his father was behind his return to Cornwall all along. It had always lurked at the back of his mind, tucked into a space he never visited because it hurt too much. But the hurt never went away and never would until he owned it.

He raised his head as sunshine flooded in through the windscreen and decided to take the improved weather as a good omen. Ten minutes later, after a quick recce in the café he set off again with a surge of adrenaline fuelled by strong coffee and two warm jam doughnuts.

Ruan meandered along on purpose to give himself the opportunity to soak up the wild beauty of the Gower Peninsula. The area's resemblance to Cornwall made it easy to see why Tree might have settled here. It had the same sense of apartness from the rest of the United Kingdom. A similarly rugged coastline with wide, golden beaches shimmering under picture perfect blue skies and a familiar collection of small villages and communities scattered across the undulating countryside.

He couldn't completely shake off his sadness over Essy but for some inexplicable reason he refused to accept their story was over. Even now, in the cold light of day, he didn't regret speaking bluntly to his mother.

A signpost pointing out he was now in Rhossili stopped his mind from wandering. Brynmor Road shouldn't be far but he wasn't quite ready to find it yet. He scanned the narrow street and manoeuvred his small car into the first available parking space. It was hard not to compare the large number of people walking around this small village to the dwindling number who visited Herring Bay. Why was this area so much more popular? Ruan spotted a decent outdoor shop, several cafés and a pub that even from the outside put The Smugglers' to shame with its gleaming white paint and colourful hanging baskets.

Doughnuts didn't provide much in the way of staying power and his stomach was rumbling. That seemed a sign to take his time and eat a late lunch in the Drunken Duck. A few minutes later he was stunned when the friendly landlord set a pint down in front of him and asked if he was Tree Pascow's son.

'You're the spitting image of him. Good man, Tree. Talks about you all the time.'

Talks about him? Was the man joking? He mumbled something innocuous to satisfy the man and was left to drink in peace while he waited for his food to arrive.

Was she about to do the most foolish thing ever? A smile quirked Essy's mouth and she wondered if that honour should go instead to the night she lost her virginity?

At college she got tired of all the other girls boasting about their own experiences and picked on Quinten Brooks to help her out. The quiet, unassuming young man with John Lennon glasses and a thick Cajun accent sat in the back row of their history lectures and rarely spoke to anyone. She plucked up the nerve to invite him to a party given by one of their fellow students and he'd been too shocked to turn her down. After several glasses of punch containing God knows what they drifted upstairs to a recently vacated bedroom. It turned out Quinten was equally clueless and they soon gave up on their fumbling attempts as a bad job. Strangely enough they managed to laugh about the gruesome experience and later became good friends. Not foolish then after all.

Essy stared at the freshly painted turquoise door that immediately reminded her of Ruan. Before she was able to ring the bell a couple of lanky teenage boys ran up the path of the narrow terraced house and almost bowled her over.

'Oops.' The older boy grabbed her right arm to stop her from falling and the scattering of pimples on his round face turned crimson. 'You okay?'

'Of course she isn't, you ape!' The second boy gave him a jab and flashed Essy a wide toothy smile.

'What trouble are you pair causing now?' A man's gruff voice boomed from somewhere inside the house and as soon as he appeared she needed no other proof of making another successful 'find' than watching a slow, familiar smile crease the man's craggy face.

'I'm sorry if my boys startled you. I'm afraid Dan and Petie are like wild animals let loose when school is over.' He gave the teenagers an indulgent smile. 'I'm still trying to teach them a few manners.'

The words 'my boys' reverberated in her skull while Essy stumbled over trying to reassure them she was fine.

'You're American!' The red-faced boy had eyes the size of dinner plates. 'Have you been to New York? What about Los Angeles?'

It gave her a chance to regroup when he babbled on about everything he loved about the United States and his plan to go there and live one day. Essy finally managed to give him a few brief answers while keeping one eye on her quarry. Tree Pascow was scrutinising her as if he guessed she wasn't a simple tourist looking for the nearest beach.

'That's enough. Get yourselves a snack to take upstairs while I talk to this lady.' The new sterner tone to his voice caught their attention. He waved them away, then turned back to her with another charming smile. 'Are we playing a game where I guess who you are or is there any chance you might introduce yourself?'

She shifted her weight from one foot to the other and shoved her hands in her pockets. It would have suited her better to talk inside but he was hardly going to invite a complete stranger into his house. 'I'm Essy Havers. My mother's maiden name was Paula Barnecutt.' For a moment he didn't react.

'I see the resemblance now.' He puffed out a weary sigh. 'Something about you was nagging at me. You're Paula all over again. You'd better come in.'

The house was cluttered with the detritus of family life. Coats and shoes abandoned by their owners. Teetering piles of books covered the dining table and a deflated football had rolled into one corner of the living room.

'They're a messy lot, I'm afraid.' He swept a pile of magazines off the sofa and gestured for her to sit down. 'Messy, but good kids. On the whole anyway.' The smile re-emerged and for her mother's sake she wished she could resist the urge to return it.

'How many do you have?'

'It varies.'

'Varies?'

Tree burst out laughing. 'Oh they're not mine.' The humour faded. 'That's not right. They are in every way that matters.'

How could she ever break it to Ruan that his father had fathered what appeared to be an indeterminate bunch of children? Essy couldn't hide her horror.

'Will this exonerate me?' He passed over a framed newspaper

cutting and the hint of devilment in his bright green eyes stirred her anger.

Local man fosters child number 100!

A flush of heat zoomed up her neck. Tree Pascow had devoted his years in Wales to taking care of children, some for a single night and others for far longer periods of time. He always chose the ones who were hardest to place. The oldest. The most troubled. Those who were burdened with extra problems on top of parents who were unable to cope.

'Why?'

'Why do I do it?' He stretched out his hands on his thighs and their recognisable well-formed, elegance made her heart contract.

'Because I failed my own son.' A shudder ran through his large loose-limbed frame. 'This doesn't come close to putting right the way I neglected him but it helps me to atone.' He swept a hand over his eyes. 'You didn't come all the way to Wales to hear all this.' Tree's sharp gaze bored into her. 'What did you come for anyway and how did you find me?'

A sharp knock on the door saved her from answering.

Chapter Twenty-Nine

Ruan stared at the bright turquoise paint. He should ring the bell or knock on the door but either simple task appeared beyond him.

'Tree always brags about his boy back in London. Fancy architect and all that. You're lucky to have such a fine father. What he does for all those poor kids is nothing short of heroic. We weren't sure he would keep taking them in after he lost his partner a few years back but he's soldiered on.'

By the time he'd listened to Gareth Jones at the Drunken Duck praising up Tree for all the children he'd fostered over the years he couldn't hide their estrangement any longer. For his own sake as much as anything he skimmed over the reasons behind it. A deep, acerbic bitterness gnawed his insides knowing that his father had freely given to strangers what he denied his own son. The better part of him understood that attitude was mean-spirited but the nugget of jealousy still lodged there. Was a man who abandoned his own son the best person to take care of other people's troubled children?

He thumped on the door and the loud noise echoed back at him.

'I'm coming there's no need to bang the house down.'

The door flung open and his thirty-year odyssey ended.

Ruan stared at the older, thinner version of his father, sporting horn-rimmed glasses these days and no beard. The sandy blond hair of his memories was now pure white but still thick and grazed the collar of his red check shirt.

'Hello, I'm—'

'Oh, my boy.'

The raspy whisper tore at him and he had to avert his gaze from his father's tear-filled eyes.

'Will you be coming in?' A hint of Welsh overlaid the soft Cornish burr.

'Uh, I suppose so.'

'I've got another visitor... I don't mean you're a visitor... well, you are, but...'

Seeing his father's awkwardness didn't give him any pleasure. 'I can leave.'

'No!'

If his mother saw him stepping in over the doorstep she'd have a fit. And Essy? He hoped she'd be proud but he was doing this for himself not anybody else.

'This way.' His father loped along in front of him. 'I believe you two know each other.'

He couldn't imagine what Tree was getting at but followed him into an untidy living room.

'Essy?' Ruan tried to make sense of why she was sitting on the well-worn red leather sofa, colourful as ever in a lime green shift dress, soft white ankle boots and her trademark scarlet lipstick. He registered her wary smile.

'You have yourself quite a young woman here.'

Wishful thinking. He didn't *have* her at all.

'How about a cup of tea?'

He caught the twitch of Essy's smile.

'Your dad and I have had an awesome chat.'

It was incredible to hear her smooth, warm drawl again. 'Really?'

'Yeah.' She held out her hand. 'Sit down.'

Ruan flopped next to her, temporarily giving up the effort to wrap his head around the whole bizarre scene.

'I'll fix us all a hot drink while you talk to your daddy.' The brush of her soft lips on his forehead and wisp of vanilla scented perfume drifting his way helped him pull back together. 'I'll take me a good long while so don't hurry.'

When the kitchen door closed behind her he wasn't sure how to start the conversation. 'Gareth Jones at the pub couldn't say enough good things about you.'

'He doesn't know me like you do.'

The resignation running through his voice shouldn't have stirred an iota of guilt but it did. 'He mentioned you lost your partner quite recently. I'm sorry. You must miss her. Were you together long?'

Tree reached for a framed photograph on the oak Welsh dresser behind him. A wary look crept into his expression as he held it out to Ruan. 'That's Huw. This was his house and we had nearly twenty years together.' He wiped at his eyes. 'Wonderful years.'

It felt like someone pulled the rug out from under him. 'I... sorry, I'm trying to wrap my head around all this.'

'That's okay.'

'Don't get me wrong. I couldn't care less that you're gay, it's just... it never occurred to me.' Ruan stared at the rugged, dark-haired man in the picture with his bright blue eyes and a broad engaging smile. 'What happened to Huw?'

'Motorbike accident. It'll be three years in November.' A visible shudder ran through his father. Tree took back the photograph and stared longingly at it before placing it carefully back on the dresser. 'How is Vera?'

It was on the tip of his tongue to ask why he would care one way or the other but the words died in his throat. 'She's all right.' Another silence fell between them. 'Did she know?'

'No.' His father shrugged. 'I'm not sure I did either... not exactly.' A tinge of pink coloured his cheeks. 'I tried fitting in at school. I wanted to be "normal", I suppose. Your mum and I always hit it off and it suited us as teenagers to be boyfriend and girlfriend. Vera was always a bit wary of the... physical side of love so she was relieved when I didn't pressure her. I shouldn't have married her though because it wasn't fair on either of us. I loved her as well as I could but she deserved better.'

'Mum told me about the separate rooms and everything,' Ruan admitted. 'She wouldn't be happy to know I'm here. She didn't have any interest in finding you.' His father sunk into a chair clutching his head with his hands, his shoulders heaving with emotion.

'I don't blame her.'

Then he remembered the foster children. 'Your parenting record isn't exactly stellar so I don't understand how the authorities let you care for all those kids?'

'I was honest with them when they did my background check. I don't have a criminal record and I'm financially stable thanks to my landscaping business. I was drawn to helping older boys who've fallen through the cracks. Huw was wonderful with the children too. He understood better than most what it was like to desperately need a safety net. His uncle was the only person on his side when the rest of his family rejected him after he came out to them.'

He almost asked where *his* safety net had been growing up.

'I wasn't there for you and I can't put that right.' He dragged his fingers through his hair making it stick up in the exact same way as Ruan's. 'This is a small way to balance the scales.'

It was hardly a small thing his father had done but he couldn't give Tree any credit, not out loud.

'Was there a lot of gossip after I left?'

'Yes, but believe it or not enough people respect Mum and the... good things you did around the village that not a lot of dirt stuck to you. Paula Barnecutt got most of the blame for your supposed affair. They say she led you on.'

'Rubbish,' Tree scoffed. 'For a start I never laid a finger on her. I swore that at the time but no one would believe me. We used to talk for hours on end and swapped dreams about starting our lives over somewhere far away from Herring Bay.'

'But not together?'

'No. Never that.'

His father vehemently shook his head.

'I can tell you've turned out good. That's your mother's doing.' Tree looked wary. 'What do you want from me anyway?

Any attempt I make to apologise would be an insult. I get that.'

'I'm not sure. Maybe the chance to understand how you could abandon us and never get in touch so we'd no idea if you were alive or dead?'

'The simplest explanation is that I was weak.' The trace of a smile flickered in his sad eyes. 'I loved you so much and your mother too in my own way. I rationalised that it would rip you all apart if the real truth came out. Of course I see now that what I did was far worse.' His father huffed out an exasperated sigh. 'At the time I thought that my leaving was the best gift I could give you both.'

Ruan cleared his throat. 'Reverend Worthington said almost the same thing. He's a wise man so I'm taking a guess that he knew your whole story?'

'We talked around it but I'm sure he saw right through me. The old chap's still alive?'

'Very much so.' For the first time in days he laughed. After that it didn't seem as hard to say the things he wanted his father to hear.

Was it eavesdropping to leave the kitchen door cracked open? She looked on it as insurance to prevent a bloodbath taking place in the other room but had to bite her lip to stop from crying when Tree took all the blame for the so-called affair with her mother that scandalised Herring Bay. If only Paula could hear him say that. Ruan must be reeling inside from all of his father's revelations. So many things made more sense now.

If she lurked out here any longer they would start to wonder. Essy banged around a bit and gathered up their three drinks. No doubt the tea wasn't up to British standards but she guessed they wouldn't complain.

'Here y'all go. Tea with milk and no sugar for the pair of you.' She handed them their mugs and sat back down herself. 'I've given up on the whole hot tea thing. I'm sticking to coffee.

Good chat?' Both men gave her a wary look. 'Is anyone goin' to answer or do I have to guess?'

'If you weren't listening at the door I'll eat my hat.' Ruan gave her a quirky smile.

'You're not wearing one today.'

'We're… okay.' Tree finally spoke, but his weak smile faded as he glanced towards his son. 'At least I hope we are?'

Ruan managed a slight nod. Not the enthusiastic response she might've hoped for but her mother always claimed she had unrealistic expectations of people and life in general.

'I hate to break things up but I've got to drag Dan and Petie away from their video games and drive them to football practice.' His laughter was slightly forced.

She squeezed Ruan's hand when he stiffened against her and lowered her voice to a whisper. 'I've got a room at the pub. You're welcome to join me. We could come back here in the morning?'

'Thanks.' The words sounded as though they were dragged over rough gravel.

'Is that okay with you?' Essy turned her attention back to Tree.

'Of course. Whatever you want.'

All Essy ever intended was to track down the man, tell him a few pertinent truths and leave. Instead she had found herself unconsciously responding to his charismatic smile and gentle manner. It was hard not to feel regret for all the years he'd spent living a lie.

'Did you bring Suzy Sunshine?' She caught his dad's confusion and explained her pet name for Ruan's car. 'He must have gotten his love of colour from you.' A deep rush of crimson flooded Tree's cheeks. The room's vivid turquoise and yellow colour scheme and the man's red and white shirt and Bermuda shorts combo were absolutely spot on too.

'I didn't used to care for…' Tree's voice faded and he stared down at his feet.

'You laughed at me. A small boy. What was up with that? I mean you knew more than most what it was to feel different.' The sadness running through Ruan's voice was more poignant than if he yelled. 'And what's with all the books?' He gestured at the overflowing bookcases lining one of the walls. 'You never read me a single story.'

'My father was… a hard man. For the longest time I struggled to be the sort of son he'd be proud of.' His Adam's apple bobbed up and down. 'I realised far too late that was never going to happen.'

'It's time we left.' Ruan's expression was unreadable.

All three of them scrambled to their feet and Essy stifled a gasp when his father grasped Ruan by the shoulders.

'I'm sorry. So bloody sorry you can't begin to imagine.' A hitching sob escaped his lips.

'You should be.' He shook himself loose. 'I've got a lot of thinking to do. We might be back in the morning or we might not.'

'I understand.'

'Let's go.' There was no point prolonging things. In a way they had both got what they came for and more. Perhaps that's where it needed to end.

A silent walk to the car was followed by the short drive back into Rhossili where they parked close to the pub.

'How about a walk on the beach?' Her tentative suggestion received a snort and a disbelieving stare. 'I'll apologise again if you want.'

'What for?'

'Where do you want me to start? Comin' here alone to track down your dad? Storming off like a teenage girl when I saw you kissing Julia?'

'For loving me?' His husky whisper made her shiver. 'Please tell me you still do because I love you and can't imagine my life without you in it.' He stroked his thumbs down to cup her chin. 'You mentioned a room. Is the offer still open?'

'Hell, yeah, but what about...' Ruan's eyebrows rose but she shook her head. 'Forget it.' She trailed a finger down to his chest. 'Someone's heart is beating pretty damn fast.'

'Can't imagine why.'

'Me neither.'

They were neither young nor dumb. The serious conversation they needed would come when the time was right. She leapt out and laughed when he couldn't get out of the car fast enough.

Essy tugged on his belt buckle. 'Come on, cowboy.'

'Cowboy? I think you're mixing me up with one of your Tennessee hillbillies.'

'Bless your heart, as my sweet mama would say. There's no chance of that in a million years.'

'Are you saying I'm not manly enough?' He flexed his biceps and struck a strongman pose.

'Oh you're manly enough for this woman. Trust me.' Essy toyed with the lapels of his pale pink jacket. 'I love a confident man.'

Ruan's smile lost its vibrancy. 'This is surface. Underneath isn't as straightforward.'

'Nobody is. It's what makes us human.' She made a determined effort to recapture the mood. They needed this now. 'You gonna talk or take action?' After a quick flicker of indecision he swept her up in his arms and raced into the pub faster than Usain Bolt out of the starting blocks.

She loved a man who listened.

Chapter Thirty

'Are you too worn out for that walk?' Ruan twirled the ends of Essy's hair around his fingers.

'Whose fault is it if I am?'

'I don't remember hearing any complaints.' He nuzzled kisses into her neck and nipped her warm skin. 'If I recall it right someone was begging me for more at three o'clock this morning. Don't blame me if you didn't get enough sleep.'

'Oh yeah, like you were reluctant?'

'A martyr. That's me.'

'And don't we all know it.' She rolled her eyes at him. 'You'll have to feed me first if you expect to walk far.'

'I spotted a couple of cafés. We could check one out.' He sensed her hesitate. 'What's up?'

'Why should anything be up?' Essy played her own teasing game with his chest hair but he eased her hand away.

'The truth.'

'Fine.' Her sigh rumbled right through him. 'Things ended up… off with your dad yesterday. What are you gonna do about it?'

'Do?' He frowned. 'I'm leaning towards drawing a line under the whole episode and going back to Cornwall.'

'That's it?'

'What do you want me to say?'

Essy fixed him with the kind of stare that suggested he couldn't seriously expect her to believe that nonsense.

'Well, let's see. I thought you might explain how meeting him again made you feel? Maybe share what exactly you're goin' to tell your mom and what I'm supposed to tell my mom? A few minor details like that.'

Her flippant tone didn't fool him. 'Let's walk.' Ruan leapt out of bed. 'I can't talk about all this… heavy stuff with you like *that*.'

'Like what?'

'Naked.' He allowed his eyes to roam over her gorgeous curves and a certain uncontrollable part of his anatomy sprang to attention.

'A walk it is then.' She uncurled like a satisfied cat and strolled towards the bathroom, making sure to give him a killer view of her pert bottom.

The damn woman knew he'd follow her and what would happen next. Brunch would work as well as breakfast.

Much later, when they'd worn each other out for the time being, they decided to behave like responsible adults in a mature relationship who could keep their hands off each other for a reasonable amount of time. After they got dressed they settled on trying out the Hiker's Heaven Café where the waitress promised them a traditional Welsh breakfast. When he'd wolfed it all down Ruan continued to have reservations about the local additions to the regular bacon, sausage, fried eggs, mushrooms and baked beans. The Cornish enjoyed eating cockles too but not usually for breakfast and he couldn't see the Welsh tradition of mixing seaweed purée with oatmeal and frying it to make something called laverbread ever catching on.

'Did you enjoy all that?' he asked and Essy wrinkled up her nose.

'It was pretty good but I've gotta be honest. Give me a good ole slice of country ham, a couple of over easy eggs, a bowl of grits and a couple of big fluffy biscuits slathered with apple butter and I'd be a darn sight happier. And decent coffee.' She pointed to the weak brew she'd allowed to go cold in her cup. 'Sorry, but y'all might be good at tea making but this doesn't really cut it.'

'I'm not sure what half of the stuff you mentioned is – make that most of it – but I suppose we've all got our food quirks.' He caught her smirk. 'Is that smug look implying I've got more than food quirks?'

'*Moi*? I'd never say such a thing. I've been called a little quirky myself so I guess we're a good pair.'

'I'd have to agree.'

'With the part about me being quirky too or the description of us as a good pair?'

'Both?'

Essy cocked her head to one side and gave him a searching look. 'Yeah, I'm good with that.'

'Really?' He thought his heart might burst out of his chest. 'Let's get out of here.'

'Is it impolite behaviour on the beach time again?' The twinkle in her eyes magnified to supernova proportions. 'I've never fooled around on a Welsh one before.'

'Me neither. Come on.' Ruan grabbed her hand, thrust far too much money at the waitress and whisked them out of there. 'Rhossili Bay is supposed to be stunning. It's topped some of the lists of European beaches before now. It's about three miles long so there's plenty of space for...' The fizz went out of him.

'Hey, stop that. There's nothin' wrong with having a bit of fun. It's not disrespectful to me or whatever other baloney you're gonna spout.' He didn't resist when she pulled him closer for a kiss. 'I'm not that dumb woman who screwed you over. You need to put Helena Carter in the past where she belongs.'

All of the warmth and colour disappeared from the day. Knowing she was right and following through with her order were two completely different animals.

So much for her new softly-softly approach. That went the way of the dodo.

'Let's walk.' Essy grabbed his hand and they plodded along in silence. 'What's that place?' She stopped by a large building where a lot of people were going in and out.

'According to the sign it's the village hall.' Ruan gave her a watery smile. 'You're bound to find out so I might as well tell you.'

'Tell me what?'

'According to the landlord at the Drunken Duck my father led the campaign for its renovation. The community raised money to extend and modernise the older building. It's run as a non-profit and there's a meeting room, kitchen and community hall. They hire out the hall for anything from weddings to keep fit groups. There's a bunkhouse too, a sort of hostel for visitors.'

Essy treated him to an interested smile but kept her mouth shut. Let him dig a deeper hole for himself.

'And, yes, the old Herring Bay Chapel could be turned into something similar.'

It took every atom of self-discipline she possessed not to grin from ear to ear. Leading Ruan horse-like to a water trough would be pointless, he needed to realise he was thirsty of his own accord. Thirsty for a new challenge. One of more value than churning out large, overpriced houses for rich people.

'Do you know how many bloody obstacles there are to your crazy idea?'

'If I said that to my clients I wouldn't stay in business long.' Her observation made him scoff.

'You can't compare the two.'

'Yeah, I can.' Time to move in for the metaphorical kill. 'You're not a coward. You've proved that your whole life so why do you have a blind spot when it comes to this? And don't spout a load of garbage about Jackie Webb or the struggling community that can't afford to help. If enough people were stirred up I truly believe it could be made to happen.'

'But why do you care about it so much?' His voice took on a new hard edge. 'You've made it clear you're going home to Tennessee soon so what difference does it make to you?' He shook off her hand. 'We need to be realistic.'

'You've never bothered to ask if I might've changed my mind about returning to Nashville. If maybe *I* need something more rewarding than collecting bottles of sand for homesick old men... there's nothin' wrong with doing that and I know

Gordon Snell will be thrilled but... oh what's the point.' Essy turned away and marched off down the road.

Nothing between them was straightforward, except for the sex. Remembering last night, and this morning, sent a rush of heat coursing through her body but she was old enough to take that with a pinch of salt. To make the relationship work long-term they needed a lot more than physical compatibility. Ruan wasn't the only one to be shocked when she put into words the dissatisfaction that had been nibbling away at her life for a while now.

Essy slowed down to a gentle trot when she realised she was almost down to the beach. Spread out in front of her was a sweep of golden sand, arcing around the dramatic coastline and bathed in sunshine. A gentle, salt-tinged warmth caressed her skin instead of the typical relentless sticky heat of a Tennessee summer day which only a blast of air conditioning could alleviate. She picked up a signpost for the coastal path and strode off.

An hour later she flopped onto the grass, rested her hands behind her head and waited.

Ruan stomped along and only realised he was on the coastal path when the sea breeze blew away the angry haze clouding his eyes, and possibly his judgement. Essy seemed to enjoy tangling him up in knots until he didn't know if he was on his head or his heels. It was impossible to ignore the stunning view a minute longer and he fought an almost overwhelming urge to race down to the sparkling blue water and dive in. An unbidden bubble of laughter spouted out of him when he pictured her dragging him out of the sea, furious and frightened for him in equal measures.

Had she meant what she said about considering a complete change in her life? He'd tried to take it with a pinch of salt because visitors to Cornwall often fantasised about chucking everything in and moving to what they saw as an idyllic spot.

Of course when they did their research and found out the soaring property prices and the dearth of year-round jobs it was another story.

When he was brusque to Essy it came from a place of fear. Fear of how he would cope when she left. Which he was convinced she would.

As he ambled along Ruan thought about the Rhossili Village Hall. Only in a hypothetical way, of course. *Right, who are you kidding?* The irony didn't escape him. When Essy pushed him he'd turned the idea down flat and here he was mentally redesigning the old Wesleyan chapel in his head. It would need a two-stage plan. One for the initial conversion and another for when they had the financial wherewithal to expand. The number one priority was a meeting space for the villagers to use along with a way to make money to plough back into the venture. A café and a few local craft offerings struck him as a good way to start.

The choice he needed to make, and no one could do this for him, was whether to go back to regular architectural work or change direction? Interior spaces interested him more these days especially coming up with creative ideas of how to utilise existing buildings, giving them a new life and purpose.

Rather like him.

'Well, look who it isn't. Long time, no see.'

Essy's cheery voice broke through his imaginary list of pros and cons. She lay sprawled out on the grass and gazing up at him, shading her eyes from the sun.

'I thought even a slowpoke like you couldn't be much longer.'

He realised he'd walked the complete length of Rhossili Bay noticing nothing outside of his own thoughts.

'I'm surprised you don't want to toss me in the ocean and leave me there this time.' He cracked a wry smile.

'Have you come to your senses yet?'

She plucked a blade of grass and idly chewed on it.

'You know the obvious next move if we're gonna consider a plan for the old chapel?'

Ruan took that as a rhetorical question and kept his mouth shut.

'You need to ask your dad's advice.' She patted the ground next to her.

He flopped down and stretched out his legs. Her suggestion made sense but he still wasn't sure how to form a new, more adult relationship with his father.

'The two villages are different and Rhossili is more on the tourist radar but Herring Bay's got a ton goin' for it if you can make folks see past what it *doesn't* have. If you can help to build the community back up and draw the sort of visitors who would appreciate its uniqueness, wouldn't that be awesome?'

He ached to tell her she'd nailed it but the lingering remains of his pride, or stubbornness, wouldn't let him.

'If you want me to I'll do it alongside you.' She grabbed his hands and he couldn't avoid her searching grey-green eyes a moment longer. Ruan picked up on the tremor running through her apparent brashness. They were equally nervous. She was simply better at hiding it.

'Don't even start on all the how's and why's. That'll come.'

It might be outright crazy but he believed her. 'I'm in.'

Chapter Thirty-One

'The boys get out for the summer holidays tomorrow and I've been thinking of taking them away for a week at some point. I'm always telling them about Cornwall but neither of them have ever been so I wondered... do you think I'm crazy to consider bringing them to Herring Bay?' Two round red splotches of heat blossomed in Tree's cheeks.

Essy sneaked a sideways glance at Ruan but his blank expression gave little away. Until this point their visit was going well. They had spent another night at the pub before Ruan finally made up his mind to see his father again. It had clearly taken Tree by surprise when they turned up after the boys had been packed off to school. She supposed when they didn't come yesterday he gave up hope. Since they arrived they had been sitting around the kitchen table, still littered with breakfast dishes, while they talked amicably about the ideas they had for the old chapel in Herring Bay. They were interested to hear how Rhossili had gone about doing a similar thing and been given some excellent ideas how to kick-start the plan.

'I'm not sure that's a good idea.'

She struggled to come up with something to soften Ruan's tight-lipped response but deep down agreed it was a recipe for disaster. A lot of people would be horrified if Tree Pascow reappeared with two teenage foster children in tow. If the full story behind his defection emerged Essy wanted to believe the village would be more broad-minded than it was thirty years ago, but who could say?

'Of course I can't stop you.'

Yeah, but you'd like to, Essy thought.

'I only meant to offer my help getting the chapel plan off the ground.' Tree's gaze dropped to the floor. 'I should have thought it through more.'

'Might not have been a bad idea.' A twitch of good humour showed in Ruan's face.

'Forget I suggested it.'

Before she could consider whether it was overstepping the mark Essy took a chance. 'We're going back to Cornwall today and obviously we're goin' to tell our families we've seen you.'

'I don't want you to try and hide about Huw and I. I'm done with all that.'

'I'll put in a good word for you,' Ruan said.

'Really?'

She watched Tree's eyes fill with tears.

'I've hated you for so long it became an insidious part of me.' Ruan's attempt to clear his throat did nothing for the gravelly rasp in his voice. 'Now I know the fuller story I want to move past all that. You've obviously got regrets but we all do for one thing and another.' He reached for Essy's hand. 'You can thank this amazing woman for my... change of heart.'

The quiet, gentle speech brought her to the verge of tears.

'Thanks, son. If I say any more I'll bawl and neither of us want that.' Tree's brows creased into an anxious knot. 'Do you have time for me to write a couple of notes?'

'Yeah, of course,' she answered for them and was reassured when Ruan squeezed her fingers three times in his special I-love-you message. With her head resting on his shoulder they sat in comfortable silence while his father tracked down writing paper and a pen in one of the overflowing drawers. Tree began to scribble away furiously and his distinctive spidery print reminded her of Ruan's own scrawl.

'Would you give your mother this, please?' He passed the first envelope over to her before handing the other to Ruan. 'This one is for Vera.' His shoulders raised in a dismissive shrug. 'It's not much after thirty years but I could write for hours and still not say everything so it's the best I can do.'

'We'll pass them on.' Thank goodness she rarely lost the ability to talk because Ruan appeared to be mute. 'Ready?'

He lumbered to his feet so she scrambled up too.

'Thanks for coming, son.' Tree's outstretched hand wasn't quite steady.

'I'm glad I did... I mean, I'm glad *we* did.' The loving glance Ruan threw her way warmed her down to her toes. 'I'm sorry if this embarrasses you.' Out of nowhere he threw his arms around his father. A rush of pride swept across Tree's face and he tightened his arms around Ruan's back.

'Feel free to embarrass me the same way anytime you like.' The jesting tone was at odds with his shaky voice.

'Will do.'

When the two men stepped apart Tree gave her a challenging smile.

'I thought you Americans were great at hugging everyone?'

'We sure are.' Essy treated him to one of her best southern girl hugs and kissed his smooth cheek, the beard he wore in the old pictures she'd seen of him was obviously part of the past too. 'This isn't the last time you're gonna see me.'

'I hope not! It's a long drive, you ought to get going.'

Prolonging the moment wouldn't do anyone any good. 'You're right, come on my trusty chauffeur.'

When they made it outside Essy was pulled into another warm hug.

'You okay?' she asked.

'Yep. You?'

Essy was suddenly inexplicably shy.

'It's all good, sweetheart.' Ruan stroked a kiss over her mouth, his tongue lingering long enough to set off the familiar, wonderful tingling. 'Let's go home.'

When he tilted her a quizzical smile she swiftly pressed a finger to his lips. 'Don't ask yet.' She was grateful when he didn't question her.

In the car the lack of sleep caught up with her and she passed out like a weary toddler, trusting her lovely man to take care of them.

Ruan had turned off the main road to head down Pengolva Hill before Essy stirred and stretched in the passenger seat. She had woken up briefly when he stopped for petrol and a toilet break in Exeter but then she returned to the same comatose state she had been in since leaving Rhossili.

'You want me to take you to Molly's?'

She rubbed her eyes and frowned. 'Yeah, or maybe no, I'm not sure.'

'It's time I met your mum.'

'Yeah, I know, but after me takin' off like a bat out of hell and only sending one text to tell them not to worry I'm pretty sure that turning up on the doorstep might not be the best way to break the news about us.'

'Fair enough.' He was pretty sure Molly would've filled her sister in on everything but the suggestion might freak Essy out.

'Oh, it didn't occur to me. As if they haven't been talkin' about me and us non-stop by now. How dumb am I?'

Answering that would be a death wish and he wasn't keen to be hung, drawn and quartered.

'Maybe your aunt was discreet and thought it best to leave it to you?'

'Yeah, right, and little pink pigs are as prolific as seagulls in the air over Herring Bay.' Essy's caustic response made him laugh.

'So Molly's or my place?'

'That's like asking if I'd rather face a firing squad or sizzle in the electric chair!' She let out a tired sigh. 'Let's go to my aunt's and get it over with.'

'I prefer if my girlfriends are a little more enthusiastic when they introduce me to their families.'

'Oh do you, Romeo?'

'If you were paying attention in English Lit class you'll

remember that particular warring families' story didn't end well. You sure you want to use that comparison?' While they were talking the car seemed to arrive by its own volition outside Number Twenty-Five Tregrehan Road.

'Forget about that for now, I must look a wreck.'

Essy's complaint made him smile because to Ruan she was always drop-dead gorgeous. 'Fishing for compliments again?' His buoyant humour faded. 'There's a whole lot of strikes against me before we even step inside the door.'

'Yeah, I know but your mom's never gonna be my biggest fan so we're even.' Her resigned smile took the edge off his flutter of panic. Ruan killed the engine and pulled her across for a kiss. A bolt of desire shot through him when he ran his fingers through her soft messy hair and a searing image of her gazing up at him in bed this morning, flushed with loving filled his mind.

'The curtains are twitching.' Essy pointed out of the window. 'Putting this off won't make it any easier.'

They were a silent pair walking up the path and before Essy could stick her key in the lock her aunt flung the door open.

'Well, look what the cat's dragged in.' Molly's scathing gaze swept over them both. 'Were all the flights to America full? Or maybe you took a detour over the Welsh border?'

Ruan fought to hide his shock. Essy hadn't talked to her family about where his father might be which left one possible source. His mother.

'So who's this? As if I didn't know.'

Essy admired the way Ruan faced down her mother without flinching.

'You're the spittin' image of your daddy.'

'Pleased to meet you, Mrs Williams.' He stuck out his hand and Paula hesitated briefly before shaking it.

'I'm sure you are.' She turned her attention back to Essy. 'I thought Molly had lost her marbles but she was right about you pair. I'm disappointed that you felt you had to run around with him behind my back.'

'Let's all go in and I'll put the kettle on,' Molly suggested.

'The Cornish answer to everything.' Paula mitigated the sharp remark with a warm smile. 'Come on.'

'How did you know where we were?' Essy asked as they followed her aunt into the living room, pretty sure she knew the answer.

'I went over to see Vera, didn't I, to see if she had any idea?' Her aunt turned pale. 'Got the shock of my life I did when Dick opened the door. That's something else you "forgot" to mention.'

'It's not Essy's fault.' Ruan stepped in to rescue her and explained about his uncle's accident. 'He didn't want the news shared around. Was he pleased to see you?'

She couldn't believe he said that out loud. They knew there was some sort of history between Molly and Dick and clearly it hadn't ended well.

'That's neither here nor there.' Molly brushed the question away. 'More to the point is the fact Vera told us young Ruan scarpered a few days ago, the morning after you did, and she had a pretty good idea that he'd gone to find his father.' Her eyes narrowed. 'Was she right or wrong?'

'Absolutely right.' The defiant tilt to Ruan's chin made it clear he didn't intend to apologise.

'Diggin' up the past doesn't do any good. Everyone knows that.' Her mother made another attempt to shut him down.

'We don't happen to agree with you.' Essy reached for his hand. 'I'd say it did us both good, wouldn't you?'

'Definitely.'

'Do you want to give them the full rundown?'

'Might as well.' Ruan's voice turned raspy.

It they didn't it would be dishonest and there had been enough of that over the years. Essy listened while he got the easiest part over with, about them arriving separately in

Rhossili and meeting at Tree's house. Next thing he eased into talking about his father becoming a foster parent in an effort to make up for abandoning Ruan. After an almost imperceptible hesitation he ploughed on.

'Most of the children he fostered with his partner, Huw Morgan.' Ruan planted his hands on his thighs. 'They lived together for twenty years until Huw died in a tragic accident three years ago.'

There was dead silence in the room as his words sank in. Out of the blue her mother burst out laughing.

'Oh boy. Talk about ironic. I should've guessed.' Paula rolled her eyes. 'No one believed me when I said he didn't touch me. I guess I wasn't the only one he took under his wing. Your father was an awesome friend to me when I needed it most.'

A whole raft of new questions swirled in Essy's mind. 'So you only left because of all the gossip?'

'Don't be silly.' Her mother shook her head. 'Things were bad at home and I was fed up. Dad had put his foot down and said I could get a job in Truro like my sister when I left school. Mum backed him up.'

'So did I,' Molly admitted, 'but only because I was jealous.'

'Of me?'

Essy got the impression the sisters had never talked about this before.

'Oh, Paula love, you were young and pretty and had all the boys wrapped around your little finger. You were full of big ideas for taking on the world. I was boring and unimaginative in comparison.'

'And I got revenge by ruining things between you and Dick.'

Ruan caught her eye. At last they might get to the root of the whole sorry mess.

'I had a few drinks with my friends one night down on the beach and bumped into Dick on my way home.' Paula's voice wobbled. 'Just for a bit of fun I flirted with him, but he pushed me away. I told him an outright lie and said you weren't at home like you'd told him but had gone on a date with another man.'

'Then you spun me a yarn that he came on to you.' Molly spoke in a strangled whisper. 'I dillied and dallied about asking him to explain himself, then Vera stuck her oar in. She told her precious brother I wasn't good enough for him and that my sister was nothing more than a tart.'

Ruan's fingers dug into the palm of Essy's hand. She wished she could've spared him this.

'If it's any consolation she bitterly regrets that now.' He tried to apologise for his mother.

'Have you been to see her yet?' Molly asked.

'No we came here first.'

'She won't be happy when you tell her about Tree.'

'Do you think perhaps she knew deep down?' Essy ventured.

'I suppose it's possible.' Ruan's shoulders drooped. 'I'm pretty sure she won't want him coming back here for a visit.'

'Visit?' Molly and Paula said in unison.

Essy leapt in to explain and then fumbled around in her bag for the envelope from Tree. 'This is for you.'

Paula stared at it for a moment then took the envelope from her.

'I'd prefer to read this on my own. Excuse me.' Her mother left the room.

Essy wasn't certain what to do. 'Should I go after her?'

'I'd leave her be, my 'andsome.' Molly's expression softened. 'If she don't come down in a little while I'll see how she's doing. You ought to go to your mum, Ruan. She were a bit shaken up when I saw her, with you leaving that way and everything.'

'You'll come with me.'

His assumption lifted Essy's spirits.

'Of course.' A new burst of confidence surged through her. Romeo and Juliet be damned.

Chapter Thirty-Two

'Come here? Back to Herring Bay? Oh, no, I'm not having that.' This was exactly how Ruan predicted his mother would react but he still experienced a flicker of disappointment.

Vera hadn't blinked an eyelash while he ran through the whole story of their visit to Wales. Afterwards she had simply nodded and made a brief comment about everything making more sense now.

'If he thinks for one minute he's coming back here to embarrass me all over again he's sorely wrong. It would be worse than the first time around because people will feel sorry for me and I couldn't bear that.' She shuddered. 'They'll all wonder how I could have been stupid enough not to realise my husband was gay.'

'I don't expect this will change your mind but he asked me to give you this.' Ruan pulled the envelope out of his jacket pocket. 'He wrote one to Essy's mum too.'

Like Paula she made no move to take the letter from his hand.

'He seemed genuinely remorseful.'

'You're a good lad and I'm sure old Tree was proper pleased to see you.' His uncle's unexpected vote of confidence made his eyes well up.

After a couple of deep, steadying breaths he attempted to explain how it felt to face his father again for the first time since he was a small boy. When he struggled to put into words the frightening extent of his jealousy as he heard about all the troubled children Tree and Huw had fostered over the years Ruan's voice cracked.

'It's okay, honey.' Essy wrapped her arms around him. 'Don't be too hard on yourself.'

'To Dad it's a way of making restitution. To me. To us.' Relief swept through him as he realised he meant every word, he hadn't spouted them simply because he thought it was the right thing to do.

'Oh, give me the letter. If it makes you happy I'll read it.' Vera snatched the envelope and ripped it open. The sight of her husband's handwriting leeched all the colour from her face. She sensed them all watching and kept her expression blank while she read the short note. Without a word the single sheet of paper was refolded and returned to the envelope.

'What did your mother say after she read hers?'

'Nothing... well, what I mean is she took it upstairs to read and hadn't come back down when we left, even though we waited for ages.'

'Mm, I'm not surprised. Poor girl.'

Essy flashed him a surprised look. They'd never heard his mother express any sympathy for Paula before. Whatever his dad said made her reconsider that rigid stance.

'Do you think she'll turn me away if I pop around now to see her?'

'See her?' Essy's voice rose.

'Good idea, Vera love.' Dick nodded. 'And long overdue. Do you want me to come with you?'

'Thanks.'

'We can all go in my car,' Ruan suggested. 'We don't want your ankle crocked up again. If the two of you want to go in on your own we're happy to wait outside.'

'All right.' His mother never believed in using ten words when two would suffice.

'I'll get the car open so come out when you're ready.' He made a swift grab for Essy's hand and steered her towards the front door.

'Is this crazy or what?'

'They're respectable grown women. They're not going to have a catfight.' He encouraged her to climb in the front passenger seat.

'Here they are.' His mum and uncle were walking out of

217

the house arm in arm, with their heads bent together talking quietly.

'Great.'

He surreptitiously crossed his fingers.

As soon as they stopped outside the house Essy jumped out of the car and beat everyone else to her aunt's front door.

'Hello, lovey. Why're you knocking? Have you lost your key?' Molly glanced over her shoulder and turned pale.

'I sure am sorry but—'

'I want to have a word with Paula.' Vera nudged her aside. 'What I mean is that I'd like to speak with her, if she doesn't mind.'

'Well, I don't know.'

'Long time no see.' Her mother sauntered out to join them, looking and sounding totally unconcerned. 'Aren't you goin' to invite them in, Molly?'

'If you want.' Flustered was a polite way to describe her poor aunt.

'Ruan and I weren't plannin' on staying.' Essy tossed in her two cents' worth. 'We thought we'd be in the way.'

'In the way? Oh Lordy, don't be idiots.' For the second time in as many hours her mother dragged her into the house.

Once they were all scattered around Molly's tiny living room a heavy silence stretched out between them.

'I came to say I'm sorry.'

Essy couldn't believe how composed Vera seemed after her earlier outburst.

'What brought this on?' Paula sounded bemused and the words 'after all these years' hung in the air.

'This did.' The letter they'd brought back from Wales reappeared. 'Also I listened to what our children had to say about Tree's... partner and everything. I don't mind admitting it shocked me at first, but then everything fell into place.' A slash of colour set her pale cheeks on fire. 'Tree understands why I misinterpreted your friendship and he wishes he'd been honest with me from the start. It would've saved us all a lot of pain.' Vera's voice cracked.

'I was no saint,' Paula said. 'Y'all know that. I sure am sorry for the way I behaved to you, Dick... and Molly.' The admission clearly cost her mother and even her immaculate make-up couldn't hide the years she normally carried so lightly. 'I don't know what got into me and I've regretted it ever since. That's one of the main reasons why I never came back. I couldn't bear to see first-hand how badly I wrecked your lives.'

Essy caught Dick and her aunt in the middle of exchanging tentative smiles.

'I played my part in all that too.' Vera grabbed her brother's arm and encompassed Molly in her apology. 'I've not always been a kind woman. If I'd been different Tree might've found it easier to talk to me.' Her eyes glazed with emotion. 'Some lessons are hard learned.'

'Don't I know it? It's taken me almost thirty-two years and four husbands.' A wan smile brightened Paula's face. 'I'm a slow learner.' Her mother pulled out her own letter. 'I didn't realise I needed this until I read it... but I sure did.'

'Mum, do you think now you would be all right if Dad comes back for a visit?' Ruan's question caught Vera off-guard but after a very brief hesitation she nodded.

'Yes.' Her chin tilted. 'People will talk for a bit but then they'll find someone and something else to gossip about. He can bring the children too but I'm afraid he'll have to find somewhere for them all to stay because we don't have any room.'

'Thanks. You won't regret it.' He squeezed his mother's arm.

'I reckon we should all go down to The Smugglers' and brighten up everyone's evening.'

'Jackie Webb will get his knickers in a right old knot.' Vera chuckled.

'Um, I'd prefer to stay here.' Dick cleared his throat and turned pink. 'If Molly doesn't mind.'

'Mind? I'll mind more if you go.' Her aunt blushed like a teenage girl. 'We've a lot of catching up to do and I'm not doing it in public.'

'Don't do anythin' I wouldn't do!' Paula winked at her sister across the room.

'That gives her plenty of leeway then, Mom,' Essy joined in.

When everyone laughed a sudden sweep of emotion coursed through her.

'It's all good, sweetheart.' Ruan kissed her cheek.

'Yeah, you might actually be right. For a change.' Her time in Cornwall had been one long rollercoaster ride and Essy craved a chance to simply breathe and take it all in.

'We'll hang in there together.' His gaze latched onto hers.

God, how well he understood her. Surely if she clung onto that all would be well?

Chapter Thirty-Three

'Seriously?'

His father put on a light-hearted front on the phone when he rang him this morning to explain how things went down. He even asked whether Wakeham's Bakery was still in business meaning he could indulge in his favourite custard tarts again, but the gruffness to his voice betrayed his emotions.

'You should've seen heads turn when we all went down to The Smugglers'. More than a few people will have sore necks this morning.'

Julia and some of the old school gang were there and he joined them for a few minutes. It was energising to hear the enthusiasm she'd stirred up for the old chapel project, already including the local shopkeepers who were firmly on their side. Maybe he shouldn't have felt relieved that Paul wasn't there but a truce between them could wait for another day.

The main hitch in his father's tentative plan of coming to Herring Bay was finding somewhere inexpensive to stay. A sudden brainwave hit him. Reverend Worthington. Conan was rattling around the three-bedroomed cottage on his own so was it outrageous to think he might welcome the company? The four of them made a plan last night to meet down on the quay this morning and walk over to see him anyway, which gave him the perfect opportunity to broach the subject.

Yesterday Paula gave his mustard trousers and jaunty green blazer a sideways glance before a smile curved the edges of her mouth. He'd taken that as approval and considered now whether to test her a little more today. Ruan hesitated with his hand on the shoulder of a peach cotton jacket. Did he need to keep pushing the boundaries with people where his appearance was concerned? He would never follow most men's slavish obedience to the social norms where fashion was concerned, but the urge to shock appeared to have left him. A few minutes later he checked the result in the mirror. Tapered linen trousers, a bright blue Cuban shirt patterned with palm trees and regular blue and white trainers. He hadn't slicked back his hair recently or kept up his usual once a week sharp, designer trim. Both were a hangover from his London days that seemed out of place here.

'Ready, Mum?' He breezed into the kitchen. 'Are you all right?' She was hunched over at the kitchen table still in her nightdress. When she lifted her head Ruan spotted dried tear tracks snaking down her cheeks. 'This is all a bit fast, isn't it?'

'Fast? Shouldn't be after over thirty years. I'm glad to have made peace with Paula but... the idea of seeing your father again? Today I'm not so sure.'

'No one's going to force you.'

'Oh, love.' Vera's slow headshake hinted at her uncertainty. 'All these years I've imagined in my head what I'd say, and now...'

'I understand, up to a point.' It wasn't fair to compare their feelings because they came from two very different places. Ruan pulled out a chair and sat next to her. It was a struggle to explain the gamut of mixed emotions he had experienced, from hatred to jealousy and much later a freeing level of acceptance and relief. His inept, stumbling efforts appeared to do some good and she straightened up with a faint half-smile.

'Dick's right. You're a good boy. That's enough of feeling sorry for myself.' Slowly she slid off her wedding ring and stared at it for a moment before wrapping the worn gold band safely in a tissue. 'I'll be ready in a few minutes and we'll see what Conan has to say. He's a wise old man.'

If it wouldn't reduce her to tears again Ruan would try to express how much he admired her. One day he'd make sure to have a box of tissues handy and go for it.

When they finally left the house they were running late but still slowed down outside the old chapel.

'You really think there's a chance we could do something like they managed where your dad is?'

'I don't know but I'm going to give it a try.' The decision popped out and he hoped Essy wouldn't be cross that he told his mother first.

'Oh, my boy.' She touched his cheek. 'You can do anything you put your mind to. Always have done.'

In a minute he'd be the one bawling, tissues or no tissues.

'I might've guessed we'd find you loitering here,' Essy yelled out to Ruan as they rounded the corner onto Wesley Street. She skipped away from her mother to kiss him but noticed him blinking hard and swiping at his eyes. 'Is something wrong?'

'Not at all.' A broad smile lit up Vera's narrow face. 'He's just this minute told me the good news about the chapel. He's going to try to save it for the community.'

'He is? That's wonderful!' An incredible lightness filled her heart. All the hours they spent hashing out the pros and cons of renovating the old building had paid off. Essy flung her arms around his neck and kissed him hard on the mouth.

'Come on, you two, or poor Reverend Worthington will be wondering what's happened to us,' Vera chided them, but there was a definite hint of amusement in her voice.

'Let's go.' Ruan seized her hand and tugged her out ahead of their mothers. 'Are we okay?' He sounded worried.

'Why wouldn't we be?'

'I thought you might mind that I told Mum first about the chapel. It honestly only came to me when we were standing in front of the old building on the way here and I couldn't keep it to myself.'

'Don't be so daft.'

'Daft? You're sounding more English by the day.' Ruan's teasing laugh made her blush.

'In case you're interested I'm pretty sure we're always goin' to be okay.'

223

'Is it my job to get you to the hundred per cent mark instead of "pretty sure"?'

'I won't be much of a challenge.' Her admission brought back the full extent of his smile and they strolled along hand in hand up to the cottage. 'Our mothers seem to have plenty to talk about.' Vera and Paula were chattering faster than they were walking. Essy allowed the sun to warm her back and her eyes were drawn to the shimmering blue ocean spread out in front of them. 'Beautiful, isn't it?'

'Yeah, you must've missed this.'

He took a moment but then gave a slow nod.

'I didn't realise how much. I know Herring Bay needs more thriving businesses and visitors to survive but I'd hate to see it turn into a replica of St Ives or Newquay. I won't be a part of that.'

She sensed a word of warning there, a hint to go slow. Ruan knew her hard-charging nature sometimes raced away from her. 'I won't either.' That simple promise earned her another kiss.

'Leave the girl alone for a minute and open the gate for us.' Vera's order came with a smile.

'About time.' Conan sounded testy when they all trooped in. 'I thought you'd all forgotten about me.'

'We sure didn't.' Essy waved a paper bag in the air. 'These are a present from Molly. It's more of those weird buns you're fond of.'

'You young people don't know what you're missing. He doesn't like them either.' Conan's eyes twinkled as they landed on Ruan. 'Probably thought I didn't notice him hiding it in his pocket.' He peered out around her. 'Where's Paula?'

'I'm here.' Her mother crouched down and grasped the old man's gnarled hands. 'Bet you didn't think you'd ever see me again.'

'Bad pennies have a habit of turning up.' The obvious humour in his voice smoothed over any hint of disapproval. 'Still pretty as ever, I see.'

Paula's warm chuckle filled the room. 'They tell me you're half-blind so that's not much of a compliment.'

Essy hoped he wouldn't take her mother the wrong way but he smiled, pinched her cheek and told her she was a wicked girl.

'Is Vera here too?'

'I certainly am.'

'Sit yourself down, my dear, and tell me how Tree is getting on over there in Wales?'

A whole lot lay behind the casual question. Vera didn't immediately respond but when she started the words tumbled out and the old man looked thoughtful. 'You knew the truth about him all along, didn't you?'

'Yes, but your poor husband was torn. He hated the idea of wrecking his family but keeping up the façade was tearing him apart. Tree understood why you misconstrued the friendships he had with other women but—'

'It helped him to listen to other people's problems and try to help them.' Vera sounded unbearably sad. 'You did the right thing encouraging him to leave, although I wish it had been done differently.'

'Thank you. It's worried me something awful all these years.' Conan reached for Paula's hand. 'Now I want to hear about you.'

'Oh, life's been up and down, like most people, but I've got the best daughter in the world and a good husband.' The colour rose in her face. 'Although I've got to admit it's taken crossing the ocean to make me see I haven't been the best wife. I hope it's not too late to put things right with him.'

'Some of us make things hard for the man up above.' Conan's shrewd observation made everyone smile. 'If you're honest I think you'll be all right.' The light faded from his pale eyes. 'You didn't have an easy time of things back then.'

'No, but I caused a lot of the problems myself. If nothing else it gave me the kick I needed to get out of here.'

'And now?'

'I'm happy I came back to visit and it won't be the last time y'all see me, but my home is in Tennessee now.' She threw a wry smile Essy's way. 'Not so sure about my baby. She seems to have taken a likin' to Cornwall a whole lot and the folks here. Certain ones in particular.'

The gigantic grin on Ruan's face rendered it pointless to argue with her mom's pertinent summing up.

'We could do with a bit of new life breathed into the old place,' Conan declared. 'What is it you want to ask me, boy? You look like you've got ants in your pants.'

She hadn't noticed Ruan shifting awkwardly around, the old man was far too observant.

'Uh, it's a bit of a cheek really. When Dad comes he's bringing his two foster sons with him and they need… he can't afford a hotel for them all and I wondered—'

'Can he cook?'

'Cook? I suppose so.'

'Tell him they're welcome to stay with me if he makes us all some good home-cooked food and they tidy up after themselves. I don't like a lot of clutter.'

'It's too much for you. They're noisy teenage boys and bound to be a handful.' Vera's protest made the old man chuckle.

'With my hearing aids turned off I won't hear a thing.' His shoulders slumped and the faraway look returned. 'It'll be small payback on my part. Now enough of that, I want to hear about the old chapel. Have you come to your senses yet, Ruan?'

'Yes. It took a while but this lady is pretty persuasive. Or maybe that should be pretty and persuasive?' He tightened his arm around her waist to tug Essy closer. Everyone laughed apart from her because she didn't know quite where to look. 'We'll give it our best try.'

'You might consider having a quiet word with Ruby Webb.' Conan nodded towards Vera. 'Weren't you friends years ago?'

'Well, yes, but we haven't spoken much in ages. Jackie's a bit of a bully and discourages her mixing up.'

'What makes you think she might help?' Essy asked.

'I spend a lot of time here sitting and thinking and it's been on my mind. It's as though I heard somewhere that Mr Webb bought the chapel in his wife's name… something to do with taxes, I'm not very good on that sort of thing. I could be mixed up though, my mind's not what it was.'

'Come on, if you were any sharper you'd cut yourself.' The sly comment made Conan preen.

'Ruby comes from a staunch Methodist family and was one of my regulars even after she married. Jackie didn't have any time for religion but that was one of the few things she stood her ground over.'

'Wow!' Essy's brain raced. 'Would you be willing to sound her out, Vera? Pave the way for us to talk to her, if the reverend's got it right?'

'I suppose I can.' A touch of satisfaction lifted Vera's smile. 'I might happen to need something in the shop tomorrow morning. Ruby always stops in around nine o'clock on Saturdays to pay their newspaper bill.'

'That would be great, Mum,' Ruan joined in and his mother's cheeks turned pink.

'I expect to be told what's happening.' Conan wagged his finger at them all. 'Don't you forget!'

'We sure will,' Essy promised. 'We'll need your help to stand a chance of pulling this off.' It wasn't said to pacify him, they genuinely did need his backing for this to stand any chance of working. She was a complete outsider in Herring Bay and many of the villagers were still sitting on the fence where Ruan was concerned.

'Off you go. You've worn me out.' The glimmer of a twinkle brightened his tired eyes. 'But in a good way. I haven't felt this useful in a long time. This might be my swansong but what a way to go out.'

'It sure would be.' She caught a hint of dismay from her companions but what was the point of denying the absolute truth of the older man's remark? Essy caught Ruan's eye and gestured towards the door. The next step was to get him to herself and by his broad, sexy smile he totally got her meaning.

Outside he caught hold of her hand again. 'We're going to run on.' A mottled flush darkened his neck. No doubt he was racking his brains how to be honest without offending their mothers. 'I need to ring Dad to plan out his visit and...'

'You have things to do and so do we.' Essy leaped in to help him out.

'What're we going to do with them, Vera?' Paula shook her head.

'Leave them be, I guess. I suppose they know what they're doing.'

That might be the closest they'd ever come to an endorsement.

'I'll beat you down to the harbour.'

Before the challenge left Ruan's lips she took off sprinting. Essy kicked her speed up a notch when he yelled at her to give him a fair chance. No way.

Chapter Thirty-Four

'Ruby admitted that Conan was right about the chapel.' Vera couldn't hide her satisfaction. 'She wants you and Essy to be on the outer quay at eight o'clock tomorrow morning. Jackie always has a lie in on Sunday while she goes for a walk. It's been their routine for years so he won't think anything of it. Make it look like a casual conversation in case anyone sees the three of you together.'

'We're not MI5 arranging a meeting with a Russian spy, you know.' His mother's expression hardened when Ruan dared to smile.

'It's all right for you with your fancy degree and comfortable pile of money in the bank. Ruby relies on that man for the roof over her head and she's taking a huge risk agreeing to meet you.'

'Sorry, Mum.' Love and economic necessity had a lot to answer for. 'Thanks for tackling her.'

'I didn't "tackle" her.' The note of censure returned to her voice. 'She was one of my best friends and I've always felt bad for letting that slip away.'

'You had your own troubles.' It surprised him when she didn't argue. 'I spoke to Dad and he's coming on Tuesday. He plans to stay until Friday but that might change...'

'Depending on the village gossip mill and me, I suppose?'

That was the first time she'd ever cracked a joke about the situation before, or anything much else come to that. As he'd matured it was easier to see why in his memories Vera was usually frowning and worried about something.

'I wish you wouldn't care so much what other people think.'

'Oh, that's rich coming from you.' Her voice softened. 'I've watched it eat you alive for years. You even left Cornwall and took up a job you didn't much like to prove to your father you could manage fine without him.'

He slumped down on a kitchen chair.

'Am I right?'

'Yes,' he whispered. 'I never admitted that to myself until I ended up back here... and that wasn't by choice to start out with.' This was clearly a day for confessions so he might as well get the last one out. His mother never said a word while he poured out the whole story of his personal and business relationships with Helena Carter. 'I felt emasculated. A loser.' He held up his hand to hush her attempt to protest. 'Essy helped me to see that was a load of rubbish.' Tears stung his eyes and he frantically blinked them away. 'She's an incredible woman.'

'Yes, she is.'

The admission stunned him. He'd concluded weeks ago that grudging acceptance was the best they could hope for.

'I didn't want to like her.' The colour rose in his mother's face. 'You know I tried my hardest not to, but the silly girl wore me down in the end. She's good for you. You're good for each other.'

Neither of them spoke. They weren't that far along the new path of laying their emotions out in the open.

'Are you seeing her later?'

'Yes, we're going to Falmouth for dinner.'

'Let me guess, you won't be back until the morning?' When he hesitated his mother burst out laughing 'Good grief, Ruan, you're nearly forty and Essy's a grown woman. What you do is your own business.' She cracked a wry smile. 'I know that's not what I said the other day but I've come around since. Now get on with you and do something useful. This house is a tip and someone's got to clean it.'

They had wildly different versions of what constituted a dirty house but he held his tongue. If he was idiotic enough to offer any help the job wouldn't be done to her standards. No wonder she had a waiting list for her housecleaning services.

'I'll go pack my bag and clear out from under your feet.'

Making his escape while the going was good seemed like a smart move.

Essy loved his impatience. The text message was short and to the point.

Be ready in ten minutes. Please. Can't wait any longer.

It meant forgoing a manicure but she was pretty certain her new, gossamer thin peach silk underwear would distract him away from chipped nail polish. A trickle of heat pooled in the base of her stomach at the thought of running her hands all over his warm, solid body again. Ever since they made the plan to run away from Herring Bay for the night she'd been bubbling with anticipation. For fun she sent him messages every hour on the hour spelling out every delectable thing she wanted to do when they were alone. He called her a wicked tease before making her blush by responding with his own 'wish list'.

'Knock, knock.' Her mother breezed in and swept her gaze over the piles of rejected clothes strewn over the bed. 'Someone's gonna have fun.'

'That's the plan.' Essy continued to toss make-up into a bag. 'Sorry but I need to be out of here in about five minutes.'

'No worries. I just wanted to tell you to enjoy yourselves.' Paula sounded breathy. 'And one more thing. I might not hang around until Tuesday. It'll be easier for Vera and Tree if I'm not floating around the village like an unwelcome ghost.'

'When would you leave?'

'Monday. There are flights available on Tuesday but I haven't booked yet.'

'Are you goin' to be okay if I...' She wasn't sure how best to phrase the question. They weren't at the stage of making long-term plans yet but she knew in her gut Ruan was the man she'd been searching for without even realising she was looking. For someone who found things for a living the idea amused her.

'Hook up permanently with Ruan Pascow? Yeah, I'm good

with that.' Her mother's eyes glistened. 'He's a decent guy.' The breath audibly hitched in her throat. 'I can tell he has his father's kindness in him. Tree picked up on the fact that I needed support and guidance and gave it... at a huge cost to himself. I see that now.' Her voice turned raspy. 'I hope you understand now how much I regret hurting an awful lot of people and I know I should've come home when my folks passed away. They tried their best with me as far as they saw it. Poor Molly got the roughest end of the stick but I've got my fingers crossed that she'll seize her second chance with Dick.'

Essy's mobile pinged and she glanced at the screen.

Where are you? I'm outside.

Essy quickly tapped in a plea for him to wait. She couldn't rush off now.

'You'll be late.' Paula glanced at the small travel clock on Essy's bedside table.

'It's okay Ruan will wait.'

'Yeah, I'm sure he will.' She sounded envious. 'Did you know Molly worked at a bank in Truro and she'd just been promoted to assistant manager when I threw a grenade into all our lives?'

Essy shook her head.

'When her engagement fell apart Dick left Herring Bay and then I went as well. Neither of our parents were in great health to start with and all the stress made them worse so Molly chucked in her job to help out more at home.' Her fingers plucked at her short denim skirt. 'She fell into doing a few bookkeeping jobs from the house to keep her hand in and by the time Mum and Dad were gone and she was free to try for another bank job she was out of the loop with all the new technology, so that was that really.'

'That wasn't all your fault.' Essy hated to hear her mother beating herself up. 'Molly and Dick could've hashed things out between them and stood up to Vera or anyone else who tried to criticise them. And she could've tried harder to keep up with things and gone back out to work if she really wanted to.'

'I suppose.'

Her mother jumped up and straightened out her skirt. 'Off you go and have a good time. I'll see you tomorrow.'

Essy worked on finishing her packing while the conversation with her mother mulled around in her head. She and Ruan had a lot to talk about.

He struggled not to resent the fact she wasn't one hundred per cent with him. Essy kept staring out of the car window as though she might find an answer to whatever was bothering her in the mellow early evening sunshine. He didn't connect her distracted mood to any problem between them but it still niggled at him that she couldn't share it.

'I'm spoilin' things, aren't I?' Essy huffed out her frustration and scowled across at him. 'Don't deny it because I'll call you a liar.'

'There's a decent pub in about a mile. We'll stop for a drink.'

'That's your only reaction to me being a misery?'

He suppressed a smile. 'Hey, I'm driving and these roads are narrow because I chose the scenic route to please my lovely lady. I'd prefer not to wreck the car or ourselves.'

'Fair enough.'

She held her tongue until they arrived at The Crown and he asked whether she wanted to sit inside or out in the beer garden.

'Definitely out.' Essy didn't hesitate.

A few of the wooden picnic benches arranged on the oval of grass were already occupied by families enjoying an early evening meal so they picked a seat as far away from them all as possible. The soothing sounds from the tiny stream running along the bottom of the garden added to the peacefulness and the air was perfumed by the abundance of sun-saturated brightly coloured flowers set in blue glazed planters around them.

'This is perfect.' She tilted her head up to the sun. 'Y'all don't realise how lucky you are to sit outside in the middle of summer without being eaten alive by bugs and sweating like pigs.'

'Sounds miserable. There must be an upside to the Tennessee weather?'

'I guess the winters aren't usually too bad and spring and fall are real pretty.' She screwed up her face, deep in thought. 'I've got to say fall in the Smoky Mountains is damn hard to beat. I'll prove it to you one day.'

He squeezed her hand. 'I'd love to see it.'

'Really?'

'Yes, really.' Ruan drew her close for a kiss. Breathing in her warm scent stirred him and he shifted awkwardly on the wood bench. The last thing he wanted was for her to think he was some sort of crazed sex-maniac when they were supposed to be having a serious conversation.

'Don't ever hide your feelings for me.' Essy nuzzled into him and sighed when he stroked her soft dark hair.

'I can't.' He sounded resigned but in a totally good way. 'Now tell me what's up. I know it's not us so I'm guessing it's your mum?' It hardly surprised him when she admitted that Paula couldn't face seeing his father again. The situation was awkward enough anyway so maybe it was for the best. 'But she's fine with... us?'

'Yeah.' Her mouth stretched back into a smile. 'Can't imagine why but she's under the impression you're a good guy.'

'Fooled her, didn't I?' Laughing together was the best thing. 'What else did she have to say? Nothing about Molly and my uncle, I suppose?'

'Are you some sort of psychic?'

'Just lucky. In so many ways.' He cleared his throat.

'Mom told me a bit more about my poor aunt.'

Ruan listened closely as she explained. 'I agree totally with you. They were two adults who could've stood up for themselves, but sometimes that's easier said than done.'

'I suppose.'

A mischievous giggle popped out of her. 'It seems they're doin' pretty good now without anyone's help. Molly's invited Dick over for Sunday lunch tomorrow and promised to make his favourite apple pie. She looks all misty-eyed when she says his name. It's really sweet.'

'My uncle is definitely less grouchy and we used to hear all the time about what his plans were when he went back to Newquay. He hasn't mentioned it now for days.'

'Sounds promising.' Essy trailed her finger along his bare forearm. 'I vote for getting back in your sweet little car and trackin' down our love nest for the night.'

'That gets my vote too.' He planned on relishing every inch of her. Worrying about all the other problems in their lives could wait.

Chapter Thirty-Five

Essy slammed her hand down to silence the jingling alarm clock, knocked it off the bedside table and broke a nail in the process. 'Damn.' A large warm body pressed against her back and Ruan's searching hand snaked in over her hip. 'We don't have time for that.'

'Oh yes we do.' He continued exploring. 'I set it to go off early on purpose.'

'Why? Are you stark raving mad?'

'I wanted time for this.'

Essy exhaled an unconscious moan when his stroking fingers found their target.

'We've got fifteen minutes before we need to leave.'

'Not planning to dilly-dally then?'

His rumbling laughter coursed through her. 'I'm ready. You're clearly ready. What's the hold-up?' Ruan gathered her to him. 'That's much better. Much better.' His rough voice aroused her, making her skin burn and tighten.

'Hurry.' Her desperate urging dragged a deep groan out of him and he didn't waste any more time. Last night they lingered over each other for hours but now she relished the new rough edge to their lovemaking. Essy urged him on and soon they collapsed in an exhausted, sweaty tangle. 'Wow, you sure do listen well.'

'We aim to please.' He brushed her hair out of her face and lowered his mouth to hers, luxuriating in a slow, deep kiss before rolling off her. 'Damn the chapel and the lot of them.'

'You don't mean that.'

'Not really, but it's frustrating.'

She teased her fingers through his thick, dark hair. 'Yeah, definitely more grey ones than when we met.'

'Can't imagine why.'

'Me neither.' They snuggled together and made no effort towards getting up.

'I'd be happy with a headful of white hair if it means keeping you around.'

Essy jerked out of his arms, her heart racing. 'What exactly are you saying?'

'I'm not sure… yet. Are you?'

'Are you asking if I'm sure about you or staying in Cornwall?'

'Either. Or.' Ruan tilted a smile her way. 'Both.'

'About ninety-five per cent sure about you and me and I'm definitely stayin' a while longer. Does that work?' After what seemed like an eternity he nodded. 'That's it? That's all I get?' He caressed her cheek and his warm, gentle touch brought her back to stillness. 'Sorry.' She lowered her voice to a whisper. 'I'm being pushy again.'

'Never apologise for being you.' The quiet statement of solidarity made her eyes sting with unspoken emotion. 'It's the myriad of things which make up the essence of you that I love. The spark in your eyes and the magical way they change colour to reflect every one of your moods. There's also your insatiable curiosity. You refuse to let me be a bad-tempered grouch, and succeed most of the time.' Ruan cupped her face so she couldn't avoid his dark, shining eyes. 'We're not done with this conversation but we'll be good citizens and put it on hold for now.' He gave her bum a playful smack. 'No time for showers or preening today.'

'Oh my Lord how will we cope? I'll beat you to it.' Essy sprang off the bed and raced into the bathroom. After the speediest freshen-up ever she hurried back to him. 'Your turn.'

Ruan was gazing out of the bedroom window, their landlady had grossly exaggerated its distant view of the Fal River. Fully dressed already he turned to her with the faintest hint of smugness lingering around the corners of his mouth. 'I'll brush my teeth and we can be off.' Strolling past he fondled her breast, making the nipple stand to attention through the sheer white lace bra. 'You might want to throw some clothes on over that. I don't object, far from it, but Herring Bay isn't quite as open-minded.'

'You're impossible.' She made a grab for her dress.

'Yes, I know, great, isn't it?'

When she stuck out her tongue it only made him laugh harder.

The edge rubbed off Ruan's good mood when they drove into Herring Bay and down onto the empty harbour. The inherent sleepiness of a quiet Sunday morning enhanced the impression that nothing much ever happened here.

'If this was Padstow or one of the other popular places visitors would be wandering round already, going into cafés for breakfast and buying tickets for the first boat trips of the day.'

Essy gave him a quizzical smile as he pulled into a parking spot outside the shop. 'Do the people here want that?'

'Maybe.' His frustration seeped out. 'I've been away too long, how should I know?'

'Ask them? The ones who stayed. You said Julia and a few of the others are interested in the community centre idea. Go on from there and find out.'

Ruan sensed she wanted to say more. 'Keep going.'

'Strikes me y'all need to find a happy medium. Lure in those visitors who prefer somewhere low-key and along with that perhaps discover a way to attract a few small businesses with year-round jobs.' Her eyes narrowed. 'You think it's all pie-in-the-sky, don't you?' Before he could open his mouth she rounded on him. 'We're gonna be late to meet Ruby if we aren't careful. We'll keep this discussion for later.'

He admired her dogged persistence.

'Come on.' Essy leapt out of the car. 'Ruby's out there already.'

He yanked down the hand she was wildly waving around.

'We're supposed to be bumping into her accidentally, remember?'

'See, this is why I need you.' A smile curled her mouth at the edges. 'To temper my wild enthusiasms.'

'I never want to temper the one you've got for me.'

'No chance.' Essy slipped her arm through his and they set off across the road. 'God it's beautiful here.'

The gentle early morning sunshine bathed the village in a soft light, blurring the starkness of the shabby buildings and skimming over the scarcity of boats in the neglected harbour. Despite everything Herring Bay held a special place in Ruan's heart that no amount of practical dissection could eradicate.

'And don't bother tellin' me it's cold, dark and dreary in winter. Most places are. You look ahead to the spring and get through it.'

The woman had an answer for everything.

'Well, hi! It's Mrs Webb, right?' Essy amped up her honeyed drawl as they walked slap bang into their quarry.

'Uh, yes.' Ruby's pale eyes, magnified behind old-fashioned oversized glasses, flitted anxiously around as though her husband might jump out of the harbour wall.

'We sure appreciate you coming.' Ruan searched for the right words to reassure her.

'I promised your dear mother I would but that was a mistake.' The lines deepened around her eyes and thin mouth. 'Jackie will be... let's leave it that he won't be happy if he finds out.'

'He won't discover it from us,' he promised.

'We visited with Conan Worthington a few days ago,' Essy said. 'The sweet old guy had a whole lot of good stuff to say about you.'

'That was kind of him.' Two pink circles bloomed in Ruby's pale, hollow cheeks. 'He's a good man. I miss the chapel.' She bit her lip. 'I've done a lot of thinking since I spoke to Vera and

I can't have anything to do with whatever silly idea you've got. What's over is over. That's life.'

The bitterness threaded through her unsteady voice tugged at him.

'Does it have to be? We can't turn the clock back but wouldn't it be a huge benefit to the community if the chapel could be revived in a different form?' He caught Essy's attention and she seamlessly took over. She ran through the various ideas they had and at the end brought his father and the centre at Rhossili into the picture.

'And you think I'm going to give you the chapel, or sell it at a greatly reduced price?' She stared at them in horror. 'Have you any idea what my life would be like if I did such a foolish thing?'

'What's it like now?' Essy's forthrightness surprised him. 'Sorry. I'm really tryin' not to be so blunt these days but it's a work in progress. What I wanted to say is that I know standin' up for yourself is hard but wouldn't it be worth it?'

'I need to go home or Jackie will wonder where I've got to.' Ruby tugged a threadbare blue cardigan in around her thin shoulders.

'Will you think about it some more?' Essy softened her tone. 'Perhaps you could try a different angle and convince your husband he'd be a hero in the village. Emphasise what the centre would mean in the way of increased business at the pub. Maybe that would bring him around.'

'Oh, my dear, I wish it would but you don't know my man the way I do.'

He saw Essy's shoulders sag. This incredible woman hadn't hesitated to plunge right in but he was like a scared child dipping a toe in the edge of the water because he didn't have the guts to plunge into the cold sea. *Here goes*, he thought.

'I'm going to spread the word that we're holding a meeting in the pub on Wednesday evening and anyone who's interested in discussing the future of the chapel should be there. My dad will be in the village by then so we'll get his input.' Essy stared as if he'd grown a second head and Ruby Webb's jaw had gaped open. 'It's easy for anyone to find out that you own the building so Mr Webb can't accuse you of revealing something that's a matter of public record.'

'I can't stop you.'

He knew Ruby's reluctant concession was the best he'd get. 'If you change your mind, we'd be happy for you to join us.'

Ruby gave him a weary smile. 'I've kept my promise to your mother, now you need to leave me alone.' She walked away with her head bent and shoulders hunched.

'That was a complete failure.' Gloom reverberated through Essy's voice. Maybe she had higher hopes than him so now it struck harder. Deep down he'd always thought it unlikely that the woman would come through for them. Ruan hated the idea of reporting back to the old minister.

'Let's put off seeing Conan again until after the meeting.'

Her razor-sharp insight shouldn't surprise him. 'That's fine with me. How about we go back to my place and cook breakfast?' He gave her waist a quick squeeze. 'Can't have you fading away.'

'Yeah, it'd be a shame if either of us did.' Essy gave his stomach a quick jab.

'True. You okay with me calling Julia to round up some supporters for Wednesday? I don't want to be sitting and looking at each other like idiots when no one turns up.'

'Why wouldn't I be?' Essy gestured to her face. 'You don't see any jealous green streaks, do you?'

They burst out laughing and strolled back along the quay hand in hand. Deep down he was still afraid of getting used to this.

Chapter Thirty-Six

The breeze whipped Essy's hair around her face as she dragged her feet along the cobbles. Occasionally she kicked a small stone but then she'd spot scuff marks on the toes of her new red and silver sneakers. The nauseous flutter in her stomach refused to settle so she couldn't imagine how nervous Vera must be feeling. Conan had invited them to his house for a late lunch after insisting it would be the perfect neutral ground for the reunion. The envelope Paula had begged her to pass on to Tree was burning a hole in her skirt pocket. For two pins she'd rip it open now but that would break her mother's trust, something she couldn't even contemplate.

Yesterday sucked big time. After they'd talked it through some more her mother made the decision to go ahead with her plan to leave. Despite Paula's promise to return again soon the sisters were both in floods of tears when the taxi arrived. Molly blushed like a teenager when she was ordered not to let Dick Menear escape a second time. Essy couldn't see that happening because Ruan's uncle was either at the house or Molly was scuttling off to meet him out somewhere. His ankle seemed perfectly well enough to walk around the village but there was no mention of him returning to his own home.

'There you are.' Ruan rushed out of the house and flung his arms around her. 'I was afraid you weren't coming.'

'I wouldn't let you down.' The promise brought his smile back out and lifted her own spirits. 'I'm nervous for your mom.'

'Me too.' It was painful to hear him explain that poor Vera hadn't slept all night. She had paced her bedroom until dawn when Ruan made her tea and steered her back to bed. 'Is this all a huge mistake?' He shoved his hands through his hair, careless about the way it looked. It would be tactless to tell him she found the new less fussed over look intensely appealing because it implied he had more important things filling his mind. She'd scraped her own hair back in a simple ponytail and only bothered with the barest scrap of make-up.

'I guess we'll find out.' She kissed his soft mouth and wished that enjoying more of the same was all they had on the agenda today. 'Let's get it over with.'

'I've changed my mind.'

They sprang apart as Vera marched down the path towards them. Essy would bet her bottom dollar that the smart black and white polka dot skirt and crisp white blouse were new for the occasion.

'Dad will be disappointed.'

'Did I say I wasn't going to see him?' They weren't given a chance to answer. 'You two can go on over to Reverend Worthington's and ask Tree to come here instead. On his own. You're allowed back after you've eaten.'

No one brought up the fact that although Vera understood why her estranged husband left in the first place she had been adamant that he wasn't coming to the house. It wasn't really her place to respond but Ruan appeared to be struck dumb.

'Sure, that's not a problem,' she answered for him. Luckily his mother appeared content with that and hurried back into the house. 'What's up with you?'

'You don't think she's got a carving knife ready, do you? Or a gun I don't know about?'

If she laughed he'd be offended but Essy couldn't help thinking he'd lost his marbles.

'Okay, I'm overreacting.'

'You said it, babe. Is your uncle home at the moment?' A hint of amusement sneaked into his dark eyes. 'Let me take a wild guess, he's out romancing my aunt again?'

'You're right.'

'Then I reckon your mom's come to her senses and realised it'll be a hell of a lot easier for them to chat without a room full of people listening in.'

'Makes sense. You're good for me.' Ruan gathered her into

his arms and rested his forehead against hers. 'Apart from anything else you stop me being a miserable, paranoid old git.'

'Hey, less of the old.' She chuckled. 'You're mature, which I totally appreciate because I'm not into boys.'

'You didn't argue with the rest of my description.'

Essy laughed some more and dragged him towards the street. 'Save it for later we've got work to do.' She checked out what he was wearing – black shorts, a white linen shirt and black trainers. 'Race you.'

'I hate running.'

'Yeah, but you love catching me.' She managed a decent head start before he got his brain in gear and set off after her.

The disappointment on his father's face would stay with him a long time. When he and Essy walked into Conan's house alone and without Paula and Vera, Tree had crumpled in on himself.

'They couldn't face me.' His head drooped and he swiped at his eyes. 'I can't blame them.'

'It's not that.' Ruan still had reservations but he followed orders and trotted out his mother's instructions for Tree to go to the house. 'Where are the boys?'

'They're off exploring. I gave them money to buy lunch, they'll be back later. After being cooped up in the car over four hours they're like puppies and need a good run around.'

The thoughtfulness of keeping his new family under the radar shouldn't have surprised him.

'Before you rush off this is for you. From my mom.' Essy thrust an envelope at his father. 'I hoped she might stay but she said she needed to get home to my stepdad and...' Uncertain and awkward weren't words he associated with her but they fitted her now as she stared at the carpet and smoothed her hands up and down her vivid yellow and white check sundress. 'Mom guessed it would be hard enough for you and Vera meeting again without having her underfoot.'

'That was thoughtful.' Tree thumbed the envelope open to

pull out a square card with a picture of a red sports car. 'Well I'm damned.'

'What is it?'

A tiny smile pulled at his father's mouth. 'A memory.' His eyes clouded over. 'Paula always had guts and determination.'

'She still does.' Essy sounded proud. 'Will you tell me what she said?'

Ruan noticed Tree's uncertainty.

'I may be speaking out of place but it is my house and I'm old so you have to indulge me.' Conan's cherubic face creased in a mischievous smile. 'It might help our young American friend to achieve that modern thing she no doubt calls closure. In the old days that was simply accepting something that couldn't be changed.'

'Please read it if you'd like.' Tree offered Essy the card.

'Why the car?' She examined the glossy picture. 'It's the same as the one she has back home in Tennessee.'

'When she was seventeen she swore she'd own one when she was older. I encouraged her to believe it was possible despite everything her family said to the contrary.'

She held the card open so Ruan could read it too.

I did it! Bought a little beauty like this on my fortieth birthday with money I'd earned myself and boy did that feel good. I bitterly regret that I hurt a lot of people but thank you for always believing in me.

'Oh, Mom.' Tears trickled down Essy's face onto her mother's neat, precise handwriting. 'Things are never black and white, are they?'

He was painfully aware she'd come to Cornwall to find answers and ended up discovering a whole lot more questions along the way.

'Mum will think you've stood her up if you don't hurry up and get going, Dad.'

'You don't mind, Conan?' His father's polite question made the old man smile.

'Don't be daft. I'll mind more if you don't get a move on. The young ones can entertain me. We've plenty to talk about.'

Essy gave a small worried headshake behind the minister's back after Tree left. She knew they weren't smart enough to avoid the subject of Ruby and the chapel.

'If you don't mind we're going to bail out too. This lady saw a kite festival advertised over in Newquay and was disappointed we wouldn't be able to go. We'll pop up to see you again later in the week.'

'Oh you will, will you?'

They hadn't fooled him for one moment.

'I could fix you a bite of lunch before we leave?' Essy offered. 'How about some of the vegetable soup and sandwiches we were goin' to have?'

Conan snorted and issued prompt instructions for her to butter two thick slices of the homemade Bara Brith fruit cake his father brought from Wales and make a mug of strong tea to go with it.

She threw Ruan a helpless look.

'I'll do it. She's not to be trusted near a teapot, I'm afraid.'

'You'd better teach her if she's going to live here.' The minister's pithy comeback made them both blush. 'Give her a lesson.'

It was pointless to argue so he gave up and pulled her into the kitchen.

'What's Bara whatever it is and what's a kite festival?'

Ruan kept his voice low in case Conan was having a good day with his hearing. The fruit cake made with cold tea was something he'd sampled on a visit to Cardiff years ago. Judging by Essy's turned up nose she wouldn't try a slice anytime soon. He'd had the idea to use the kite festival as an excuse to leave because of a sign he spotted in the village shop window earlier in the week. While he rattled through the explanations he stayed busy and grabbed the plate of cake and steaming mug of tea – their escape passes. 'This should do him.'

A few minutes later they stood outside the house and debated what to do next.

'Are we really trekking to Newquay to see a few kites?'

'We can if you want or I could take you out for lunch before we check on my parents.' That sounded strange to his ears because he hadn't described them that way in forever.

'A pasty on the beach works for me.'

'You're not suggesting more impolite behaviour I hope.'

'I sure am. Got any objections to that?'

Of course she knew damn well he wouldn't. First he needed to make certain of something. 'Are you sure you're okay? All that stuff with your mum, I mean?'

'Yeah.' She sounded thoughtful. 'Yeah, I am.'

Ruan let it go. He wrapped his hand around hers and gestured down the hill. 'Come on then.'

On the beach they messed around like a pair of teenagers but when the sun retreated behind the clouds anxiety crept back into his face. They trudged along the road barely speaking and when they reached his house Ruan stopped dead outside.

'Don't promise me it'll be okay. We know that's not how things work.'

Essy swept her hands up either side of his face and wedged her fingers in place so he'd no choice but to look at her. 'You might believe I am but I'm truly not a mind reader. Vera could've tossed Tree out hours ago or they could be laughing over a cup of tea and sharing happy memories. My guess is somewhere in between but we won't know unless we go inside.'

'In other words don't be a coward.'

'Did I say that?'

'You don't need to,' he groused. 'What's all that?'

Raucous laughter drifted out through an open window.

'Want to find out?'

'I suppose so.'

'Hey, lighten up. No one is screaming. We're not in a live

247

episode of that *Midsomer Murders* programme my mom's obsessed with so I doubt anyone has been skewered with a poisoned pitchfork.' Essy inwardly cheered when her warped logic made him smile.

When he opened the front door the smell of fried food assaulted her nose, reminding Essy that they never did get a pasty because the shop and bakery were both sold out. 'They better have some leftovers, I'm starving.'

'There you are. Come and join us.' Tree beckoned them into the kitchen.

It only took a quick glance around to work out why the room was extra cramped today. They'd only expected to see Vera and Tree but Dan and Petie were squeezed around the table as well. In the narrow space in front of the sink Molly and Dick were perched on a couple of extra chairs. The remains of their fish and chips lunch was scattered over the table and she caught a mixture of emotions skittering across Ruan's face. It wasn't that he hoped to find his parents at loggerheads but the cheerful family scene hurt him.

'These vultures have eaten their weight in chips but there's plenty left.' Vera sounded indulgent. 'I suppose you've eaten?'

'No.' Ruan's gruff response startled his mother.

'Your mum wanted to meet the boys so I rounded them up.' Tree fixed his gaze on Ruan. 'This wasn't planned.'

It struck her as ironic that the father who barely knew him had realised how difficult this was for her lovely man rather than his doting mother.

'Sit down and I'll fetch you a plate,' Vera pleaded.

'Well, I...' Essy wasn't sure how to reply although she longed to get her hands on the chips that were yelling her name.

'Why don't you clear off for a bit boys and get yourselves some ice cream?' Tree yanked out his wallet and thrust some money at Dan. 'Be back in an hour and behave.' He shooed them away.

'We'll stop cluttering up the place and leave you all to it.'

Dick nodded at Molly and an understanding look passed between them.

When only the four of them were left Essy claimed one of the vacated chairs and crammed a couple of chips into her mouth to stop her stomach rumbling.

'Your mum's a very understanding woman,' Tree said gently. 'We've had a good old chat and I'm not forgiven for deceiving her or disappearing that way...' He twitched a wry smile. 'But we're ready to draw a line under the past. We'll go ahead and divorce but we're friends again. That's right, love?' There was no argument from Vera. 'She's okay with me coming back here occasionally to visit.' His steady voice wavered. 'I hope we're not going to lose touch again either, son.'

'I don't plan on it.' Ruan smiled.

'My other boys come and go, that's the nature of fostering and I love them while they're with me but you... it's different.' Tree's voice cracked. 'I want to play a part in your life. Be there for you. If you'll have me?'

'Yeah, that would be more than okay.'

Essy caught Vera wiping her eyes and swallowed down her own rush of tears.

'Good, now tell me more about the chapel project. Your mum says you've been busy stirring things up?' Tree's smile broadened. 'That's what I like to hear.'

Chapter Thirty-Seven

He shouldn't be nervous but found it hard to trust Julia's promise that things would be different tonight.

'I told Paul he was a prat. When he's had a few drinks he doesn't think before he opens his mouth. He's really not a bad person.'

Ruan decided to reserve judgement until after the meeting.

'Come on, let's find where they're all sitting.' Essy swished through the door and he almost walked into her when she stopped dead. 'Oh Lord. Either Jackie Webb's givin' away free beer or we've put the cat among the pigeons.'

At his most optimistic he hoped maybe a dozen people would turn up but the pub was heaving and there was barely room to move.

'I'll try to get us a couple of drinks.'

'Good luck with that,' Essy grimaced. 'Jackie's givin' you a daggers look. I guess he knows why they're all here.'

Julia was waving at them over the crowd and trying to mouth something at him. 'I think she said she's saved us a seat.'

'One? You mean I've got to perch on your lap?'

'Could be worse.' Ruan squeezed her waist until she laughingly pushed his hands away. 'Go on over and join them I'll be with you soon as I can.' He started to elbow his way to the bar and made it halfway before someone tapped on his shoulder.

'Can I buy you a drink?'

'Oh, hi, Dad.' The offer sounded odd coming from his father. He supposed it was because seeing Tree back in Herring Bay made him feel like a child again. 'Thanks. A pint of Tribute will work and a large glass of rosé for Essy.'

'Well, look who it isn't. Still stirring up trouble are you, Tree Pascow?' Jackie hitched his trousers up and gave them the evil eye. 'Did they get fed up of you over there in Wales?'

'Good to see you too, Jackie.'

The landlord ignored the sharp comeback and switched his attention to Ruan. 'Next time you plan on rounding up a mob, warn me first.'

'I thought you'd appreciate the extra trade. Anyway, if we had a proper space to hold community meetings we wouldn't have to bother you.'

'I paid good money for that bloody chapel and I'm not a fuckin' charity. You couldn't wait to clear off to London because Herring Bay wasn't good enough and now you turn up with your useless degree and fancy clothes trying to tell us how to live our lives. Why don't you bugger off?' Jackie growled.

'Don't you dare talk to my son that way!' Tree's face turned to thunder.

'I'll talk to him anyway I want. It's not like you've given a damn about the lad all these years. You were too busy playing house with your "boyfriend".'

Ruan rested a hand on his father's arm. The silent gesture should make it clear whose side he was on.

'That's quite enough, Mr Webb. We'd all appreciate you keeping your uncharitable thoughts to yourself.'

He was shocked to hear the minister's voice by his shoulder. 'What are you doing here, Reverend?'

'I brought him.' His father gave a 'what-could-I-do look'.

Essy would say they should've expected nothing less. Conan's web of informants rivalled MI5, so of course he'd heard about the meeting.

'It's time to start.' Conan tapped his watch. 'People won't hang around if you dawdle.'

'Uh right, okay.' Ruan snatched their drinks off the bar and started the battle to rejoin Essy.

'Here's your spot, that way everyone should be able to hear you speak.' Julia gestured to an empty chair that faced the crowded room.

The landlord's words still resounded in his head and he wondered how many others shared his old-fashioned views.

Paul Bonny lumbered up on his feet and clapped his hands until the noisy hum of conversation died down. 'Ruan's got some smart ideas you should listen to and we're all a hundred per cent behind him.' He pointed around to his friends. 'We love this place same as he does.'

He plastered on a smile and managed to mutter some sort of thanks. It wasn't easy to block out any negativity but he zeroed in on putting the skills he'd acquired in his professional life to good use. There were a decent number of frowns when he explained who he was and when he made a reference to his infrequent visits to Herring Bay over the last twenty years that elicited a lot of grumbles.

'The way I see it there are two main problems. I don't think I'm the only one who believes the Herring Bay community has lost much of its heart?' There were rumblings around the room but he ploughed on. When he asked what there was to bring people together, especially in the middle of winter, the general consensus was very little. No arguments bubbled up when he raised the need to bring more jobs to the area so all the young people weren't forced to leave. 'The other challenge is how to attract more visitors.' That earned him more than a few headshakes and dark looks. 'Don't worry, I've no desire to see us turn into another overcrowded Newquay or St Ives.'

A ruddy-faced man he didn't recognise jabbed a finger at Ruan. 'All these ideas about turning the chapel into a community centre are well enough but where's the bleedin' money coming from?' He jerked a thumb at Jackie Webb who was polishing glasses behind the bar and struggling to ignore them. 'That old skinflint won't sell at a price we could afford. He'd rather see it fall down.'

'Perhaps he might but I certainly wouldn't.'

Ruan stared at Ruby Webb who had appeared out of nowhere, red-faced and defiant.

'That chapel belongs to *me* and it's falling down over my dead body.' The halting declaration wobbled out of her. One woman at the back of the room clapped and then another joined in, until everyone was stamping their feet and cheering.

A trickle of unease ran through him. Jackie Webb's bark might be worse than his bite but he didn't want to be responsible for Ruby finding out otherwise. He scanned the room for Essy and found her squeezed between Julia and Heather Bunt on a wood bench by the window. The blatant admiration plastered all over her face did nothing to alleviate his concern.

You go girl! Essy almost yelled out her support but caught a glimpse of the landlord's scowling face and held back. That cowardice only lasted for a few seconds. Ruby had found the guts to stand up for what she believed in so she should do the same. She ignored her thudding heart and sprang to her feet.

'I know I'm a foreigner here and not just from up in Devon either.' That raised a few whoops of laughter. 'Feel free to tell me to sit down and shut up if you want but I reckon y'all need to hear Reverend Worthington's opinion.' The suggestion drew attention away from Ruby and the old man looked thrilled when several people encouraged him to speak. The room fell silent when he glanced around with a satisfied smile.

'Community is everything,' his voice shook with emotion, 'but we've let ourselves forget that. When the tourists aren't around we must be able to rely on each other. These young people will explain the ideas they've come up with. They have plans how to fundraise and turn the old chapel into a centre run by us and for our benefit.' He nodded at Ruan and the group gathered around him. 'I'll leave that to them now and my old friend, Tree Pascow, who's helped with a similar project in Wales.' His sharp blue eyes, magnified behind his bottle-top thick wire-rimmed glasses, swept around the room.

Essy craned her neck to see who the reverend was focusing on.

'Mr Webb, your wife is a brave and generous lady. She needs your support.'

The frail ninety-four year-old had more guts than the rest of them put together.

'You have the chance to do something great for the village.' He spread out his arms. 'Picture it in big letters on the front of the building – The Ruby and Jackie Webb Community Hall.'

A sliver of indecision shadowed the landlord's face.

'We'll talk it over.' Ruby nodded at her husband and linked her arm through his. 'Won't we, dear?'

Jackie looked blindsided. 'I suppose.'

The gruff response shocked everyone and a murmur of surprise ricocheted around the room. No one had expected any concession on the landlord's part.

'I reckon we all need another drink before we talk through some of the nuts and bolts,' Ruan yelled over the noise. 'My round.' That elicited another loud cheer and brought the twitch of a smile to Webb's sour features. Business was business.

She worked on wriggling her way through to him. 'Have I told you recently how much I love you?'

'Yes, but feel free to say it as often as you like, sweetheart.' Ruan tightened his arms around her waist and drew her into a deep kiss. Surrounded by his delicious clean scent she tingled all over. 'Never gets old.'

'Good, 'cause you're goin' to be hearing it a lot. Can you believe the way tonight is going?'

'No.' His gaze smouldered. 'You knew I needed this before I did.'

'What can I say, I'm a genius!'

'It still might not happen.'

'We've got to be positive and if for some reason it doesn't come off at least we've tried. Not giving a hundred per cent to things you believe in is the worst crime in my book.'

'We've still got a lot to talk about too… and I don't mean community centres, parents or any of that extraneous stuff.'

'Yeah I know, and the middle of a crowded pub is an awesome place to kick it off.'

'I didn't mean now, you daft woman.'

'Daft woman!' Essy threw him a fake glare. 'You're such a charmer. Of course I know now where you get it. I really love your dad.'

'Me too. It's great seeing my parents reconnect and I'm relieved everything's out in the open. Your mum's doing better now too so it's all good.'

What a turnaround, she thought. When they first clashed over the supposed affair that split up his family and led to Paula emigrating to a new life in America it seemed beyond the bounds of possibility that they could ever be friends, let alone something far more.

'If you two have finished eating each other's faces is there any chance of getting on with this meeting?' Paul Bonny's broad smile mitigated the sharp remark. 'Are we okay now?' He looked sheepishly at Ruan. 'Julia had a go at me after the other day and told me I was an idiot.'

'I heard she called you a dick?' Essy's question made him cringe.

'Look, I'm sorry.' His face reddened. 'I'm really trying to make some changes. My ex won't let me visit our boy if I don't get a handle on my drinking. Julia's helping me and I'm doing the same for her. Neither of us are happy drunks.'

'Good luck.' Ruan grasped Paul's shoulder. 'Let's be honest, I was a bit of a prat too. I used my clothes to get attention and stick the middle finger up to people.' He nodded across to his father. 'I stupidly saw it as a way to pay my dad back but he wasn't even around to see it.' He clutched her hand. 'Let's get on with this. Conan's flagging but he won't go home until we're done.'

Neither will I, and I don't plan to be "done" with you for a very long time. Essy kept the thought to herself but the radiating smile lines around his eyes told her he caught every word.

Chapter Thirty-Eight

Ruby brandished the chapel keys in Ruan's face and her pale blue eyes sparkled in the early morning sunshine.

Last night Ruan could hardly believe it when she rang and casually informed him that he could round up anyone interested to meet her at the old chapel the next morning.

'Eight o'clock sharp or Jackie will complain I'm not pulling my weight at the pub.'

'Is he... agreeable?'

'Agreeable? Let's say he's resigned to the idea. Dear old Conan hit it on the nail by appealing to his ego.'

After that he didn't ask any more questions and simply obeyed her instructions. Now their motley group was gathered outside the chapel and waiting for Julia and Paul to arrive. Ruan spotted Jane Moody and John Wakeham deep in conversation and their obvious enthusiasm for the project cheered him no end. They had the foresight to see that if the project was successful it could help to save their own businesses. 'Are those your ideas for the place?'

His father pointed to the sketchbook Ruan was carrying. He'd been working on them since his first foray into the building and wasn't sure why he felt so reluctant to pass them over. Essy was the only person he'd shown them to and of course she said they were incredible but she wasn't exactly unbiased. He nibbled his lip while Tree flipped through the book.

'They're good. Incredibly good. I'd no idea you were so talented.'

Why didn't Tree's effusive praise impress him? His mother was right when she claimed a huge part of his choice to go into architecture was to prove to his father that his artistic leanings could lead to a responsible, well-paid job. And now? It no longer seemed important.

'Thanks. This sort of work interests me. I'm tired of

designing massive houses for people with more money than taste.' Several of the people milling around him were listening too and giving him sideways looks.

'You're capable of anything, son, go for it.'

Tears pricked the back of his eyes and if Essy hadn't squeezed his hand Ruan would've broken down. Reconnecting with his father was worth it for those few words alone.

'Are we going to stand out here all day... or sit in my case?' Conan's voice rose above all the chatter. Someone had found him a wheelchair when he insisted on joining them today and the old man had grudgingly accepted the perceived indignity after balancing his pride against a fear of missing out.

'Sorry we're late.' Julia ran up the street to join them looking flustered.

'It's my fault.' Paul was red-faced and out of breath. 'She was waiting on me.'

Ruan caught Essy's smug smile and knew they'd both seen the new arrivals hastily letting go of each other's hands.

'You haven't missed anything we're just about to go in.' He raised his voice to make sure everyone could hear. 'Please be careful inside. Until it's been checked by a structural engineer I recommend not going up into the balcony and choir loft. Everywhere else should be okay if you watch your step.'

Ruby pushed Conan in first and everyone else trailed along behind them. At a rough count there must be about twenty people, which struck Ruan as an incredible turnout. It still struck him as strange to see his parents walking along together and chatting amicably.

Once they were inside the noisy chatter died away and everyone went eerily silent. No one had set foot in the place for decades and some of the group were too young for anything more than vague memories. The beautiful, neglected space spoke to them all. He took notice of Conan's bowed head and struggled to imagine the emotions flooding through the older man right now.

'I'll spread these drawings out along here.' Ruan began to arrange the sketches on the front row of chairs. 'They'll give us some ideas to start from. Wander around. Get a sense of what might be possible. I've never worked on anything like this so I'm no expert.'

People split up and there was a general hum of conversation, finger pointing and general poking around.

'We got married here, you know.'

He almost let his mother's wistful tone upset him but the new sense of acceptance she carried like a warming cloak stopped him from indulging in self-pity.

'I'm sure you were a lovely bride,' Essy said kindly.

'No, she was far more than that. She was beautiful.' Tree shook his head. 'When we made our vows to each other I truly thought I could be the man she believed I was. Of course I was trying to fool us both so it was always doomed to failure.' His breath hitched. 'I still can't regret it though because of Ruan. You were everything to me, son, and always will be.'

'We both made mistakes.' Vera's quiet assertion surprised his father. 'Come on, let's have a look around. We haven't got long. You've got to get those boys back home.' Her eyes sparkled. 'Do you know I've never been to Wales?'

There was dead silence. His father was probably afraid to answer the wrong way and Vera had turned pale, perhaps wishing she could take her words back.

Ruan gave his dad's arm a playful jab. 'In case you didn't get the hint, you're supposed to suggest Mum comes to visit you.'

'Oh, right.' Tree's face lit up. 'I'd love that. You're welcome anytime, Vera love. It'll be quieter if you wait until after the kids go back to school in September.' The implication that he'd have more time to devote to her then made his mother turn pink.

'I'll think about it.'

'If we're not interrupting could you round everyone up? I'd like a few words.' Conan jabbed him with his walking stick.

He'd been determinedly hobbling around his old stomping ground holding on to Ruby's arm.

'Of course. I'll clear them out of the annex and I expect Essy will be happy to round up the rest?'

'Yeah, no problem.'

As he headed towards the old Sunday school rooms the sound of her soft, warm drawl drifted through the air and lifted his spirits. Sometimes the realisation of how much he loved and wanted her was overwhelming in the best possible way.

She couldn't believe they had the choice of two houses to themselves without being forced to pack a suitcase and check into a hotel for some privacy.

'Eeny, meeny, miney, moe, pick one quick and off we go.' Her joke brought out Ruan's sexy grin.

Vera was eating lunch with Tree and the boys at Conan's house before the Welsh brigade started the long drive back home. Molly and Dick had taken the bus to Newquay to 'pick up a few more of his things' as her aunt put it. She had a wicked twinkle in her eye when she promised Essy they wouldn't be home until at least five o'clock.

'Yours. Mum will be home again around three.' He tightened his arms around her waist and rocked against her, leaving her in no doubt how he planned to pass the time.

'Perfect.'

He clasped her hands to his chest. 'First I'm going to love you boneless and then… it's time for that chat we keep promising ourselves.'

The nervous knot invaded her stomach again. She hated the reminder that this wasn't real life. Real life was her loft apartment in Franklin, Tennessee. It was Eureka! The weight on her shoulders grew heavier when she threw in sweet iced tea, salty country ham and fried okra. Two months. Did sensible people make life-changing decisions that fast? Every time she came to that conclusion, in the middle of another sleepless night, it struck her as ridiculous. But when her hands stroked his beautiful face again and their mouths sought each other out, when they laughed and loved in a way she'd never done with anyone else, she couldn't picture life without him.

'Don't panic.' He tilted a reassuring smile her way. 'This is me. Remember?'

I could never forget. I tried when we first met and the idea of you, us, was impossible. But it was always a miserable failure.

A gentle laugh rumbled through him as he read her thoughts.

'Oh, love. I'm not going to railroad you down the aisle tomorrow or even next week…' His eyes shaded to that impenetrable dark of a starless night. 'Do you think you might consider the idea one day?'

'Of being railroaded down the aisle?'

'No, you—'

'Daft woman? Isn't that the insult you normally toss at me?'

'God you're making this hard.'

Essy wriggled against him. 'If we go to my aunt's we can do something about that… and the other stuff.'

'You're a temptress. Speed walk.' He seized her hand and almost dragged her along.

'I know its off topic but wasn't Reverend Worthington awesome earlier?' Everyone at the chapel hushed when he challenged them all to step up. 'This venture could be only the beginning. You've got the power to bring Herring Bay back to life. Make it a thriving community again. Or you can let it die. It's your choice.' She repeated his powerful words. 'It did a number on me and I'm not even a local. I saw several folks cry and try to hide the fact.' She slid a sideways glance at Ruan. 'The smart ones didn't bother.'

'Yes, well, I'm that weird artistic kid so I'm allowed. Real men don't blubber.'

'Please don't say things like that.' Her plea made him jerk to a full stop. 'You're my totally real, one hundred per cent manly man and I wouldn't have you any other way.' Essy tilted him a smile. 'Even Paul Bonny thinks you're okay now.'

'I'm sorry.' He sounded mad with himself. 'That was a minor relapse. It won't happen again.'

Of course it would and she wouldn't stop her own irritating habits overnight either. They'd both had too many years of practice for that to happen.

'No, I'm sorry for pushing you.'

'It's what you do best. Don't ever change.'

This man appreciated facets of her personality others saw as faults, another reason she loved him.

'We're not going to make the most of that empty house if we don't hurry up. We've got a ton of work to do next week. Heather Bunt's husband has offered free legal advice about setting up a charitable Community Benefit Society. Once that's done we can put into motion buying the chapel from Jackie Webb at a reduced price. She works for the local Member of Parliament and has been bending Kyle Hunkin's ear about the project. Apparently she's got him interested in getting involved.'

'Doesn't your head whirl thinkin' about everything needs to happen for this to fall into place?'

Ruan gave her a steady look. 'I thought you were all in? I can't do this unless you're alongside me every step of the way.'

'I am. I'm not perfect either remember. You know I love you... and Cornwall. I didn't know what I needed until I found it all here.' She gave a wry smile. 'That's a lame thing for someone in my profession to admit.'

'Not lame at all. We've a lot more in common than we thought to start off with, that's for certain.' There came the teasing smile again. 'Hey, look where we are.'

Somehow they had walked all the way from the chapel to her aunt's house without being aware of anything but each other.

'I vote we test out your bed first then make our plans.' Ruan grinned at her.

'Love the order you put those in.'

'Thought you might.'

His smug expression made her laugh. 'You are so cocky.'

'Come upstairs and I'll prove that.' Ruan chuckled.

'Promises, promises.' She ran off up the path, stuck the key in the lock and flung the door open. 'Hurry up, Prince Charming before Cinderella turns back into a poor downtrodden drudge.'

Out of nowhere he swept her off her feet and ignored her protests that he would hurt his back after the amount of pasties she'd consumed recently. After a lumbering race up the stairs he deposited her unceremoniously on the bed and proceeded to strip off his clothes in record time. From where Essy lay the sight of Ruan with his hands on his hips, staring down at her with burning eyes was a glorious view.

'Do you want to know my first plan for you?' The most evil grin she'd ever seen him wear was spread all over his face.

Essy wriggled out of her own clothes and tossed them willy-nilly on the floor. Under his sweeping, intense stare her body heated and she struggled to string a sentence together. 'Stop talking and show me.'

'Willingly.'

She moaned with pleasure as he sunk down into her and what seemed like hours later they fell asleep wrapped around each other. When she stirred it took a moment to realise his heavy, muscular body was almost crushing her.

'You still breathing?'

'Barely. You?'

'Maybe.'

A loud banging noise echoed through the house. Essy turned her head and groaned at the bedside clock. 'Oh Lord, it's nearly five o'clock. They're back. Get off me, for heaven's sake.'

'Damn.'

She sprang out of bed and made a wild grab for her clothes then tugged them on any which way. 'How's that? Be honest.'

'Bedraggled?' He dragged his own on then raised an eyebrow at her. 'Do I look much better?'

'Not really.' His clothes were creased and his hair resembled a startled skunk.

'They're goin' to guess what we've been up to anyway so we might as well brazen it out.' Essy shrugged and threw open the bedroom door. 'Time to shock the natives.'

His heavy footsteps followed her down the stairs.

'We're some glad you're here, my loves.' Molly beamed at an obviously embarrassed Dick Menear standing next to her. 'You can be the first to hear our good news.'

In the light she picked up the glint of a diamond ring that definitely wasn't on her aunt's left hand this morning. Essy let out an ear piercing shriek. 'Wow! That's awesome. Congratulations.' She flung her arms around Molly before doing the same to Dick. 'When's the happy day?'

'Soon. He doesn't want to wait long.' A hot blush lit up her aunt's cheeks.

'We're not exactly spring chickens so what's the point.' Dick's eyes glazed over. 'I've wasted enough years and I'm not wasting any more. I'm going to sell my place in Newquay and move in here with my Molly.'

'We should get a bottle of champagne to celebrate,' Ruan suggested, kissing Molly on the cheek and shaking his uncle's hand.

'Don't bother with that.' Molly blew him off with a smile. 'We're gasping for a cup of tea. Stick the kettle on and then we want to hear what you've been doing today.'

Essy felt her face go up in flames.

'After we've done all that I must give your mum a ring. If she doesn't come back for the wedding I'll never forgive her.'

Oh, you will. You can forgive a lot for love. When she met Ruan's gaze she blushed again. They'd had a whole bunch of forgiving to do and now they had laid all that to rest nothing could hold them back, unless they allowed it to.

Chapter Thirty-Nine

Late October – three months later

'For goodness' sake, Molly, stand still.'

Essy stifled a giggle as Paula fiddled with the back of her aunt's hair.

'There. That's the best I can do.' She grasped her sister's shoulders and angled her towards the full-length mirror standing in the corner of the bedroom. Its antique mahogany stand gleamed from a recent coat of polish and Essy wondered how many other brides had smiled at their reflections on their wedding day with the same surprised awe.

'Oh!'

'Don't you like it?'

Paula had swept Molly's hair back into a sleek French pleat fixed in place by a delicate spray of freesias. They had banded together to take her shopping and managed to wrench her out of her normal stretchy leggings and baggy tunics. After a lot of to-ing and fro-ing they talked her into buying the first dress she'd worn in years. The soft chiffon floated around her in a tantalising rainbow of soft pinks and purples and her mother had reined in her natural tendencies to keep her sister's make-up light and flattering.

'It's... Dick's going to be some flummoxed when he sees me all done up like this.' Molly's eyes glistened.

She heard her mother sniff and guessed all of them were within a hair's breadth of breaking down. The last week since her mother arrived had been one long see-saw of emotions surrounding the wedding.

Her step-father had been invited but Brad couldn't get enough time off work so they were planning to make his first visit to Cornwall together next summer. The couple had reached a new level of understanding and Essy had her fingers crossed that her mother wouldn't be looking for a fifth husband anytime soon. Paula had been determined to overcome one final hurdle before today's ceremony.

'I'm not going to come face to face with Tree again for the first time in thirty years in a register office. That wouldn't be fair on any of us. Nothing is going to spoil Molly's big day if I can help it. Ruan said he's planning to arrive the day before so we'll do it then.'

Her mother had told Ruan to book a table for them at The Drifters last night and left a short message asking Tree to meet her there. She'd been uncharacteristically quiet when she returned and would only say that seeing him again had put the past to rest.

The last three months Essy barely had time to breathe and desperately wanted to slow down today and enjoy the moment. The two weeks she spent back in Tennessee were a whirlwind. Her first task had been to go through her apartment and put some personal things into storage before she rented it out. She would make the decision whether or not to hang onto the property long-term later. Next she took the plunge and sold Eureka! to one of her employees who had worked in the business since the beginning. They only signed the final agreement after she wrapped up her last finding job – literally – with personally designed paper featuring a map of Cornwall with Gordon Snell's favourite beaches circled in gold. Essy had taken a day out of her busy schedule to drive to Memphis and hand deliver the gift on the man's ninetieth birthday. His face when he opened the present, framed in remnants of Cornish driftwood and accompanied by a small leather bound booklet she had put together with a detailed history of each beach, would stay with her forever. The years seemed to fall away as he became that carefree small boy again playing in the warm golden sand. With all that complete Essy was set free to explore what a new version of her life might look like. She pushed through exhaustion to rush back to Ruan because they'd been forced to make the heart-wrenching decision for him to stay in Cornwall rather than come with her. Things had moved more swiftly than they'd expected and he was needed here because the official Herring Bay Community Benefit Society was now in hardcore fundraising mode. If things went well they could be the proud owners of the old Methodist Chapel by next summer.

'Did you hear a single word I said, Scarlett Caroline?'

Her mother's sharp question cut through Essy's skittering brain. 'Uh, no, sorry.'

'I asked you to go down and check on the car. It should be here any minute now.' A white Rolls-Royce was on the way, another of Molly's lifetime dreams.

'Yes, ma'am.' They would only be a small group at the register office in St Austell. As far as Molly and Dick were concerned that was a simple formality they legally had to go through before the real celebration back here in the village.

Essy ran out of the front door and crashed into Ruan. 'Oops.' He grasped hold of her elbows and held her at arms' length.

'Very nice.' The bland compliment conflicted with his searing gaze that swept over her bright purple shot silk dress, travelled down her bare tanned legs and lingered on her high-heeled purple sandals.

'Not bad yourself.' She wanted to devour him on the spot. The new light grey handmade Italian suit was cut fashionably loose and he'd paired it with an open-necked white linen shirt.

'Tame enough?' His dark eyes sparkled.

'Show me the socks.'

'Very ordinary.' Ruan hitched up one of his trouser legs.

The same purple colour as her dress and dotted with embroidered silver wedding bells and horseshoes. Ordinary they weren't. 'Oh yeah, right.' She glanced behind him. 'Where's your mom and our bridegroom?'

'They decided to meet us there.' He chuckled. 'It's sweet. Dick wants to wait and see Molly for the first time at the register office. I'll ride with you, if that's okay?'

'Perfect.' She kissed his cheek and breathed in his heady, musky cologne. God, if he smelled like that all over she couldn't wait for tonight.

Ruan slid his hands inch by lingering inch down to rest on her hips and nuzzled kisses on her neck. 'You're killing me.'

'I sure hope not because I've got plans for you later.'

'We might have to take turns. I've a few things in mind too… in fact, more than a few.' His warm breaths caressed her skin and sent shivers running through her.

'For heaven's sake get your paws off my girl, Ruan Pascow. If you mess her up I won't be happy.' Her mother stuck her head out of the door. 'While you were "busy" the car arrived. Let's get this show on the road. Get your skates on, Molly, or I'll be up there to fetch you,' she yelled back into the house.

'Stop shouting, for goodness' sake, I'm here.'

'Wow, and I thought my lady looked good.' Ruan let go of her and beamed at Molly. 'May I have the pleasure of escorting the bride to her limousine?'

'You're a daft boy.' The pithy retort didn't stop her aunt taking his outstretched hand. 'I don't know why you're all making so much fuss. I'm nearly sixty and Dick's a pensioner.'

'So what? Love doesn't have boundaries. Not for age or anything else in my reckoning.' Essy's declaration made everyone smile. 'Come on, let's get you married.'

They piled into the car, which was decorated with fluttering white silk ribbons, something she'd been assured was an old English tradition, and they set off in the sunshine.

Ruan's nervousness increased as they drove back into Herring Bay. Molly's request hadn't been easy to pull off but they squeaked in under the wire early this morning. The limousine stopped outside the chapel gates as he'd asked the driver to and there was a quick gasp from the newlyweds when they spotted the stunning arch of autumn flowers Julia had created around the rusted, old gates. Weeks earlier he was talking to his old friends in the pub about what they were trying to pull off for today's happy couple and Heather Bunt had brought out some photographs of her boss's recent wedding. Even Ruan could see that the extravagant floral displays at Kyle Hunkin's charming village church were exceptional but his jaw dropped when Heather gave Julia all the credit. He immediately booked his old girlfriend up for Molly and Dick's big day and when he suggested Herring Bay could do with a resident florist she'd turned pink with pleasure. The idea that her hobby might become a means of support for her and her daughter and be a part of the village's renaissance stirred her imagination. He liked the notion of Julia's fledgling business becoming one of the first occupants of the new community centre's planned artisan spaces, alongside Tina Cloke and a couple of her fellow artists.

'We're going on in first,' Ruan told the newlyweds. 'When you hear the music it means we're ready for you to come in.'

More fragrant flower arrangements helped cover up the peeling paint and other signs of disrepair. Although the building had been deconsecrated Conan assured them it was perfectly legal to hold an informal blessing there. Jackie Webb had grudgingly gone along with his wife's enthusiastic approval when the happy couple promised to hold their simple reception in the pub afterwards. Ruan couldn't help smiling when they went into The Smugglers' for a drink a few days ago and discovered the walls had been freshly painted and the windows cleaned until they sparkled. That was Ruby's doing.

He swallowed a rush of emotion when the old minister rose up out of his wheelchair with Tree's help. Dan and Petie were staying with friends over the weekend and his father had driven down from Wales alone. Last night he had taken Essy's mum out for dinner but was equally close-mouthed afterwards about how it went. One of the local teenagers was in charge of the music and the soaring tones of Handel's 'The Arrival of the Queen of Sheba' filled the building. Dick chose that piece because, in a startlingly romantic way for such a prosaic man, he declared that Molly was his queen.

'Oh my.'

He slipped an arm around Essy as tears streamed down her face. The newlyweds were walking down the aisle together arm in arm with eyes only for each other. When they reached the front they almost looked surprised when the minister started to speak.

'That's what I want,' Ruan whispered and when she glanced up her eyes were flooded with another sheen of tears.

The short blessing ceremony didn't take very long and then they heard Molly's music selection resonating in the air. Etta James' sultry voice singing 'At Last'.

'Oh Lord, surely I must be all cried out soon.' Essy fished another tissue out of her tiny purple bag.

I'll make you cry again later, he thought. Hopefully that would be in a good way too.

After taking a few photographs outside everyone walked back down the road to the pub. Ruan had offered to persuade Brian Martin to cater the reception but Molly and Dick politely turned him down.

'A good old Cornish spread will suit us.'

'Y'all sure like pastry, don't you?' Essy was checking out the selection of cocktail pasties, sausage rolls and mini-quiches set up on the buffet.

'We like cake too.' Large platters of traditional saffron cake, heavy buns and jam and cream scones filled up one end of the long table. 'I'll fight you for a seed bun.'

'Hey, they're all yours.' She flung her hands up in mock surrender.

'You pulled it off, son. Well done.' Tree held out a pint of beer. 'Thought you could do with this.'

'Cheers.' Ruan took a long swallow and wiped his mouth. 'That's better.'

'Sorry I couldn't get near the wine,' he apologised to Essy.

'The women were swarming around it and I couldn't get close.'

'Don't fret. I'll go and do battle myself. You two have a catch up.'

When she disappeared a touch of the familiar awkwardness settled between them.

'Your mother's coming back to Wales with me tomorrow.' Tree sounded tentative.

'Really?'

'Only for a week or so.'

'That's great. I hope it goes well.' It touched him to see the old friendship between his parents blossom again. 'I'll chase Essy down and see you before you leave.' In trying to make a swift escape he almost tripped over Conan, parked in his wheelchair by the pool table.

'Have you come to book me up for your wedding?'

'Mine! No way.' Out of the corner of his eye he caught the shock plastered all over Essy's face. 'Oh hell... sorry, Reverend.' He pushed a couple of people out of the way and made a swift grab for her arm. In his haste he knocked her brimming glass of wine over them both. 'Sorry.' Ruan yanked a clean white handkerchief from his pocket and dabbed at the front of her dress.

'Stop. You're making it worse,' she pleaded with him.

'I never meant to spill the wine... or what you heard. At least not like that.' He fumbled in his other pocket and yanked out the dark blue leather box he'd stashed there for safe keeping. 'I didn't plan on doing this here but I can't bear you to think I don't love you enough to marry you. I wouldn't say anything to Conan before I asked you.'

'I don't. I...'

He dropped to one knee. As her shimmering eyes rested on him the crowd around them melted away.

'I want us to spend the rest of our lives together. Doesn't matter if it's one day or fifty years... well, it does but you know what I mean, at least I bloody hope you do.' His rambling proposal broadened her already beaming smile. 'Marry me, for heaven's sake, and put me out of my misery.'

'Yeah, okay.'

'Okay?' He popped open the box. 'Does this make it more than "okay"?'

'Oh, you silly man.' She planted a big, sloppy kiss on his mouth. 'Okay wasn't meant to sound unenthusiastic. I'm not an expert on being proposed to so I'm sorry if I screwed up a bit. You're my first.'

'And I hope I'll be the last.' Ruan held up the ring for her approval and the breath stuck in his throat while she playfully examined it. The wide yellow gold band with inset multi-coloured stones twinkled under the pub lights.

'It'll do…' She tilted him a mischievous smile. 'Actually it's seriously gorgeous. Not in the least traditional. Exactly like us. Where on earth did you find this?'

The tips of his ears burned. 'It's made of Welsh gold. It was Dad's suggestion. The initials of the stones spell out the word *Cariad*, which doesn't have a real English equivalent but it combines Darling, Sweetheart and Lover. That covers all the ways I think of you.'

'Oh, we're gonna need a whole box of tissues in a minute if you keep this up.' She sniffed and swiped at her eyes. 'I don't recognise all the stones, what are they?'

'Citrine, amethyst, ruby, iolite, aquamarine and, of course, a diamond.'

'Isn't it bad manners to propose at someone else's wedding? You know takin' the limelight away from them?' Her shining eyes told him that wasn't a genuine complaint.

'I'd planned to do it tonight. I've booked us a room in a fancy hotel between here and St Austell. You would've had rose petals strewn over the bed and a bottle of expensive champagne on ice.' He grimaced. 'Don't know what I was thinking because that's not you or me, is it?'

Essy pressed another lingering kiss on his mouth, her eyes glittering like the jewels in her ring. 'No, but as we say in the south when we feel a tiny bit sorry for someone – Bless Your Heart. You meant well and you've totally redeemed yourself with that. Is there a chance I'll ever get to wear it?' She stuck out her hand and wiggled her finger. Finally the penny dropped in his scrambled brain and Ruan obediently slipped the ring into place.

'Hey, everyone, she said yes,' Paul Bonny shouted over the crowd. 'She's part of Herring Bay now.'

Everyone cheered as the word spread and next thing they were swamped with people hugging them and offering congratulations. As soon as he could Ruan grabbed Essy's hand and managed to wriggle her in the direction of the newlyweds to apologise.

'Don't be daft. We're some pleased for you both.' Molly seized him for a kiss and Dick nodded his quiet approval.

'Thanks.' He whispered in Essy's ear. 'Your mum next.' After a few hold ups to talk to other people they found Paula. 'Sorry. I did mean to have a word with you first but...'

'Oh Lord, my girl's a grown woman and doesn't need my permission to get hitched.' Her face softened. 'But my blessing? You have that.'

'Thanks, Mom.'

His parents appeared to join them and he scanned their faces for any hint of disapproval.

'Congratulations.' Tree grasped hold of them both. 'Always be honest with each other. Trust is everything. Learn from your old dad's mistakes.'

'That's a good lesson for me too.' Paula caught his father's eye. Whatever was said last night they seemed at ease around each other today.

'And me,' Vera chimed in. His mother nodded towards the window. 'It's a pretty day. I bet it would be a nice walk down on the quay. Quiet too. Most everyone is in here.'

It must be the day for women dropping him massive hints. 'Great idea, Mum. You have a great time in Wales.' He shook his father's hand. 'Take care of her.'

'Come on. Let's make our escape.' Essy linked her arm through his and they navigated their way outside.

The cool air on his face was a welcome relief.

'I love this place so much.' The slight shabbiness of Herring Bay didn't matter. This magical part of Cornwall was lodged deep in his heart.

'Yeah, me too.'

A frisson of worry sneaked in. 'We haven't discussed—'

'Shush. Let's walk a while to catch our breath then we'll talk.'

Ruan had no problem going along with her and when they reached the far end of the quay they snuggled together on an empty bench. He stared out to the horizon and the shimmering silver green sea reminded him of Essy's eyes.

'I love our little rented flat over the bakery but now we're getting married I reckon we need somethin' a bit more permanent. Do you think we could buy a house in the village somewhere?'

'I might be able to do better than that.' Ruan grinned. 'Jago Hawkey owns a plot of land on the right hand side just as you start up Tregolva Hill. I know Kit isn't interested in holding on to it and the Hawkeys could do with the money for their retirement but the old chap won't let it go for anyone to build a second home. I bet he'd be more than happy to sell it to us. It's got an awesome view of the sea and I could design something unique and special. Like you.'

'Flatterer. That sounds perfect. You know what else I think?' He could listen to her soft, sweet drawl forever. And he did listen as she spoke of her hopes and dreams. They would start by working on the community centre together and then start a family of their own, of whatever sort it might turn out to be. The knowledge that they thought along the same lines warmed him more than anything else.

'I sure found a hell of a lot more than I expected when I came here.'

'In a good way?'

'Searching for compliments again?'

'Do I need to?' he asked.

'Nah, I'll hand them out freely anytime you like. I came for a few vials of sand and some photos, but discovered you and all this.' She gestured around the bay. 'Pretty awesome I'd say.'

'I don't mind admitting my expectations of how this summer would turn out were way off course.' Ruan cradled her face with his hands. 'I could never imagine anyone like you in my wildest dreams... or us. I love, love, love you Essy Havers.'

'Oh I love, love, love you too Ruan Pascow.'

'That's all we need.'

Their breaths mingled in a long, lingering kiss before they made their way back along the quay. Slowly because Essy's towering heels didn't allow for hurrying even if they'd wanted to. 'Ready to call it a night?'

'No, that sounds as though we're done and I reckon we're just about to begin.'

Thank You

I'm thankful for all of you wonderful people who've read this story and I hope that it was a welcome break away from everyday life. If you've enjoyed Essy and Ruan's story and have a minute to leave a review at the retail site where you purchased your book that would be wonderful.

Angela

x

About the Author

Angela was born in St. Stephen, Cornwall, England. After completing her A-Levels she worked as a Naval Secretary. She met her husband, a US Naval Flight Officer while being based at a small NATO Headquarters on the Jutland Peninsula in Denmark. They lived together in Denmark, Sicily, California, southern Maryland and London before settling in Franklin, Tennessee.

Angela took a creative writing course in 2000 and loved it so much that she has barely put her pen down since. She has had short stories and novels published in the US. Her debut novel, *Sugar & Spice*, won Choc Lit's Search for an American Star competition and is her UK debut.

Follow Angela:
Twitter: www.twitter.com/AngelaBritnell
Facebook: www.facebook.com/angelabritnell

More Choc Lit

From Angela Britnell

Sugar and Spice

The Way to a Hero's Heart …
Fiery, workaholic Lily Redman wants more than anything to make a success of her new American TV show, Celebrity Chef Swap – without the help of her cheating ex-fiancé and producer, Patrick O'Brien. So when she arrives in Cornwall, she's determined to do just that.

What Happens in Nashville

'What happens in Nashville, stays in Nashville!'
Claire Buchan is hardly over the moon about the prospect of her sister's hen party; travelling from the UK to Nashville, Tennessee, for a week of honky-tonks, karaoke and cowboys. Certainly not Claire's idea of a good time, what with her lawyer job and sensible boyfriend, Philip.

But then she doesn't bank on meeting Rafe Castello. As he and Claire get to know each other, she realises there is far more to him than meets the eye.

Celtic Love Knot

Can two tangled lives make a love knot?
Lanyon Tremayne is the outcast of his small Cornish village of St. Agnes. Nobody knows the painful secret he hides.

But when Olivia meets the ruggedly handsome Lanyon, her trip to Cornwall looks set to become even more interesting.

Visit www.choc-lit.com for details.

The Wedding Reject Table

Once on the reject table, always on the reject table?

When Maggie Taylor, a cake decorator, and Chad Robertson, a lawyer from Nashville Tennessee, meet at a wedding in Cornwall it's not under the best circumstances.

They have both been assigned to 'the reject table', alongside a toxic collection of grumpy great aunts, bitter divorcees and stuffy organists.

Here Comes the Best Man

Being the best man is a lot to live up to …

When troubled army veteran and musician Josh Robertson returns home to Nashville to be the best man at his younger brother Chad's wedding he's just sure that he's going to mess it all up somehow.

But when it becomes clear that the wedding might not be going to plan, it's up to Josh and fellow guest Louise Giles to make sure that Chad and his wife-to-be Maggie get their perfect day.

Love Me for a Reason

Love doesn't always have to make sense …

When Daisy Penvean meets Nathaniel Dalton whilst visiting a friend in Nashville, it seems there are a million and one reasons for them not to be together. Nathaniel's job as a mergers and acquisitions manager means sharp suits and immaculate hair, whereas Daisy's work as a children's book illustrator lends itself to a more carefree, laid-back style. And, as Daisy lives in England, there's also the small matter of the Atlantic Ocean between them.

Visit www.choc-lit.com for details.

You're The One That I Want

What if you didn't want to fake it any more?
When Sarah, a teacher from Cornwall, and Matt, a businessman from Nashville, meet on a European coach tour, they soon find themselves in a relationship …

Except it's a fake relationship. Because Matt is too busy for romance, and Sarah is only trying to make her cheating ex-husband jealous … isn't she?

Christmas at Black Cherry Retreat

What if you had nowhere to call home for Christmas?
When Fee Winter books a winter break at the remote Black Cherry Retreat in the small town of Pine Ridge, Tennessee, it's with the idea that the peace and quiet will help her recuperate from her hectic life as a photographer.

But what she didn't bank on was meeting Tom Chambers and his huge, interfering yet lovable family. With them, could Fee finally experience the warmth and support that's been missing from her own life?

One Summer in Little Penhaven

Book 1 in the Little Penhaven series

Could one summer change your life?
When high-flying American lawyer Samantha Muir finds out she's lost her partnership whilst on an assignment in London, she has a dramatic reaction.

Rather than returning home, she resigns, leaves her business suits behind and jumps on the first train to Cornwall at the encouragement of a friendly stranger.

Could the Cornish village and Cadan play a part in Samantha's summer of self-discovery?

Visit www.choc-lit.com for details.

Christmas in Little Penhaven

Book 2 in the Little Penhaven series

Have yourself a little Cornish Christmas …
Wannabe author Jane Solomon is expecting an uneventful Christmas in her Cornish village of Little Penhaven.

But then super fit American gym owner Hal Muir comes to town, and suddenly the holiday season looks set to be far more interesting. Hal is keen on embracing every British tradition on offer, from mince pies to Christmas pub quizzes – and perhaps some festive romance too …

New Year, New Guy

Out with the old life, in with the new …
When Laura's bride-to-be sister, Polly, organises a surprise reunion for her fiancé and his long lost American friend, Laura grudgingly agrees to help keep the secret. And when the plain-spoken, larger-than-life Hunter McQueen steps off the bus in her rainy Devon town and only just squeezes into her tiny car, it confirms that Laura has made a big mistake in going along with her sister's crazy plan.

Spring on Rendezvous Lane

Can even the most seasoned traveller find a home on Rendezvous Lane?
As a former 'third culture kid' and now spicy street food connoisseur and social media influencer, Taran Rossi's never really stayed in one place long enough to feel part of a community. And that's just the way he likes it.

But a springtime stint house-sitting for his grandmother on Rendezvous Lane in East Nashville could lead to a long overdue wake-up call. Can Taran come to understand that sometimes it's not about the place – it's about the people?

Visit www.choc-lit.com for details.

Christmas at Moonshine Hollow

Mistletoe and moonshine: a Christmas match made in heaven?

Moonshine Hollow's famous 'Lightning Flash' might be an acquired taste, although the same could be said for moonshine distillery owner Cole Landon, what with his workaholic habits and 'Scrooge' tendencies when it comes to all things Christmassy.

But when Jenna Pendean from Cornwall pays a visit to Cole's family-run distillery in Tennessee during the holiday season, will Cole's cynicism about the existence of Christmas miracles be put to the test?

A Cornish Summer at Pear Tree Farm

Book 1 in the Pear Tree Farm series

Cornish charm and a Tennessee twist – the perfect pair?

Nessa Vivian is determined to keep her parents' business afloat, but Pear Tree Farm near the backwater Cornish village of Polgarth didn't do well as a farm, and it's not faring much better as a camp site.

Ex-musician Ward Spencer from Tennessee is certainly intriguing – does his arrival signal a second lease of life, and not just for Nessa's business?

A Cornish Christmas at Pear Tree Farm

Book 2 in the Pear Tree Farm series

Pairing up at Pear Tree Farm in time for Christmas …

Pear Tree Farm in Cornwall, owned by the kind-hearted Nessa Vivian, is known for taking in lost souls, and ex-soldier Crispin Davies is certainly one of those. Crispin soon finds himself roped into helping out with a short-notice Christmas festival, organised by Nessa's force-of-nature sister, Lowena.

Visit www.choc-lit.com for details.

Introducing Choc Lit

We're an independent publisher creating
a delicious selection of fiction.
Where heroes are like chocolate – irresistible!
Quality stories with a romance at the heart.

See our selection here:
www.choc-lit.com

We'd love to hear how you enjoyed *A Summer to Remember in Herring Bay*. Please visit **www.choc-lit.com** and give your feedback or leave a review where you purchased this novel.

Choc Lit novels are selected by genuine readers like yourself. We only publish stories our Choc Lit Tasting Panel want to see in print. Our reviews and awards speak for themselves.

Could you be a Star Selector and join our Tasting Panel?
Would you like to play a role in choosing which novels
we decide to publish? Do you enjoy reading women's
fiction? Then you could be perfect for our Tasting Panel.

Visit here for more details...
www.choc-lit.com/join-the-choc-lit-tasting-panel

Keep in touch:
Sign up for our monthly newsletter Spread for all the latest
news and offers: www.spread.choc-lit.com.
Follow us on Twitter: @ChocLituk,
Facebook: Choc Lit and Instagram: ChocLituk.

Where heroes are like chocolate – irresistible!